SHOT TO THE HART

KATELYN SNYDER

Copyright 2024 by Katelyn Snyder

All rights reserved.

No parts of this publication may be reproduced, distributed, or transmitted in any form or by any means, including photocopying, recording, or other electronic or mechanical methods, without prior written permission of the publisher, except as permitted by U.S. copyright law. For permission requests, contact the author by authorkatelynsnyder@gmail.com

The story, all names, characters, and incidents portrayed in this production are fictitious. No identification with actual persons (living or deceased), places, buildings, and products is intended or should be inferred.

Book Cover by Books and Moods

Edited by Caitlin Lengerich & Chelsey Brand

Formatted by Books and Moods

First edition 2024

To the women who thought your first would be your forever, until your forever came along and showed you what love truly was.

CONTENT WARNING

This story contains content that might be troubling to some readers, including mentions of cancer, loss of a parent, grief, on page panic attacks, PPD, and graphic sexual content.

PLAYLIST

Please Please Please-Sabrina Carpenter
Thnks fr the Mmrs-Fall Out Boy
You'll Always Be My Baby-Alan Jackson
In A Perfect World (with Julia Michaels)- Dean Lewis, Julia Michaels
greedy-Tate McRae
run for the hills-Tate McRae
Paralyzed-Sueco
1 Step Forward, 3 Steps Back-Olivia Rodrigo
To Love Someone-Benson Boone
Dandelions-Ruth B.
Let Me Down Slowly-Alec Benjamin
Anything But Love-Shane Harper
Little Life-Cordelia
Finally//beautiful stranger-Halsey
Lucky-Dermot Kennedy
Forever and Ever and Always-Ryan Mack

PROLOGUE
The Breakup

Kodi

2 months earlier

"This relationship just isn't working for me anymore, Kodi." He moves a wild hair out of my face to maintain eye contact with me. This move used to give me butterflies, but right now it makes my skin crawl. He continues, "I think we've both known that for a while, but neither of us wanted to address it. I need you to move out of the apartment this weekend."

"Excuse me. You're breaking up with *me* out of nowhere when just last week we were talking about the future we envisioned for us? Then, you give me four days to get all of my stuff together and get out of the apartment?" I reply, completely flabbergasted by this, I thought he held a little more respect for me than that.

"The future that *you* envisioned for us," he corrects.

Five years, family holidays, building a life together and

promises of a ring and a family are now just empty promises he made to me for years. Meeting fresh out of high school where he worked at our local movie theater, we were attached at the hip from the moment he asked me on our first date. His outgoing and kind demeanor was one of the things that drew me to him. He would drop everything for me if I was upset about anything, he would spend Sundays with his mom just to see her smile, he would drop by my mom's just to steal a kiss and drop off flowers. I'm seeing none of that man standing in front of me. My Andy wouldn't just abandon our relationship for no reason. My Andy would have a discussion with me about his feelings and then we would move forward together. This man is not my Andy.

"Why are you rushing this? We have two rooms. Can't you give me a little time to find other arrangements before just kicking me to the curb?" He flinches a little at the anger that has seeped into my words.

I start to panic and begin fidgeting with the hair tie on my wrist again. It would typically hold my jet black hair into place, but I decided to wear it down today, forgoing my typical messy bun.

I'm moving away from him, needing the space to keep a clear head and closing my eyes.

Maybe this is just a bad dream and when I open my eyes, we will be snuggled up in bed and everything will be okay again.

I can't break down in front of him.

Unfortunately, when I open my eyes, Andy is standing right in front of me, attempting to reach for me, speaking to me, but I can't make out the words over the pounding that's begun in my head. Running towards the bedroom, I lock the door behind me. My breaths are coming in shallow, I'm shaky, and I can feel the weight of this whole situation closing in on me. The panic, feeling heavier than my body can handle, causes me to slide to the floor and drop my head into my hands. My thoughts are running rampant; I can't organize them, making my chest tighten even more, my breaths becoming jerky.

Holy shit. What am I going to do? I have nowhere to go, no savings to cover my ass, since Andy swore up and down he would take care of me for the rest of whatever lives were ahead of us.

It was all bullshit.

I've got my job nannying for Bill and Trent, but I haven't been saving, I've been spending. I should have been putting money aside, just in case, but no, those empty promises made me believe that I had nothing to worry about. That I wouldn't need money to rent a place alone, to get a moving truck, to take on bills that have been split for years. I don't even have rental history considering Andy's name holds the lease, and our apartment complex didn't require my name to be added.

I force myself to attempt a few deep breaths.

In. *One. Two. Three.*

Out. *One. Two. Three.*

Repeating until my breathing has steadied. I pray that Andy doesn't knock on the door but secretly hope he does, and provides the comfort that only he has ever been able to provide.

He comes to the door and knocks after a few minutes, but I can't bring myself to face him. Immediately my chest tightens and I can feel my eyes getting watery again.

"Love, please talk to me. I know you weren't expecting this, but it's what's right for both of us. I think we can both be happier." His muffled voice comes through the door. The nickname burns my ears.

The tears are falling now. How long was he unhappy? Why does *he* get to decide I'll be happier without him? What lies is he telling me right now? How long was he really planning on doing this? Were there signs that he was unhappy that I missed? I attributed his change in attitude and lack of affection the past few months to work stress.

On shaky knees, I push up and turn towards the door, swiping at my cheeks and opening it to find Andy pacing back and forth, shoving his hands through his dark brown curls.

Like a predator approaching its' scared prey, Andy approaches me and pulls me into a hug that I accept. I don't know why I do, I should be mad at him, but I need this last embrace.

He held me like this for what felt like hours, when in reality it was just a few minutes to let my breathing calm again and ground me in this moment with him.

"What did I do wrong?" I can't look at him, but I feel like if I don't ask him this now I may never know.

He sighs a shaky breath as if he is on the verge of tears. "Kodi, you didn't do anything wrong. You've been a wonderful partner, but we've been together for years and I don't see us moving past this stage of life. You're comfortable where we are and don't want to go out and experience what life has to offer. I… don't think I want kids anymore either and that has always been so important to you."

"I just don't understand. Everything was fine, or I guess it wasn't. Is there anything I can do to change your mind?" A choked sob is threatening to escape me as his comment jolts me, intensifying the burning in my chest.

"No, KJ, there isn't. I'm not willing to let you change yourself to make me happy. I'm sorry," is all he says.

"Okay. I guess that's it then. Goodnight, Andy," I reply, defeated as I pull away and walk towards our bed. He watches me as I go, letting me get tucked in before shutting the door as he leaves the room,

I cry myself to sleep.

CHAPTER 1

The Sahara

Kodi

Darcy bursts through her front door like the little firecracker she is with… *OH GOD NO*. This bitch has a bottle of tequila in one arm, Harley and Sinclair on the other, and a devious grin on her face. "Get up and get ready hoe. We're drinking and dancing tonight. And before you ask, no, you don't have a choice!" she exclaims, with Harley and Sinclair looking like they will pull me off the couch if I don't willingly get up. My three best friends since high school are on a mission, and once they start, they can't be stopped. If they want to get me off my butt, it'll happen even if they have to drag me out.

"Yeah, no thanks," I say, turning my attention back to my phone where it appears, according to Instagram, that Andy has been living his best life with Lyla—his coworker. The one he told me not to worry about when we would go out with his colleagues and she'd follow him around acting like I didn't exist. The one who is now spending most of her weekends in

SHOT TO THE HART

the apartment Andy and I lived in together; sleeping in the same bed and on the same sheets that Andy and I spent our nights in. I get why he chose her, she's the opposite of me—bubbly and blonde, skinny, can pull off outfits I wouldn't dare to wear. Probably the exact girl he's always wanted. I juxtapose her in almost every way; my personality isn't big, I have some curves and don't show off all of my assets the way she typically does.

"Ko, it's been two months. I know for a fact you're on one of their pages right now, making yourself miserable when you could be out there, enjoying life with us and gaining your independence back," Darcy states, plopping back down beside me, her blonde hair pulled into a tight pony, her blue eyes crinkling in the corners as she smiles at me. "I'm going to go change and then you are too."

Two months? Wow, I guess I really have been sitting in my miserable, post-breakup mentality.

I've been on autopilot, going to my shifts at *Wake, Bake, Repeat* down the road from Darcy's apartment and then ending up in this exact spot almost every day. Not too long after my breakup with Andy, when I thought *maybe* Andy would take it all back, Bill got an overseas job and offered to move me with them, but at the time everyone was here. Andy was here, and even if we weren't together, I couldn't see myself leaving any of them. After the breakup, I needed a job and fast. Wake, Bake, Repeat was hiring immediately and was walking distance from Darcy's apartment, so I took it.

I need to pick myself up, dust myself off and move forward. I can enjoy a night out with my friends, maybe meet someone new to get under. Andy was my first and only, I fear that I won't be good enough if I give myself to someone else. On the other hand, it could be fun to experience sex with someone different. Worse comes to worst, at least I can get drunk and spend the night dancing with my best friends.

However, now I'm just feeling like a sad, single millennial with no prospects and little to no hope for my future. Sad over this breakup, which is making me feel unmotivated to do anything, including hanging out with my best friends.

If I don't hang out with my best friends then they won't want to be friends with me at all. What's worse than living on your best friend's couch? Moving home with your helicopter Mom because said couch is not an option anymore.

Oh God, being back at home with Mom, who has called almost every day to check-in would drive me nuts. She would never give me a moment of peace and no guy is going to want to date a twenty-four-year-old living at home with her parent. Speaking of Mom, my phone buzzes and I see that she's checking in *again*.

MOM
> Hey sweetie, I hope you're doing okay. Let's grab lunch soon.

ME
> Just like yesterday, I'm good Mom. We can arrange that. Love you.

> **MOM**
> Love you most.

"Ugh, you're right. I need to enjoy life and be more present in this moment." I stand with a determined stride, heading to Darcy's room to make myself presentable. Passing her as she exits in a dress akin to that of a disco ball, she does a little shimmy at me which causes us both to chuckle.

"Where are we going?" I yell in the general direction of where I left my friends.

"Lockout. That new, expensive looking club downtown," Sin says, sidling into the room behind me with two shots in hand. Just like her personality, Sin's hair is fiery red, and she's always looking for trouble. She's sporting a pair of dark wash jeans and a white crop top under a leather jacket that accentuates her chest. Unlike me, she's never been afraid to show off her body and I'm envious of that.

"What's our mission tonight?" Sin asks as I take my shot from her, throwing it back with a wince.

"You guys are the ones dragging me out tonight."

"Well babe, you need to get laid, or at least let someone dance on you. So put on a sexy outfit and let's go find you a man," she says smiling devilishly at me. *Maybe Sin is right, maybe getting under someone else will pull me out of this funk. The thought of being with someone else is scary, but what am I going to do? Be single and sad until I die?*

Even if I don't go home with someone tonight, at least I've taken a step in moving on from my breakup with Andy by enjoying life with my friends. I think back to the night that we broke up and how he said I never wanted to go out or have fun. If he knew that I was headed out tonight would he still think that I was boring, or would he think that I was just trying to prove him wrong? Sure, he was right that I didn't want to go out often—reading and reality TV always sounded like a better option than drinking and dancing—but when I would go out, especially the past few months, he felt detached, barely touching me, not including me in conversations. I should have taken that as a sign that things were not going as well as I let myself believe. I chose to live in my naivety that we were just in a place of contentment and didn't need the same type of excitement we did when we were nineteen.

"Alright, more shots." More shots turned into us killing the bottle of tequila, posting tipsy selfies to our Instagram stories before calling our uber, and giggling the whole drive as we sang off tune to *Please Please Please* by Sabrina Carpenter. Our uber pulls up to the curb of Lockout and I step out wearing a little black dress that I feel confident in, but still covers me in the places I don't typically show off. My patchwork of tattoos are on full display, my jet black hair is curled and falling over my shoulders, and black high tops are on my feet because whoever decided that heels were good for dancing and drinking was actually delusional.

Bodies are packed wall to wall, making me wonder if there's an event going on, or if this is what a Saturday night at the newest club in Tampa looks like. I've been to a few bars and clubs, but I've never seen so many bodies packed into a place like this. The blue, red, and green flashing lights illuminating the dance floor make me realize how tipsy I actually am while dim lights hang over the bar to our left that we are slowly squeezing our way up to.

I'm ready to have a good time with my friends, even though this was not my plan tonight.

Honestly, my plan was to cuddle up with my e-reader and a glass of white wine until I eventually passed out.

Harley, with her dark brown curls and bronze skin, sporting a bright pink silky tank and black jeans, leans over into a very handsome, lumberjack-looking man's personal bubble and sweetly asks, "Why is it so busy in here?"

She turns back to me with an eye roll, leaning into my ear and relaying his message, "Why are men the way they are? Tell me why he said, 'Didn't you hear sweetheart? The Tampa Bay Manta Rays took home their first win of the preseason. Everybody, including some of the players, are here celebrating.' Like dude, you don't have to call me sweetheart and act like I should know what's going on."

"Over there." She gestures towards the VIP section where multiple men are dressed to the nines and flirting with the bottle girls. They all have to be at least 6 feet tall, and some are tattooed, while others have man buns that range from dark to light in color. I can't tell from here, but I'm sure they are more handsome up close. One in particular catches my eye in a navy blue suit, I can really only see his side profile. His hair is longish, golden, and tied half up. His skin is the color of the whiskey he lifts to his mouth, and his suit is tailored to fit his body in all the right places.

I have the sudden need to go and run my hands up his arms—feel how firm they are. I shake it off. I'm tipsy, and surely a hookup with a hockey player is not what I need right now, even if I thought I could get one's attention. I'm just a plain Jane, there's nothing remarkable about my looks or my personality that would snag the attention of someone of that caliber. I'm sure they are only seeking out models or the like. More recently, Andy stopped commenting on how beautiful I was, regardless of much or little effort I put in. The only people who ever hyped me up were my best friends, and they are required to do that by friendship law.

I decide to ignore all thoughts of the men standing in the roped-off section and focus on spending time with my friends. I drag them out onto the dance floor and dodge the hands of grabby men. After what feels like hours of dancing, I grab Sin and drag her to the bar with me. While we wait to squeeze to the bar top, I pull up my phone and two notifications stick out. Andy liked my story, and I have a text from him.

ANDY

> Glad to see you're spending time with your friends, you look good. Been thinking about you.

What the fuck. I haven't heard from him once until right now and now he's suddenly thinking about me.

I don't have time to decide if I want to respond because Sin is grabbing my wrist and pulling me up to the bar. We order a round of shots, taking them back to Harley and Darcy. We throw them back, wincing as the alcohol slides down our throats, then return to dancing. The night continues on and we drink enough to know we are all waking up hungover tomorrow.

Just as we decide this is probably going to be our last song of the night, a pair of hands find my waist, and a warm body presses into my back. The feeling of someone else's hands on me after five years of only Andy's has me almost shrugging the touch off, but Sin's words from earlier come back to me. I remind myself that I need to get laid or at least have fun with someone. Instead of pushing him off, I turn away from my wide-eyed friends who are clearly shocked by the fact that I am allowing this man to touch me. I give myself over to the feeling of dancing with him and let myself enjoy the feel of his hands on me. He's handsome, probably an accountant or business man, taller than my five-four by what could be three, four, maybe five inches, and his eyes meet mine with a devious glint in them.

"Hey there, beautiful, I'm Conrad," he finally says, leaning into my ear.

"KJ," I reply in a sultry tone before turning my back to him and allowing myself to lean into him as we continue to dance with my friends surrounding us. Giving him Andy's nickname for me allows me some anonymity, he doesn't need to know Kodi because he will probably never see me again after tonight.

We dance for another five songs before I feel his hot breath against my neck and hear him over the music as he asks, "Wanna get out of here?"

I nod and signal my friends in the direction of the exit. We reconvene on the sidewalk outside of the club.

"Where are you taking her?" The first question thrown

in Conrad's direction, from Harley, as everyone orders their Uber rides home. Everyone ordering their rides makes me question one last time if I want to do this or hop into the car my friends are taking and maybe see what Andy is doing.

Nope, no, not doing that, I don't need to go down that path again. Conrad it is.

"I'm staying at The Edition about fifteen minutes away," he hesitates, "room three seventeen."

"If she doesn't come home tonight, and I don't get a text from her when you arrive at your hotel, I will find you, and I will make sure your dick is irreparable. Got it, Conrad?" Darcy smiles up at Conrad who has an arm around my waist, holding me close.

"And I'll make it look like an accident," Sin slurs from her seated position on the sidewalk, head hanging in her hands.

"She's not joking, she knows how." Darcy's smile is now more evil than sweet. My best friend likes to think she is a pitbull, but she's more of a dachshund. She can bite your ankles, but won't do much more damage than that.

"Let us see your ID," Harley pipes up beside Darcy, arms crossed over her chest. Conrad raises an eyebrow at her, but she doesn't back down.

"Alright, you win," he chortles, pulling his ID out and handing it over. Harley snaps a quick pic and hands it back to him.

"Oh, Uber's here, babe. Ready?" He gestures in the direction of the silver sedan waiting on the side of the road. I give a quick hug to my friends and slide into the car beside Conrad.

Twiddling with my hair, leg gently bouncing, I ask Conrad, "So, what do you do for work?

He laughs as if I said something funny. "I play hockey, KJ, for the North Carolina Firestorm. We lost to your team, the Manta Rays, and some of the guys wanted to blow off steam, maybe find a bunny to take back to the hotel." He eyes me up and down. *Is he insinuating that I'm a puck bunny?* "We just didn't realize Lockout was the celebration spot for the home players."

"No fucking way." My response is almost immediate. "I wouldn't know that you're a player. I don't keep up with sports."

Just as our Uber pulls up to the hotel, Conrad scoffs, almost a little offended that I didn't know who he was. Shrugging it off, I slide out of the Uber with Conrad placing a hand on my back to guide me, quickly sending a text to the girls that we made it to the hotel.

The elevator ride is quiet, Conrad subtly moving his hand lower until he's got a handful of ass. When the door dings open, he guides me to his room, scanning his card and gesturing for me to enter.

Walking further into the room, Conrad approaches me placing his hands on my shoulder and turns me to face him. Moving one hand up to the back of my neck, he hauls me to him, our lips meeting in a fevered crash as he unzips my dress with the other. He guides us backward, laying me down and spreading my legs with his.

"Fuck. You are a sight." Leaning back on his haunches to completely undress us both then rolling a condom on that he very clearly had in his pants pocket.

I'm starting to regret my decision to come back with him. *Let's hope he can make me come, that's the least he can do. Although it wouldn't be the first and probably won't be the last time a man put his pleasure before mine.*

He lines himself up with me, pushing in, and then he's moving in wild, erratic movements. He doesn't kiss me, tries to find my clit but fails miserably, and five minutes later, we are laying next to each other with Conrad's arm wrapped around me, a look of pure bliss on his face while I am drier than the Sahara.

Turning to Conrad I say,"I had fun tonight, maybe I will catch you next time you guys play in town." With a frown that he quickly shakes off, he gets out of the bed and says,"Yeah of course. I did too. Let me walk you to the elevator and grab your number."

And with an awkward side hug, I head back to Darcy's apartment, so not ready to share the details of the night but knowing full well I will have to.

CHAPTER 2

Chocowate Chip Cwookie Dough

Kodi

I wake up with a pounding headache and a dry mouth. I will never be touching another bottle of tequila in my life. Then, the orgasmic smell of bacon grease hits my nose, making my mouth water. Bacon is hands down the best food after a night of drinking, and I'm ready to devour it. I hear other groans of appreciation on the floor next to me, where Harley and Sinclair lay in a tangled mess of limbs and oversized t-shirts.

From the kitchen we all hear, "Rise and shine, biotches. Ko has a story to tell us about a certain Mr. Conrad Hoyer." I try to snuggle further into the couch only to be threatened by Darcy with no bacon if I won't share the story of my escapades.

Once we are all settled with our breakfast, I begin to recount last night. "I think I hurt his ego when we were in the uber and I asked him what he does for work. And well… The sex lasted all of five minutes leaving me with a very dry vagina."

"You're telling me that man didn't even try to get you off and then came in five minutes?" Sin mumbles from the floor, a pillow draped over her eyes, her bacon barely touched, and a huge water bottle sitting next to her. She is clearly going through it this morning.

"That would be correct," I roll my eyes thinking about last night.

Harley scoffs,"Gross, he must have been expecting you to be a puck bunny with how easily you left with him."

I throw a pillow at her. "Rude!"

Darcy chimes in at this moment. "Come on Harls. Give her a break, you know Momma never watched hockey, and if she had sports on, Ko would fall asleep."

"Thank you D. This is why *you're* my best friend," sarcasm dripping off my voice as I glare daggers at Harley.

"I have a bone to pick with all of you. Why didn't y'all tell me that I was going home with a hockey player?" I fully make eye contact with each of them so they can feel my aggravation with their move last night.

"Would you have left with him if you knew he was a hockey player with a bruised ego from losing?" Sin mumbles again, this time lifting her head slightly from the ground to munch on a piece of bacon.

"Absolutely not," I say instantly.

"Why?" That's all Darcy says, leaving the question hanging in the air. I really don't know why I wouldn't. The fear that I might not be enough maybe, the drop my self confidence took when Andy broke up with me, the worry that someone with status wouldn't actually want me.

"Babe, you are stunning and have the sweetest soul. Anybody would be lucky to be with you, to even have you look at them. Conrad sucks, and I'm sorry that last night wasn't good for you." My eyes water as she continues,"It's okay to take your time moving on. You don't have to go home with random men, you can go on dates when you're ready, but whoever you choose to give your time to is lucky. It doesn't matter who it is, hockey player, barista, hell an old man." I smile, and because I don't have words, I give my best friend a hug.

"Can I ask you something?" Harley asks from her place on the floor.

"Hit me with it, future LMHC." I grin at her, Harley is so close to finishing her licensure and she gets embarrassed anytime we bring it up.

"What do you want your life to really look like? Like without Andy, without living on someone's couch, what do you want?"

"I want to find another nanny job that I'm passionate about. One where I feel welcomed and cherished and will pay me enough that I can get my own place or provide housing. Outside of that, eventually I want to find my person and be loved and cherished the way I deserve to be." I pause. "But, most importantly, I want to be happy."

"Putting that education to work today." Sin chuckles face first into the pillow.

A few hours later, I'm hugging Harley and Sin, sending them back to their shared apartment, and I'm perched on the edge of Darcy's bed as she gets ready for a date. "You look hot, think you're coming home tonight?"

"Ehhh, probably not."

"Boo, okay. I'm going to settle into my bed with mac and cheese and wine, then start applying for better jobs. The barista gig is easy, but I miss nannying," I sigh. "If I can find another job like that I'd love to."

"Why don't you look back into teaching or finishing your childcare license?" Darcy asks, swiping eyeliner onto her lower lid. I was working on getting my child care licensure, but never went back to complete the courses after I connected with Bill and Trent on a site for nanny and family matching.

"Ugh you know how I felt about college, too much money and too much time," I respond dejectedly. I just couldn't bring myself to do it. Going to college was never really something I was interested in. "You know I was only willing to give it a chance because I've always loved kids. I don't know if I want to explore daycare again, but I loved working with the kids individually. Fostering their growth and learning new things alongside them, that's what I want to do again. It was so fulfilling for me."

"Okay babe, well if you don't get something immediately it's fine. The couch is yours as long as you need." She chuckles, sliding on black heels to go with her cream cropped sweater and jeans.

I walk with Darcy as she grabs her purse and heads to the front door, squeezing her tightly and tapping her lightly on the ass on her way out, locking the door behind her. After a quick shower to wash off last night, I throw my hair into a bun and slide on a pair of sweats and an oversized hoodie.

Making myself comfortable on the couch with a bowl of mac and cheese and some white wine, I start scrolling through a job website but stop when I see a posting for an au pair for a "high-profile client" that has a two and a half year old daughter. The listing mentions that the client needs someone to travel with the family and is hiring immediately. I submit my resume, apply for a few other odd jobs and hope that someone gets back to me soon.

When Darcy gets home the next morning, I tell her about the jobs I applied for. While she is my best friend and would never kick me out, I know that her having her own space is always something she's craved given the way she was raised. She beams at me and I assure her that we are both hopeful that I will get one of these jobs.

※

I'm standing in the ice cream aisle after the longest shift of my life, debating between chocolate chip cookie dough or sea salt caramel, when a small body slams into my legs. At first, I'm confused, but when I look down into the cutest pair of blue eyes I have ever seen, attached to two little crooked black buns and a jumper covered in sunflowers, I am no longer confused but concerned. I back up and get down to her eye level, "Hey sweetie, where's your mommy or daddy?" She just giggles at me and presses her face up against the freezer door.

Then I hear it, "Arabella?! Bella? Where are you sweetie? Daddy promises he will get you ice cream, but he can't do that if you won't come to him."

I can hear the concern in that deep, Southern timbre. So,

I grab the small hand of the little girl that I can only assume is Arabella and begin to head in the direction of the voice. We are a quarter of the way down the aisle when a man turns the corner with a look of relief on his face. His hand clutches his chest, like he is on the verge of panicking.

"Is that your Daddy sweetie?" I ask as I take in the man heading our direction. He is about six-five, with muscles comparable to those of Hercules. His blonde hair and matching full beard contrasts with his daughter's raven hair, but his piercing blue eyes are definitely a feature they share. I continue to shamelessly check him out as he moves quickly towards us, at the same moment Arabella takes off running into his arms.

He sets Arabella gently back down on her feet, but keeps her tiny hand wrapped in his. He walks towards me with a smile on his face and begins speaking, at first I don't think it's to me, but then I realize we are the only ones standing in this aisle.

"Thank you so much for grabbing her. We were standing in produce. I was trying to get some grapes because this little lady goes through them like candy, and she was asking over and over again for ice cream. I told her we had to wait a second, and she just took off. I figured this is where she would be, but I was so worried. And, well, you probably didn't care to hear all of that, but thank you so much." He's still smiling at me and I can feel myself smiling back. He looks down at Arabella with so much love. "I guess we are going to be putting you in the cart from now on little lady. Speaking of, I definitely need to go and grab my cart now that she's back with me."

"No problem, I'm glad that she ran into me, quite literally actually. She was helping me decide between chocolate chip cookie dough and sea salt caramel. Isn't that right, Arabella?" I smile fondly at the little girl and she nods enthusiastically, she can't be more than three years old.

In the cutest, smallest squeal, she says, "Chocowate chip cwookie dough! Daddy chocowate chip cwookie dough!"

I turn to the alluring man and say, "Well, I guess it's decided then."

"Yes, I think it's decided that I will be buying both you, and my little lady, a gallon of chocolate chip cookie dough ice cream." My cheeks heat immediately and I am just about to tell him that I can get my own ice cream when he cuts my train of thought off with, "It's the least I can do."

"I'm Maverick and you've clearly met Bella already," he introduces himself as I walk beside them with my basket to checkout.

"That I did. I'm KJ." Sticking my hand out for a shake but quickly retracting it because you can't shake hands, walk and push a cart at the same time. I don't know why I just gave another random man Andy's nickname for me, but it's too late now.

"Is that short for anything?" He asks as we approach the register, waiting while the cashier finishes up with the person ahead of us.

"Nothing special." I shrug, my free hand gently pulling at the hair tie donning my other wrist as we speak.

"If you say so," he gestures in front of him, "You go ahead, and we will follow behind. Full cart and all."

I set my white wine on the belt, quickly flashing my ID and swiping my card. Then I wait as he loads groceries onto the belt. I can't help but notice he doesn't have a ring on his finger, not that it matters, he could have left it at home. He hands me my bag of ice cream, and we fall into step again as we head to the exit of the store.

"We are this way," he gestures towards the right side of the parking lot as we step through the exit door into the humid night air. He pulls Bella out before dropping the cart in the corral, "Uh, thanks again for bringing her back to me."

"Oh, no problem. I wouldn't have wanted her to get even more lost."

"Bella, say goodbye to Ms. KJ." She runs to me again and I get down to her level to give her a high five. She opts to give me the biggest little hug I've ever experienced and I head left to my ten year old elantra. I find myself reflecting on our interaction and wondering if I should have offered my number to Maverick whether that be for childcare or something else entirely.

CHAPTER 3

Evergreens

Maverick

Every morning before Bella wakes, I get in a quick workout and prepare her breakfast. Today it's pancakes and fruit for when she gets up. As I'm cleaning up the kitchen, I decide to call my Dad and check in.

On the other end he says, "Maverick, son. To what do I owe the pleasure?"

"Just checking in Dad. Wanted to see if you needed anything, see how you're doing," I respond.

The silence is deafening for a moment. I know he thinks we shouldn't be checking on him everyday, but it makes me feel better. "For the third time this week, I am perfectly fine, son. I would like to see my granddaughter though."

"I know, I'm sorry. I just worry about you. I'm sure she'd love to see you too. Are you free this afternoon? I could cook a late lunch and you could play your favorite game with her."

He chuckles on the other end. "Oh right, princesses, my favorite. I could swing by around one-thirty?"

"That's perfect." Bella starts chatting on her monitor. "Oh, she's up. I'll see you this afternoon Dad. Love you."

"Love you, son." He ends the call, and I type out a quick text to my sister as I head towards Bella's bedroom.

> **ME**
> Miss you, come visit soon?

> **GRACE**
> Hoping my big bro makes it into the Stanley Cup so I can come celebrate.

> **ME**
> Me too. Love you.

> **GRACE**
> Love you. Hug Bella for me.

A few hours later, Bella and my dad are sprawled across the living room floor. Bella is clinging to Floppy and rubbing her eyes like crazy. "I think it's naptime, little lady." I open my arms for Bella to come to me.

"Let me Mav. I could use the extra snuggles," Dad requests, opening his arms to Bella. She runs right to him, making my mind up for me.

"Well, it looks like the decision has been made. Call me if you need anything," I say, grabbing my phone out of my pocket. I open social media and start scrolling; I don't post publicly, but I do keep up with some family and friends on a private page. I see Dom posted a photo of him at the gym, shirtless of course. Grace posted a photo of her, her husband Jason, and their Golden, Billy, hanging out by a beautiful lake. The Manta Rays socials posted a video of some highlights from our preseason game against North Carolina a few weeks back.

"She's out like a light." My dad startles me as he sits on the opposite end of the couch, looking down I realize it's been twenty minutes. I lock my phone and stick it back in my pocket.

"So, Mav, I wanted to talk to you about something," he grimaces and I look at him expectantly. "I think that it's time I take a step back in caring for Bella."

"Wait. What? Why?" He loves being with Bella, even gets sad sometimes when I'm home because it means he doesn't have to come spend the day with her. He and Ma moved down here when I got drafted to be close to me and to continue to help with Bella.

"Mav, you know I love and adore that little girl with my whole heart. She is a ball of energy that quite frankly I can't keep up with, and I'm old and tired." He chuckles at himself," I'm not saying that I don't want to help you with her, she is the sunshine in my life since your mother passed, but I can't do it full time anymore, especially with how much you're gone during the season. I'll still help until you find someone, I won't leave you high and dry."

Over the past seven months, I can see the changes in my dad. He looks older and has less energy. Even my sister, Grace, has noted from thousands of miles away that Dad still seems to be grieving seven months later. There's no timeline on grief and maybe Bella is the reason I haven't truly sat and processed the loss of Ma. My throat begins to clog with unwanted sadness.

"No, Dad I think it's time I bring someone in full time anyways. I've been meaning to do it since Ma died, but I could see how much spending time with Bella means to you. Plus, I lost her in the grocery store the other day, I need the extra hands. It's just the thought of bringing someone in that I don't know is scary, so I've been pushing it off." I sigh.

"Trusting someone new can be scary, but if you're thorough with who you hire and you set a standard of care for her, then everything should be fine. If you ever feel like she isn't getting the care she deserves then you hire someone new," my dad gives me a piece of that good old wisdom, he always knows exactly what I need to hear.

"You're right, I know that the team will have things in place to help me ensure her safety as well. NDAs and all of that fun stuff."

"Exactly. She will be fine and you will too. There is one more thing I wanted to tell you. . .I think I'm going to start therapy. I know that you and Grace check on me every other day because you can see I'm not myself. I've been trying hard to push through and be myself, but I don't know what I look like without your Ma beside me." My parents were together since they were fourteen, grew up together, and now she's gone. I feel my eyes begin to water and when I look into my dad's eyes, I see the same watery expression.

"Oh, Dad, that's wonderful news. I know you usually say

this to me, but I'm proud of you." And for the first time since Ma's funeral, Dad pulls me into a hug and we cry together.

"Okay, so have we gotten any applicants?" I sigh, lifting my beer to my lips. Tatum, my best friend, sits across from me watching Bella on her monitor because "she is the cutest when she is asleep". Tatum loves Bella but is firmly against having children of his own. He has been my personal assistant since I moved to Tampa and joined the Manta Rays, playing center position.

"Yeah, a few. We can start going through applications soon, I want to give it a little more time. You lost her in the grocery store last week man, you've missed every opportunity to go out with the guys, and remember when you had to call Collins to drive your dad to urgent care because Bella was sleeping and you didn't want to wake her up? You need help now more than ever, I've just been waiting for you to see it yourself, " he replies, not bothering to look up at me.

"Yeah, yeah, rub it in then why don't ya?" I exasperatedly reply, taking another sip of my beer. I'm still coming to terms with the fact that my dad is taking a step back for himself. It's bittersweet considering that he's doing it for his own well-being, but I'm losing the person that I *know* I can trust with Bella's care. "I wish you could act as a manny too."

"I can't act as a PA for you and the guys along with taking care of Bella, Mav. Having an au pair isn't a bad thing, plenty of the other guys use them. Preseason is about to end, and your media appearances and travel schedule are about to pick up. Having someone here to stay with Arabella and your dad, or to travel with us, would be useful." He finally looks up, a furrow between his brow, making eye contact with me.

"You're right. I need the help, I'm just in denial about it, especially with Ma being gone. I didn't think I would need anyone else, I didn't want to need anyone else." I clear my throat to rid myself of the emotions bubbling up my throat. "How am I supposed to trust someone I don't know to stay with her?"

"I know man, but I've got you. That's what I'm here for. It might be hard, but we are going to find someone kind and trustworthy. We will make sure to vet everyone thoroughly, then once you have some applications you like we can set up the interviews." He gives me a reassuring smile.

"Thanks, hopefully we can get some applications and get someone in before it gets too busy."

My mind wanders back to that grocery store trip, to losing Bella and the woman who found her. The jet black hair and the eyes that reminded me of evergreens, the way she interacted with Bella. It's too bad I refuse to bring a woman into my life, otherwise I would have asked for her number. After Lily though, I can't date, I won't. The next time a woman leaves, it would affect not just me but Bella too.

"What are you thinking about over there Mav?" Tatums statement interrupts my thoughts.

"Lily. What if she finds out I hired someone and comes back with the papers unsigned and in hand?" I mutter.

"That almost sounds worse than hiring a stranger." This statement confirms my thoughts that Tatum never really liked

Lily. "When was the last time Jeremy and the team reached out?"

"Bella's second birthday, it's been five months. Third time in the past two-and-a-half years. I just don't get why she wouldn't just sign them and send them back. She didn't answer my text update either." When Lily left and I let the Manta Rays legal team know, they immediately started searching for her but came up short until Bella's first birthday. They ended up finding her in North Carolina and have sent termination of parental rights papers religiously, but she's not signing them or not sending them back. She knows she can't get anything from me, the team made sure of that when we let them know I had gotten her pregnant. The open-ended possibility of her coming for Bella though, that makes me worried.

"That's so weird, it's apparent she doesn't want to be involved," Tatum wonders inquisitively.

"Yeah, but you know I've always said if she wanted to have a relationship with her, she could."

"Which I will never understand, but it is your call," he relents.

"And KJ, the woman from the store. She was beautiful dude. I wanted to ask for her number, but you know I couldn't do that," I divulged, changing the topic because I can't deal with Tate judging me for leaving that door open any longer.

"Couldn't or wouldn't?" Tatum shoots me a questioning look.

"Aren't they the same? *Can't* because it's not just my heart on the line. *Wouldn't* because I can't get hurt like that again."

Lily leaving was unexpected and while I didn't feel we were truly in love, it hurt like hell that she didn't even talk to me. Didn't say goodbye to me or her daughter. One thing I know for sure is that my feelings for her were stronger than hers were for me until Bella came, when Bella came it felt like Lily didn't feel anything for anyone. I tried to talk to her, tried to figure out why she was so distant, but she wouldn't talk to me, kept telling me she was fine until she disappeared.

"I understand why you're hesitant, Mav, but I think you deserve to be happy too. You being happy will bring so much more joy into her life." He gestures towards my sleeping daughter. "Next time you want to ask for a woman's number, just do it. Nothing has to come of it until you're ready. At least try though."

"Okay, I appreciate you, Tate. So what about you? Dating anyone?" I ask to take the spotlight off me for the moment.

"Nah man. You know me, one night stands and that's about it. I enjoy my luxurious lifestyle, I don't want to give that up quite yet." He laughs.

"Oh, right. The Porsche can't handle a passenger princess, and your 1,650 square foot, three-bedroom, two-bathroom condo on the water isn't big enough for a woman to occupy," I retort on an eyeroll. "Let's not forget about the beach bungalow, that couldn't handle a woman either."

"Oh, shut up, Maverick. If I find the right girl, maybe I'll settle down. Until then, let me live." He flashes me a shit eating grin.

"Alright dude. Get out of my house. I'm tired," I say on a yawn.

He gathers his things and makes his way towards the front door. "We'll get together when we get a few more applications. Talk to you later!"

"Thanks again!" I throw his way as he closes the door behind him. Hearing the automatic lock click into place, I head into my room.

Sitting in my bed, I can't get a grasp on my breathing, and my hands are shaking uncontrollably. I can't quite pinpoint if my panic attack started because of my discussion with Tatum about hiring an au pair, thinking about Lily maybe showing up for the first time in months, or the realization that my Ma is actually gone and won't be here to celebrate my wins or see Bella grow up; I won't have her to lean on during my times of struggle. I attempt to take in a breath, and then another, until my chest is rising and falling almost regularly again.

"Get it together Maverick," I tell myself. "I can see my bedroom door, my hands in front of my face, the picture of Bella being held by the guys and I after our first win when she was born, my hockey gear, and my pile of dirty clothes I need to wash. I can feel my comforter beneath me, the sweat dripping down my back, my feet on the cold floor, and my fingernails digging into my palm." At that moment, I remind myself to unclench my fists and relax my shoulders. "I can smell my deodorant and the detergent on my clean sheets. I can taste my mint toothpaste." After working myself through that, my breaths have completely regulated, and I find myself leaning back into my bed and closing my eyes.

CHAPTER 4

Wake, Bake, Repeat

Kodi

"Order for Grace," I call out as I set down a medium Americano on the pickup counter. I still haven't heard back from any of the job applications I submitted over the past two weeks, and while I make good tips at this coffee shop, I'm not making enough to work towards my goal of relocating off of Darcy's couch.

My shift is almost over, we made it through the afternoon rush, and just then the bell above the door chimes, and my three best friends are walking into the shop, right up to the counter where I stand already typing in their orders. Ever since I started working here, when my friends' schedules line up, they will waltz in at the end of my shift so we can have some girl time.

"Kodiiiiii," Sin drawls leaning into the counter. "Wanna take our afternoon coffee for a walk?"

"Uh, sure. I've got about fifteen minutes left, your coffee will be up soon." I wink at her and shoo them away so that I can help the next person. Once my shift is over and I've got my coffee, I meet my friends and we head towards the river. I check my phone as we stroll to see if I've got any leads, but all I see is one text. I huff a breath in frustration; when will he get the picture that I am done?

> **ANDY**
> Baby, please. I just want to know that you're okay.

"So, any news on the jobs?" Harley asks as we approach a picnic table looking over the water.

"No, I've reached out again and applied for a few more since. I hope someone will get back to me soon," I sigh.

Darcy reaches across the table for my hand, "Ko, it's no rush really. You're welcome to stay with me as long as you need."

"D, I know and appreciate that. I'm ready to be off your couch and for you to have your space back though," I squeeze her hand as I speak. "So, what's new with y'all?"

Harley is the most reserved of us, so it surprises me when she speaks up first. "I have to tell you guys something, and you all have to promise me you're not going to be upset with me." All three pairs of our eyebrows shoot up, but we keep our attention on Harley. We all nod our heads, urging her to continue. "I saw Benji last night. He called, and I was already feeling sensitive after that horrible date the other night. So, when he asked me to come over… I went," she ends with a sheepish grin. Benji is Harley's occasional hook up who felt like she was too "boring" to enter into a relationship with and has been using her for sex for months. We've all made it clear how we feel about him.

"Holy shit. That's why you came in so late last night!" Sin practically yells, and Harley shrugs.

"So you're too boring to take on a real date but not too boring to continue having sex with, and you can't even stay with him?" I chime in. Harley has started fiddling with her coffee cup, avoiding eye contact with any of us.

"Listen, I know I need to let him go. I...I just can't for some reason," she whines.

It's Darcy's turn to jump in. "Harls, we are here for you. We just don't want him to hurt you again."

"Agreed," Sin and I say at almost the same time.

"Where is everyone headed after this?" I ask as we all appear to be nearing the bottom of our coffee cups.

"I am going to shower and sleep. Last night was… tiring," Harley blushes.

"I have a date," Darcy says.

"With who? The same guy from last week? Leighton was it?" I ask.

"His name was Leighton, and yes, he asked me out again. We are going to truly test this new situationship by doing an escape room." Darcy is at a stage where she is enjoying going to the deli aisle and sampling all of the meats, not strictly sticking to one type or another for very long. Probably why she's calling it a situationship.

"Wow, I am incredibly jealous of all three of you bitches," Sin says,"I have my first twelve-hour day of three in a row this week. Sleep? Don't know her. Sex? Nonexistent. Coffee?

My best friend, no offense to you three." Sinclair works in the children's ward of our local hospital, typically three days on and four off.

"And I am headed back to take a quick shower before I meet my mom for dinner. Love you!" We all stand, disposing of our cups before heading in different directions.

※

I walk into the diner Mom chose for dinner and see her sitting in the corner, nose deep in her phone. Probably reading about current events or trying to figure out how Facebook works. The diner is giving fifties vibes with its vinyl checkerboard floor, red booths with cracking plastic, and wobbly tables. Elvis plays in the background, and I feel like I've just walked onto the set of Grease.

"Hiya Mom." She jumps, bumping her knee on the table then cringing.

"Kodi James, you scared the living heck outta me!"

"Sorry, I literally wasn't even quiet, you were just nose deep in your phone." I shrug and she stands enveloping me in a hug.

"How have you been? I feel like I haven't seen you in months." She's right, she saw me a few days after my breakup with Andy, and I've been antisocial up until the girls dragged me out.

"I'm good, Mom, just like I've told you almost every day."

"Lord help me, I care about my only child." I roll my eyes at her, knowing she's not actually upset but just being a typical helicopter mom. She doesn't have anyone else to direct her energy towards, being that my Dad is gone and I don't have any siblings. She dated here and there, but no one ever stuck. A rotating door of nice-enough men, but when it came to the meat of things, my mom didn't want me to get attached to a man that could leave, so she never brought them around. Then, she'd come home crying to my Aunt Nancy, that's how I knew she was no longer seeing someone. I should be grateful, I *am* grateful, but I also am sick of people asking me how I'm doing.

"You know that's not what I meant Mom. I love you and appreciate you for checking in. But I really am good. I've applied for some new jobs, and I went out with the girls and had a blast."

"I'm happy to hear that. . .you know Andy has texted a few times. Says you aren't answering him." He would text my Mom because I won't respond. It's not like he ever reached out to her before, so the fact that he is now is just desperate.

"That would be because I'm not, Mom, and I hope you aren't either. I don't want anything to do with him."

"I told him to leave you alone, too." She beams with pride at her statement, the superhero in my story always. I let her have it, she has worked hard to feel that way, being that she raised me alone and did everything in her power to keep me happy.

"How's work been for you?" The waitress comes by and my mom orders a BLT with fries while I go with a classic burger, chocolate shake, no cherry and fries.

"Same old crap, new day," She sighs, "I'm glad I get to see you today."

"Me too, Mom." I do miss my mom and I need to make a more conscious effort to spend time with her. "Anything else new to share?"

For the first time in my twenty-four years of life, my mom blushes, a genuine smile spread across her face. "I met a man, around my age, who runs a construction business, and he has a daughter a little younger than you. We haven't been seeing each other long, but he's been very respectful."

"That's great Mom! What's his name? Do you think I'll meet him? How did you meet?" I ask, genuinely curious if my mom gets her true shot at happiness and the man who might provide it to her.

"His name is Dale, and if things keep on this track, I think you might. Your Aunt Nancy, the matchmaker, had his company come and renovate her bathroom and then forced my number on him. He told me that he considered not calling, but Aunt Nancy kept telling him he wouldn't regret it so he took a chance."

"Ah, that's so great! I'd love to meet him if it goes that way. Of course Aunt Nancy has to play matchmaker. I'm surprised she hasn't been sending me portfolios of her friend's sons to get me back out there." Our waitress drops our food and we dig in.

"Are you ready to date again?" My mom asks, plucking a fry and pointing it in my direction waiting on an answer.

"Not at all, he would have to be really special for me to be ready to date again," I tell my mom. Mom tells me more about Dale as we finish our meals; he and his wife split after his daughter turned eighteen, and he just started dating again due to Aunt Nancy's meddling. His daughter, Callie, attends school at the New York fashion institute and will be back to visit during her breaks.

With our checks paid, we exit the restaurant together. "Thanks for meeting me tonight, I miss you," my mom says as she pulls me into another hug.

"I've missed you too. I'm sorry, I'll check in with you more often. I love you, let me know once you're home."

"I love you too, and you do the same." My mom unwraps her arms from me, and I watch her walk to her car before taking off towards my own.

CHAPTER 5

Always Has Been

Maverick

"Check out this one. Linda Gregory, in her forties, has grandchildren, nannied while she was in college, has some early childhood development education, but ended up working in corporate America, weird. She's willing to work whenever she needs to, so that's a plus. Downside is she doesn't want to live here, but we could probably make it work for the weeks where we would just need her during the day or for times you're away." Tatum slides over a resume across my dining room table as I take a peek over at my dad and Bella snuggled up, watching a movie in the living room.

"Hmm. . .sounds like she might be a good option, let's put her in the interview pile." I pick another resume from the pile, scanning it quickly. "Kodi Roscoe, twenty-four, six years with one family until they left, willing to travel and stay here. Not asking for too much pay. No education history, so that'd be something to follow up on. She listed a lot of the activities she would do with Bella's age group, which I like. Take a look and then add her to the interview pile."

"She's young, do you think she can manage the lifestyle you lead with whatever she wants as a twenty-four year old?" Tate ponders aloud.

"Another question I'd have to ask her, but being young means she can probably keep up with the Tasmanian devil over there," I gesture towards Bella who is standing in the middle of our living room spinning in circles, her small giggles filling the air. "Hey Bella, let's take a break baby. You're moving so fast and that's really cool, but I don't want your tummy to hurt." She complies, joining my dad back on the couch.

"You got it boss. Look at this one; Corrine King, twenty-six, preschool teacher looking to leave the field, babysits during summers, but has never nannied." Tatum hands it over and I eye it giving him a nod of approval before passing it back. "You feeling better about this now?"

"Marginally better. I don't think I'll feel confident in my decision until the second part of the interviews where I let the top candidate interact with Bella to see if they are a good match too."

"Doesn't Bella like everyone though? Isn't that normal for a toddler?" Tatums question makes him laugh, and I guess he does have a point.

"Seeing them interact will make me feel better though. If Bella really likes someone, that's a good sign."

"Alright then, I'll call these three pending their background checks and then let you know when they will come in. Nap time only." He waves the resumes at me before sliding them into his briefcase and exiting the house.

CHAPTER 6

Little Late

Kodi

Checking my email for the tenth time in the past twenty-four hours as I walk to my shift at *Wake, Bake, Repeat*, I still haven't heard back from any of the jobs I've applied to.

Just then, my phone buzzes with an unknown number, I quickly answer, "This is Kodi."

"Kodi, hi, this is Tatum Reed. I'm the personal assistant to Mr. Hart. You applied for an au pair position to help him with his daughter, and I was hoping you had a few minutes to chat." My stomach is in my butt, I am suddenly very nervous.

"Yeah, um yes, of course," I stammer. I need to get it together.

"After reviewing your resume, he would like to bring you in for an interview. Are you still interested?" he asks plainly.

"I am, yes, of course," I say it more quickly than I intended.

"Great! What does your schedule look like over the next couple weeks?" This response has a little more personality behind it.

We discuss my shifts at the coffee shop, trying to find a time that works for me and Mr. Hart, the potential employer I'll be interviewing with.

Before I head into work, I shoot off a quick text to my girls.

> **ME**
> I got the au pair interview *smiley face emoji*

> **DARCY**
> Awesome! When?

> **ME**
> Two weeks out. Busy people.

> **SIN**
> That's awesome. You're going to kill it.

> **HARLEY**
> *3 red heart emojis*

My newfound sense of peace immediately dissipates as I walk into my shift and see who is standing at the counter with Lyla on his arm. I try to slip past them both to duck into the back and clock in, but I'm halted by that high pitched voice, dripping in venom.

"Oh my God, Kodi, is that you?" Lyla asks, louder than necessary.

I turn around, pasting my fakest grin on, "Lyla, Andy. Good to see you."

"KJ, this is the new gig?" Andy asks, letting his eyes roam up and down my body while his new girlfriend, fuck buddy, friend with benefits, whoever she is to him, is literally standing right next to him. I'm disgusted.

"For now, yeah, and don't call me that," I make sure it comes out sugary sweet.

"Lyla, why don't you go get a table? I'll order our coffees." He pecks her on the lips and sends her to the other side of the small coffee shop.

"I gotta go clock in. Demi can take your order. Enjoy your coffee." I turn on my heel, clocking in and then coming back out to man the counter, only to see Andy is still waiting, not having ordered his coffee and moved down the bar.

"KJ," he whispers as he approaches the counter. There's no one waiting so I can't even pretend to act too busy to talk to him. "Can we talk? You never answered my text."

"I know, Andy. I purposefully didn't." My anxiety is spiking the longer he lingers, and I don't have a spare hair tie, so I grab a pen by the register and rhythmically tap it to the counter.

"Listen, I just want to make sure you're okay." He looks like he's in pain but I don't buy it. He just wants to make me feel like I did something wrong.

"Two months later? Little late. I'm fine and you can stop worrying about me now. What can I get you to drink?"

"I'm not going to give up."

"Well you should, you gave up then. You can give up now." His presence is draining my patience, "It seems like you don't actually know what you want Andy."

"I do know, and it's you. Always has been."

"While you are literally here with another woman," I scoff.

"It's… She's… I don't…" He can't even get his thoughts out, probably not used to my cold demeanor towards him. Another customer comes through the door.

"Listen, I'm sure that you're having second thoughts now but it's too late. I have more customers to help, what can I get you both?"

"Two iced coffees with cream and sugar. One vanilla and one maple," he orders, pays, and as he walks away whispers, "Thanks, I'm going to keep texting KJ."

After taking the next customer's order, I step into the back. Letting out a big breath and then returning to finish my shift. I do my best to avoid looking towards the table that Andy and Lyla have taken a seat at.

CHAPTER 7

It's Her

Maverick

ME

> Dude, these interviews have been a disaster. There's no way this last applicant can be that much better.

ME

> Linda showed up an hour late. Corinne was definitely a bunny I've seen out and about. Once she recognized me, she was more worried about flirting than learning about the job and Arabella.

TATE

> Give Kodi a fair shot, she might be a pleasant surprise. IF you don't vibe with her, then we start again. No big deal.

Just then I get a notification from my doorbell camera that Kodi has arrived and head to the door. She's looking down so I can't get a good look at her.

ME
Fuck dude. Gotta go, she's here.

TATE
Text me after.

I had Tatum schedule all of these interviews during nap time so that Arabella wouldn't get attached to someone who may not be able to stick around. I open the door and am at a loss for words staring at the woman standing in front of me. It's her. The one who found Arabella in the ice cream aisle—who was stunning in sweats and a messy bun—this absolutely gorgeous woman who I've thought more about than I should have in the time since our run-in at the store.

This has to be some sort of kismet experience, right? Raven-colored curls, black nose ring, sinful green eyes, black button up paired with cerulean jeans and high-top black converse. While not professional, her outfit is practical for someone who will possibly be caring for a small child. And today, her tattoos are on full display, the patchwork art covering her arms almost entirely, making her ten times more attractive than she was that night in sweats at the grocery store. I take note of three small daisies sitting next to each other above her right wrist; as she moves her hair out of her face, the daisies go from wilted to smiling. I want to ask her what that represents, but that's not why she's here.

When she looks up into my eyes, recognition passes over, her pale face turning tomato red while her mouth flops open and closed like she has words but can't get them out. "This has to be a mistake. I must have the wrong house." She rushes out with a sheepish grin, and it's then I remember she introduced herself as KJ and not Kodi. That has to be why I didn't piece two and two together before she showed up for her interview today.

I laugh genuinely, and she seems so confused. "No, I think you are in the right place Ms. Roscoe. I could use some help with Arabella, and my personal assistant, Tatum, was setting up interviews for me. Why don't you come inside and we can chat?"

"Are..." she stutters. "Are you sure?"

"One hundred percent positive. It's actually a relief that I recognize your face, it gives me some peace of mind being that you've already shown me that you put her safety first," I say as I lead her into the living room of my house and gesture for her to have a seat on the gray couch across from me. "Can I get you something to drink? Water, coffee, tea?"

"Um, water would be great actually, thanks." I turn on my heel and head to grab my phone and two water bottles from the fridge.

> **ME**
> Dude, you won't believe who you set up an interview with. Kodi is KJ, the girl from the grocery store last week.

> **TATUM**
> No way! Are you going through with the interview? If so, update me afterwards.

> **ME**
> Yeah, I definitely am. Talk later.

Sticking my phone back into my pocket. I question why I even told Tatum about the grocery store incident, since it's when he got his 'I told you so' moment. My Dad stepping back just sent us careening off the edge.

I return and notice that she is gently pulling a hair tie on her wrist and letting it recoil against her skin. That can't feel good. I hand her the water, give her a smile, and sit down across from her.

"So Ms. Roscoe, I guess I should tell you first that I am a professional hockey player, hence Tatum keeping details to a minimum during his phone call with you. But, based on our interaction in the grocery store, I assume you didn't know who I was anyways."

"Uh, Kodi is fine, if you're okay with calling me that. But that would be correct, I have never been much of a sports fan myself," she laughs nervously, a light pink tinting her cheeks.

"No problem there. So tell me what made you apply to be an au pair? I noticed that you previously nannied for a family with three kids for about six years, but it seems that ended abruptly."

"Well Bill, the father, got a job opportunity in another country, so although they moved I decided to stay here. They offered to take me with them, but all my friends and family are here. I couldn't move to another country. Bill and Trent were so good to me, and I loved working with them and their kids. And to be frank, the pay and living opportunity was a big selling point. I recently found myself in need of a new place to live, so this would work out perfectly," she responds with a shrug..

I hate that she feels like I don't want to hear her story, I really do, but I remind myself I don't need to know that to know if she is a good candidate to care for Bella. I can't explain why, but something about her is intriguing to me.

"I see. So, what do you feel makes a person a good fit to be an au pair?" The length of work with her previous family shows that she is capable and trustworthy enough that someone decided to keep her around for a while with their kids but it still feels necessary to ask.

"Well, honestly, I think taking care of someone's children requires a lot of patience and energy, willingness to play with the same toys or sing the same songs all day, every day. I feel like being able to pivot and adjust as a child learns and grows is also important. I will always follow whatever schedule and rules you have set because in the end, she's your baby, and I want to help you raise her the way you envision when you aren't able to be present."

I'm just about to tell her that I liked her willingness to work with me and that Bella does require a lot of patience and energy, when the monitor linked to Arabella's room lights up and her light cries drift through. I look at Kodi. "Excuse me. I need to go get her back to sleep. I am so sorry, I will be right back to continue this."

She gives me a genuine smile and says, "Of course. I'll just hang out here."

I swiftly head towards Bella's room, knowing the sooner I get to her, the easier it will be to get her back to sleep. She has always been like this. If she wakes up and you get to her quickly, she will almost immediately pass back out, but if you take thirty seconds too long, she will be wide awake, and it takes ten extra steps to settle her back in. Quietly, I creep into the room, swoop my sweet little girl into my arms, holding her close to my chest. She immediately pushes back against me with all the strength she can muster in her little body, trying to flail around, so I settle her deeper into my chest. I know this game and I won't give in. "It's okay Bella, Daddy's here. Just go back to sleep." Easing my hold just a little, I begin humming,"You'll Always Be My Baby" by Alan Jackson. It always seems to soothe her, and her body becomes lighter as she begins to relax into my hold. After a few minutes of this, her soft snores are audible enough that I can safely lay her down.

I sneak out of her room, smooth my shirt back down, and run a hand through my messy hair that I know Bella's hand had clutched to as she got comfortable. At this point, I'm not sure I should continue this interview. Can I really have this woman, who I am extremely attracted to, working and living with me? Will I be able to stop the attraction that I've had for her from going any further?

CHAPTER 8

Probably Naked Too.

Kodi

As soon as Maverick exits the living room, I grab my phone and pull up the group chat. As I begin typing, I hear Mavericks soft mumbles to Arabella and then he begins humming a tune I've never heard through her monitor.

ME

> You will not believe who I am interviewing with right now.

DARCY

> Is it Tom Hiddleston? Because if so, I need pictorial proof.

ME

> *eye roll* No, Darcy. First, why would Tom be interviewing for an Au Pair in Tampa? Does he even have kids? Anyways, It's Maverick from the grocery store. The one who was more handsome than Tom Hiddleston and had the cutest daughter on the face of the planet.

SIN

No fucking way. Are you about to live out a boss and employee-to-lovers trope?

ME

OMG, absolutely not. As much as I would love to climb him like a tree, I would love to have a job more.

HARLEY

Por que no los dos? I mean you could have a job AND climb him like a tree.

SIN

Yeah, definitely. It would be convenient considering if he hires you, you'd be living right down the hall from where he sleeps every night.

HARLEY

Probably naked too.

DARCY

Okay, but he's high profile. What does he do?

ME

He's a hockey player! Why wouldn't I know that? Shouldn't I have recognized him at the store?

HARLEY

Baby, you didn't even know you were going home with Conrad Hoyer. What is the hot new boss's name again?

ME

Maverick

SIN

Last name?

ME

Hart

Harley

This him?

A picture attachment of Maverick walking into the arena in a suit with his gear bag slung over his shoulder is attached to the text.

ME

Uh, yep, that looks like him.

SIN

> NO.

DARCY

> FUCKING.

HARLEY

> WAY.

Just as I'm about to ask why everyone is freaking out, Maverick walks back into the living room looking a little disheveled. I quickly tuck my phone back into my purse. I can't help but giggle. "You look like you went to war in there."

"She didn't want to go back down for the rest of her nap. When you arrived she had only been out for twenty-five minutes, but she typically naps for one to one-and-a-half hours. If she doesn't, well, trust me, you don't want to find out what happens." He grimaces.

"Noted. Although, I'm sure if you hire me, I will find out at some point. I'm glad she went back to sleep for you."

"Now where did we leave off? I guess I should tell you a little more about Bella's schedule and what I would be expecting during your time with us. I have cleaners come once a week, so if hired, you wouldn't be required to clean except for tidying up and helping with dishes and laundry. I'd have her full schedule written up when you start, but I would just expect you to make sure she is safe, fed, bathed, and when needed, put to bed. I say 'when needed' because if I'm home, I like to do her bedtime routine." This makes my heart flutter a little bit, I can tell he really loves his daughter. "We are still working on potty-training, she's in pull-ups but doesn't always tell us when she needs to use the toilet, so ideas on that would be great. I don't really monitor her screen time. She can have sweets, but not after nap time, or she will be a literal demon when bedtime rolls around. She goes to a tumble class for toddlers twice a week in the mornings so she can get some of her energy out. You would be more than welcome to drive her in your car or my spare, and you could take her to do any activities on my dime, I'd be giving you a card. I just ask that you keep Tate and I updated on where you will be going and when. Does all of that sound okay?" I nod, encouraging him to continue. I have ideas on potty-training but I will mention those and help implement them if I'm hired.

"You'd have your own bedroom and bathroom and free usage of anything in the house. If you ever found yourself or Bella needing anything, I will keep a list on the fridge or you can let me know. I would like you both to travel with me on occasion; I prefer for Bella to maintain a routine, but I also don't enjoy being away from her for too long. Does that all sound okay as well?"

He's asked me that question twice in the last three minutes, is he worried I can't handle the job, or is there a candidate that he would prefer over me? I have a few questions I would like to ask, some of them inappropriate like where Bella's mom is and why he is hiring an au pair. Instead, I take the safer route. "Sounds pretty simple. Does she have any allergies or medical issues I should know about? Any quirks?"

He smiles, but it's a specific smile. I have noticed in my few interactions with him that spreads across his face when thinking or speaking about Arabella. "No medical issues or allergies but she does have a stuffed stingray she got from the arena named Floppy, or as she says 'fwoppy', that has to travel with us and go to sleep with her always. It's a little stuffed version of our mascot."

I smile back at him, "That's good to know, I can't wait to meet Floppy."

"Well, I think that about sums it up. While I think you're a great candidate, I'd like to see you interact with Bella before extending an offer and moving forward. Would you be willing to meet somewhere, like a park or a museum, sometime next week?"

My heart skyrockets with excitement, "I absolutely understand wanting to see how we do together. I work the rest of this week, but I'm free Sunday morning."

"Sunday morning works. How about we meet at the Children's Science Museum downtown around ten-thirty?"

"That's the one downtown right? I used to take the littles there all the time, they loved it. Honestly, so did I."

"It is a pretty neat place, they just recently added a bubble exhibit and I think Bella will have a blast with that. Do you have any other questions for me?" he asks.

"Not that I can think of. If anything comes up, I'll reach out to Tatum. Otherwise, I will see you and Bella on Sunday."

"Let me walk you out." He stands and leads me to the front door, opening it up.

"Thank you again for the opportunity, Mr. Hart." I stick a hand out to him and he shakes it.

"Maverick is fine. Mr. Hart is my father." He smiles at me

and I return it before turning and going to my car. I notice that he waits until I'm in my car before waving and closing the door behind him.

※

"Are you ready for today?" Darcy asks as I scurry around the apartment trying to get my things ready to head over to the children's museum to meet Maverick and Bella.

"I think so. Have you seen my gold studs?" I throw in her direction as I pull on and tie my black low tops embroidered with flowers tucking my dark wash jeans into them. I need to be out of the apartment in the next ten minutes and my earrings are missing.

"Right here babe. Take a breath. You look great, you're fucking awesome, and you know that museum and how to play and interact with kids." I turn to Darcy as I pull a matching shirt over my head and she's holding my studs in the palm of her hands. "You are a blessing, I could kiss you but I have to go." Looking at my watch, I begin panicking, "Like, right fucking now. Bye, love you!"

Then I'm running down the stairs, hopping in the car, and taking off towards the museum.

CHAPTER 9

Scetti Time

Maverick

"Bella, sweetie, we need to go." I glance at my watch noticing we should have left ten minutes ago, but Arabella has decided to give me a run for my money this morning. Her yogurt bowl ended up all over her head and the floor because it wasn't what she wanted after she asked for it, resulting in an unplanned bath. We've been working on potty-training, but instead of telling me she needed to go potty, she pooped in the bathtub, leading to a bath in my bathroom and me spending twenty minutes cleaning her tub. Now she's running circles around the house in nothing but her pull-up, Floppy in hand, as I sit in the middle of the living room feeling defeated.

I pull out my phone to call Tate because he never gave me Kodi's contact information, and I need to call her and let her know we are going to be late. I finally stand and chase after Bella, swiftly placing her on my hip so I can finish getting her ready, and she begins screeching like those monkeys at the zoo do when it's feeding time.

"What the fuck was that shriek?" Tatum asks upon picking up my call.

"Your niece is acting like a gremlin this morning and we are running late to meet Kodi. I need her number because you never sent it, please." I place Bella on the floor, and she attempts to run again, but I gently hold her still pulling her shirt that says "daddy's main squeeze" with a juice box on it. I lift her quickly onto the couch to get her legs in her black cotton shorts before sliding her bright pink sneakers on because those are the shoes she picked out. They don't match her outfit, but I don't have the energy to fight with her today.

"Alright, sent it over, sorry about that man. Let me know if I need to get with legal about the paperwork afterwards."

"Thanks dude. Will do. Talk later. Bella, say bye to Uncle Tate," I directed at my daughter holding the phone to her face.

"Uncle Tate bye bye bye bye bye bye," she sing-songs, her mood suddenly rainbows and sunshine.

"Go grab Floppy and then we need to get in the car seat." Her little feet clobber across the floor while I grab the backpack full of pull-ups, spare outfits, and snacks. She comes barreling into my legs with an "mmph". I pick her up and we head towards the garage, letting her press the start button on the Bronco and getting the air on before circling back to the rear passenger seat to get her buckled in.

Once I'm in the driver's seat, I see we should have left twenty-five minutes ago. My phone is connected to bluetooth, and I click on the contact Tate sent over, calling Kodi as I back out of the garage. After a moment, a breathless "Hello?"

comes through the speakers.

"Kodi, it's Maverick."

"Oh hi! I just pulled in, are you all waiting on me?" Checking the clock I see that she's right on time.

"Nope, someone gave me trouble this morning. We are just now leaving, I'm so sorry. We should be there in about twenty minutes," I sigh, checking on Bella in the mirror facing her car seat. Her little ponytail is falling to one side and she somehow still has yogurt in her hair.

"It happens to the best of us. I ran out of the apartment, so it sounds like we were both having a moment. Drive safe, and I'll see you both soon." She ends the call and I get "Bella's Jams" playing as we make the drive downtown.

When Bella sees Kodi standing outside of the museum, she immediately takes off running towards her. Kodi crouches down and opens her arms to Bella, who excitedly throws her little body into them.

"Good morning!" Kodi acknowledges me as I approach them. "Ready to go see the bubbles?" she asks Bella as she stands with her in her arms. Bella nods her head enthusiastically.

"Good morning," I smile at her, holding the door open.

"Thank you. How was the drive?" Kodi seems to be taking in the museum to see if anything has changed since she was last here. The first floor typically holds specialized exhibits like the bubble one, as well as the "Crawlers" exhibits for the guests under three. Bella loves to go in there, but we usually head upstairs first where a play grocery store, doctor's office, firetruck, vet office, and camping area all sit. The bright colors of the museum stairs and walls can be overwhelming to the eyes, the vibrant bright lights making sure you can see everything with absolute clarity.

"It was fine. You know parking down here though. Not super great, but we found a spot eventually," I answer her as we wait for the clerk to call us up to the desk.

"Kodi!" Bella says, looking between my face and Kodi's.

"Yeah, that is Kodi. Are you going to show her around the museum today?" I ask her.

"Next," a gruff male voice calls from behind the sterile looking white desk.

"Bubbles please," Bella tells the man. He doesn't smile or even acknowledge her, and I can see Kodi roll her eyes at the man for being so standoffish.

"Here's my membership card. We also have an adult guest today," I tell the man, flashing the barcode for him to scan, then pulling out my card to pay the fee for Kodi's entrance.

"Fifteen seventy-seven." He doesn't look away from his computer screen, and I'm starting to get aggravated with his lack of people skills.

I scan my card, then cough because he hasn't asked if I want a receipt or offered to tell us about the bubble exhibit—which I know about—but it's still typical of the receptionist to ask if we've heard about it. His eyes leave the screen and find mine, "Is there anything else I can help you with?"

"A receipt would be appreciated, sir," I smile at him. He prints and hands it over but doesn't say anything else.

"Alright, have a good day," I knock on the desk and lead

Kodi and Bella away. She sets her down once we are away from the desk.

"So, bubbles first?" I ask, and Bella nods her head before grabbing my hand and guiding me to the exhibit. Kodi follows slightly behind us.

Upon entering the exhibit, the floor feels slippery from all the bubble liquids, and the room is absolute chaos. Kids running in all directions, all of the sensory tables surrounded by more kids blowing bubbles into each other's faces and spilling liquid everywhere, the little circle for kids to "stand inside a bubble" has a line a mile long, and I immediately regret entering this space. As I look at Kodi, she seems calm as she waits for Bella to lead us where she wants to go. Instead of heading further into the room as I expected, Bella lifts her gaze to mine, "I don't want bubbles. Let's do grocery store please."

"Oh thank God," Kodi lets out a breath. "I was going to do it because she seemed excited, but I was not ready for it."

"Me too," I chuckle and we head towards the elevator. Bella presses the up button and then presses the level two one as well. The elevator doors open, and this level is already much calmer than the environment downstairs. Bella heads over to the grocery store area, grabbing a cart and beginning to pull a variety of play foods off the shelf.

"What are you going to make with all those ingredients Bella?" Kodi asks her as she follows her around.

"Scetti," Bella states firmly.

"Oh, it sounds delicious. Do you put cheese on top of your spaghetti?"

"Mmmm. . .no cheese."

"Okay, no cheese. What about garlic bread?" she asks, crouching down beside her, eyes wide. Her tattoos are on display again today as she flails her arms around, having an animated conversation with Bella about garlic bread and ice cream for dessert. Her face is so expressive, letting Bella know when she likes something she said, is confused, or sad that Bella won't let her put cheese on her own spaghetti.

"Are you ready to check out with your groceries?" I ask Bella, noticing her cart is going to start overflowing soon.

"Yep. Scetti time," she says, doing her little happy wiggle. She started doing that when she was excited, about the time she started sitting up on her own. Her upper half moves side to side in a fast and dance-like fashion whenever she's really happy about something. It's one of my favorite things she does, aside from when she's sleepy and cuddles into my chest when she gets tired.

"Can Daddy play cashier?" I ask her.

"Yes, please." She and Kodi load all of her groceries onto the belt, and I begin scanning her items, making the beep sound each time I pass an item over the little red light.

"That'll be eighty-two fifty-seven." I tell them sticking my palm up to get their payment. Bella looks at Kodi expectantly, waiting for her to pay me for the groceries, "So usually I pay for the groceries so she's waiting for you to pay."

"Oh gotcha. One second." She pretends to dig in her black cross body that rests over the curves of her breasts perfectly before handing me her debit card. I pretend to slide it through the machine before handing her a fake receipt and telling them to have a nice day.

We spend the next hour or so playing together. Kodi is actively involved in every exhibit with Bella, once in a while we let her play alone and would chit chat casually about the weather or the silly things Bella would be doing. Now I've got Bella tucked into her carseat, and she's already passed out.

"Thank you for meeting us today. It was helpful for me to see you interacting with her."

"Of course, if given the opportunity to work with Bella I want you to feel comfortable."

"She seems to really like spending time with you," I say, and it's true. Bella doesn't often warm up to strangers this easily.

"The feeling is mutual." She smiles, and I can tell she means what she says.

"So, your background check came back clear, and I would love to extend this job offer to you, but we do need to get some paperwork settled, standard NDA's and other legal jargon. It's to protect mine and Bella's privacy. All that being said, I think Arabella would love to spend more time with you, and I feel like I can trust you with her safety and happiness when I'm not around."

"Absolutely, thank you again for the opportunity. I can already tell that taking care of Bella is going to be an adventure in the best way." Her smile brightens even more as she once again sticks her hand out for me to shake.

"I'll have Tatum get with the legal team and find a time where we can meet down at the arena to solidify everything. Cross all the I's and dot all the T's." I let her hand go, missing the warmth just a little, then slapping myself mentally because *what the fuck*. She's going to be Bella's nanny, and that's all she can ever be.

CHAPTER 10

You Did It!

Kodi

I did it! I got the job! After Maverick and Bella pull away, I do a little happy dance in the front seat of my car then text the group chat that I got the job. Before driving away, I turn on my pop punk playlist and blast "Thnks fr the Mmrs" by Fall Out Boy. The whole drive home my phone is pinging with notifications that I can only assume are my friends freaking out about me working for Maverick and congratulating me.

I get a message as I'm pulling back into the apartment complex.

TATUM REED

> Think you can swing by the stadium on Wednesday to meet with the team lawyers and Maverick to get all of the paperwork out of the way?

SHOT TO THE HART

> **ME**
> Sounds good, do I need to bring anything? Is after 12 okay?

> **TATUM REED**
> Your ID is all you need. Think you can make it by 12:30?

> **ME**
> Definitely.

As soon as I step into Darcy's apartment, squeals erupt from the couch. Darcy, Sinclair, and Harley are all huddled on the couch, wine and charcuterie spread across the small and wobbly coffee table. As I get closer, I see a cake in the middle of the table that says, 'You did it!' in wobbly letters.

I roll my eyes but join my friends on the couch, laughing at their shenanigans.

"Okay, first, hot hockey player, I get why we freaked out. But what I really need to know is if you've heard anything about Bella's Mom or his dating life?"

Harley immediately jumps in. "He just got moved to Tampa from Carolina this year. His social media is private, and no one has figured out where her mom is. It doesn't seem like he dates or goes out much. Aside from a celebration here or there."

Sinclair pipes up with, "He is also the hottest player on the team, and according to every Instagram post on him, no puck bunnies can get or keep his attention."

Harley nods her head in excited agreement, "You sure you

don't want to climb your new boss like a tree, Ko?"

Well, of course I do, but I can't let them know that, I would never hear the end of it. I lift my chin and make eye contact with each of them before saying, with a little uncertainty in my voice, "I absolutely do not want to climb Maverick like a tree."

I know for a fact my cheeks have blushed and Darcy scoffs, "Babe, you are such a bad liar. I give it a month before you're sleeping in his bed."

I gasp in shock. "*Excuse me?* I am classy, it will be at least three months." Knowing in all seriousness that I can't let anything happen with Maverick if I want to keep this job and not end up back on Darcy's couch. We all laugh and spend the rest of the night enjoying each other's company before sprawling out around Darcy's apartment for sleep, wine drunk and giggly.

※

I've never been to a hockey game, but parking at the Tampa arena is a bitch. I approach the entrance that Tatum gave me directions to via email after our text message conversation, and a brooding man stands by the door raising an eyebrow at me as I approach. My tattoos are on display, but I've dressed up a smidge for this occasion. Trading my typical jeans for a pair of slacks that I swiped from D's closet and a button up shirt.

I paste on my biggest grin as I get closer, "Good afternoon. I'm supposed to be meeting with legal today."

"ID?" he asks, skipping over the pleasantries I suppose.

"Here ya go." He cross checks it with a list he has next to him, hands me a guest pass, and then opens the door.

"Up the stairs, left down the hall, check in there." He points towards the giant set of stairs down the hall.

"Thanks, have a great day." I find myself at a reception desk once I make it up the stairs, there an older brunette woman sits behind a computer. "Hello, my name is Kodi Roscoe, and I am supposed to be meeting legal."

"Kodi, you made it," Mavericks voice drags my attention away from the woman in front of me to a conference room a little further down the hall. "Betty, she's here for me. Come on in Kodi." His look is a little more casual today, wearing sweats that cling to his thighs, a black athletic shirt and backwards hat. A small sheen of sweat on his face makes me wonder if he was working out or had practice before our meeting.

I offer the woman a smile before heading towards Maverick. He pulls out a seat for me in front of a stack of papers, heading around the table and sitting down beside the man I assume is the lawyer.

"Ms. Roscoe, thanks for coming in today. I'm Jeremy, one of the attorneys for the Manta Rays, and I'll be going over the paperwork with you. It's nothing crazy, an NDA to ensure that Bella's safety is intact; for example, this NDA prevents you from telling anyone where she is or where you're working unless Mr. Hart gives explicit permission. Another will ensure that if you happen to hear any private Manta Rays business that it will stay private. I will need to borrow your ID for our files, and you'll have a form to give us some basic contact information to fill out. Do you have any questions?"

Jeremy speaks rapidly and leaves no room for argument, not that I was going to argue. This is information I would have kept private regardless, but I'll sign my name on the little dotted line if it means I can secure this job.

"Nope, no questions. It all sounds reasonable to me." I smile at Jeremy, pulling my own pen from my purse as he slides me the stack of papers. I read over each one just to make sure everything he said was clearly stated and I didn't miss anything before filling out and signing each one.

After Jeremy has received the papers back he says, "Alright, Mr. Hart, you all should be good for the date that you had set for her to start. If anything comes up that gives me pause, I'll call you. Did you need anything else today?"

"Nope, I think we are all set. Thank you for your help." Maverick hasn't said a single thing, sitting quietly beside Jeremy as he went over the paperwork and checking his phone every minute or so like he's waiting for a message. It leaves me wondering if he's checking in on Arabella, or he has somewhere else to be, but I imagine making sure the person you're hiring to care for your child is pretty important. "Kodi, can I walk you out?"

"Sure, thanks Jeremy. It was nice to meet you, but hopefully we don't have to meet again." I laugh lightly, but it appears my joke doesn't land because neither of the men even smirk at me. Maverick stands and I follow him out of the room past Betty.

"Thank you for swinging by at such an odd time today. I wanted to get everything in order ASAP, but now is the only time I could get Tatum to watch Bella since she's napping."

"He'll only watch her during nap time?" I ask.

"Yeah, Tatum doesn't particularly want kids, but he adores Bella—even though he would probably never admit it. My Dad had his wellness check today, otherwise I would've asked him to watch her, so Tatum only agreed to watch her if she was asleep."

"Ah, gotcha, that makes sense. I feel like my friend Sinclair is similar; she looks at kids and goes 'ew' now, but she literally works in the childrens ward at Tampa Health Hospital." We pass a coffee cart that smells heavenly, and I think Maverick notices that I've slowed down.

"Coffee for the road?"

"Uh, yes please. I need an afternoon pick me up," I respond as we pivot and join the short queue. Once it's our turn, Maverick orders his caramel macchiato and I order a vanilla cold brew then we continue towards the exit, silently sipping our drinks.

"Can we sit and chat for a moment?" he asks me, gesturing towards a table to the left of the doors.

"Of course. About?"

"So, I realized after your interview, I wasn't super clear about what your schedule would look like. Additionally, those NDAs are pretty tight, but I have a few exceptions to them."

"Okay, let's hear it."

"So I am thinking that Monday through Friday will work from six a.m. to between four and six p.m., depending on the day. Bella typically sleeps until eight or nine, but I have to leave pretty early for practice most days; so, you should still be able to sleep past six as long as you have her monitor on your phone, which I will set you up with. Once I get home, I will take over, but it really will depend on how practice is, if we have any media stuff, meetings, etc," he tells me. It sounds manageable enough. "Now, obviously, when I am out of town, you will be with Bella twenty-four seven. When you travel with us, I will have the team handle hotel arrangements for you two, and you'll still be on your normal schedule, unless I have a day off, then I will hang out with her."

"Okay, all of that sounds good to me. What about the NDA stuff?"

"So, I know the NDA prevents you from letting people know where you are with Bella or bringing her around people. My dad is here and will want to see her sometimes, so I don't mind you bringing her around him. I also assume you have family and friends that you will want to spend time with, but if I'm on the road I don't want to prevent you from seeing them, so I just ask for that communication. The only thing that I ask you to do is not post her on your social media. I barely post about her myself and my page is very private."

"Absolutely. I appreciate you letting me bring her around my friends and Mom so that I can still see them. As far as social media, that will never be an issue." I smile at him before taking another swig of my coffee.

"Okay, perfect, we better get going," he says as he stands, gesturing to the right of the building,

"Well, I'm this way, got to get home to my lil' lady. I will see you in two weeks, text if anything comes up."

"And I'm that way. Thanks for the coffee and have a good afternoon." I smile at him before turning and heading to my car.

CHAPTER 11

Dinosaurs

Kodi

Two weeks later, I'm typing in a gate code before pulling into Maverick's neighborhood with my car full of my belongings. I find myself thinking that this is not the home I expected a man of his caliber to own, but I also have come to realize that he is much more down-to-earth than I expected. While the house is large, it's not big and luxurious or on the Bay like you'd expect. It's got character, made of brick, with a wrap around porch and fenced-in backyard. There's what looks like a two-car garage and three sports cars, plus a motorcycle, parked on the road out front. Maverick didn't tell me to expect anyone to be here, but it's possible he had family come in at the last minute, or maybe something came up with the team.

I pull into the driveway, grab my purse and a box, and head to the front door. It swings open and Maverick comes out greeting me with a smile and takes the box out of my hand. I turn around to grab a few more, but from behind me hear, "Don't worry about those boxes, a couple of my teammates are here. I totally blanked that Bella and I were hosting family dinner this month."

Oh great, I'm wearing leggings and an oversized shirt, and my hair is pulled into a messy bun. I probably look like I just rolled out of bed, and I'm about to meet who knows how many of his teammates. "So we can grab them and take them to your room."

With a shrug and a, "thank you", I head inside with just my purse and emotional-support water bottle. I almost get bowled over by a brick of a man covered in tattoos and a thick black bun sitting on top of his head, walking backwards towards the front door. At the last minute, he turns around and stops before he can knock me over. An appreciative look passes over my body as he eyes me, pastes on a shit eating grin, sticks a hand out, and says in a thick Russian accent, "Well aren't you a pretty thing? I'm Niklaus, and it is fully my pleasure to meet you."

I feel my cheeks heat and hear Maverick behind me, "Nik stop flirting with my child's caretaker and get your ass out here to help me unload these boxes."

I shake his hand quickly, ignoring how much I liked the assertiveness in Mavericks tone, mumble "Kodi", and rush inside.

I slowly make my way down the hallway covered in photos of Bella, the team, and a man and woman who I assume are Maverick's parents. Fidgeting with the hair tie that lives on my wrist, I continue into the living room where I'm greeted by Arabella surrounded by three other men, who

I assume are also Mavericks teammates making dinosaur noises and chasing her around the room. This makes me laugh loud enough that all eyes turn to me. I awkwardly wave as Maverick sidles up next to me.

"This is Kodi. She'll be staying here and helping me with Arabella. You cavemen are to stay away from her."

I giggle, and while I shouldn't like that he has made the decision for me on whether his teammates are an option or not, it makes me feel like he wants me here and to be comfortable in his home.

A few groans erupt throughout the room, and the man acting like what I can only imagine is a T-rex mumbles, "Way to ruin the fun." Maverick shoots daggers his way and the man replies, "Sorry. . .I'm Dom. It's nice to meet you."

Dom is smaller in stature compared to the other guys, seems younger and more muscular, with a full head of curls and deep tan skin. Pterodactyl stands up and introduces himself as Maverick's personal assistant, Tatum. Dirty-blonde hair perfectly swept to the side, hazel green eyes that I just know Darcy would be entranced by, definitely works out, but it isn't super pronounced. I make a mental note to keep those two away from each other.

The last man peeks up from behind a pair of glasses, gives me a shy smile and says, "What's up? I'm Collins." He is definitely more reserved than the others, has dark red hair, is covered in freckles and is absolutely adorable. Being less burly than the other men in the room, Collins doesn't look like he would play hockey.

Dom pipes up with, "Don't let Collins fool you, he isn't

as shy as he's acting. I think it's just cause you're like really pretty." He's raising his eyebrows at me, causing me to roll my eyes and stifle a laugh.

"Well, on that note, I think we should eat before dinner gets cold." Nik comes out of the adjoining kitchen, clearly having dropped my boxes somewhere, presumably my room. We all make our way into the dining room.

I end up sandwiched between Arabella and Dom who chats my ear off, asking rapid-fire questions like, "Favorite color?"

"Purple."

"Favorite ice cream flavor?"

"Chocolate chip cookie dough."

"Dude, this isn't twenty questions," Tatum cuts in.

"I'm just trying to get to know her. Favorite music genre?" Dom glares at Tatum across the table.

"Ummm, probably pop punk."

"Favorite flower?"

"Ooo, daisies, but sunflowers are a close second."

"That's enough, Dom. Let the woman eat," Nik demands.

"Fine, Dad. Last one, I promise, and this one is the most important. Favorite food?" Dom asks with a huff.

"I can't pick one dish. Favorite cuisine though, Mexican."

He turns to me with a confident grin. "I'll have to host the next family dinner and make my moms famous tacos."

Maverick chuckles, "By making his moms famous tacos, he means he will bring the ingredients to his Moms house and she will make them." This gains some laughs around the table.

Dom turns red and focuses on his food before I lean over and whisper, "Regardless of whether you or your mom make them, I'm sure they will be delicious. Can't wait." This earns a smile, and he immediately is back to his bright and bubbly demeanor.

The guys are great and I'm kind of glad I got to meet them, but I'm beat. Once Nik and Collins are clearing the table, I look to Maverick and ask, "Do you mind showing me to my room? I'm tired, and I think I could use a shower and sleep."

"I was just about to put Bella down for the night, would you like to see her bedtime routine first?" he replies.

"Yes, of course." He scoops Arabella up after the guys pass her around the room for hugs and forehead kisses. This is the cutest thing I've ever seen, and I am in awe of how loved this little girl is. It puts an ache in my chest, unwanted feelings creep their way to the forefront of my brain.

I begin following them down the hallway where we take a right into Arabella's room. Along one wall is a sun mural that says, "You are my sunshine" painted into it, and below lays her small bed with sunshine and daisy sheets that match her mural. Toys litter her floor, and my eyes immediately find Floppy in the corner. I grab him and place him in her bed.

Maverick catches my attention, leading me into her attached bathroom and guides me through her night time routine. "She doesn't enjoy getting her hair brushed, but if you brush it while she's 'brushing' her teeth it makes it easier. Or, in the mornings, while she's watching TV. It's curly, so I definitely recommend you braid it before bed," he mentions as he expertly french braids her hair then helps her finish her teeth. "So, when needed, she loves a bath, she has a ton of toys as you can see, but we are going to forgo that tonight. Alright, Bella, go pick two books and we can show Ms. Kodi how you read." I watch in awe from the opposite side of Bella's bed as Maverick reads The Rainbow Fish and Llama Llama Red Pajama, Bella finishing some of the lines for him, and I can't help but smile at them. He turns her nightlight and sound machine on once he's read the books. Simple enough. I think she and I will be able to manage that.

The last step brings that ache back to my heart, those unwanted feelings and thoughts from earlier come boiling back to the surface with a vengeance. Maverick leans down, placing a gentle kiss on Bella's forehead, and she giggles, beaming up at him. My father worked so much that I never got these experiences, my mom did everything for me. And then one day, when I was about eight years old, he left us. He has a whole other family out there, getting the love and time that Mom and I never did. It leads me to wonder if my half-siblings got this sort of bedtime routine from him. At least that's what I see on his social media, the only way he ever bothered to let me into his life since he left. Bella is one lucky little girl to be so loved and cared for.

CHAPTER 12

Man, Am I Fucked.

Maverick

A few thoughts ran through my head during dinner and I'm reflecting on them as Kodi follows me quietly out of Bella's room and down the hall. I don't like how close she was when she was speaking with Dom, I found myself wishing she was leaning into me and laughing as I asked her all of her favorite things. I don't like the suggestive glares she received from everyone when she walked in. I definitely logged all of her favorites in my brain for a later time, just in case I need them. *Even though I definitely shouldn't need them.*

I selfishly put her in the bedroom closest to mine, even though I should have put her across the hall from Bella to make her job easier.

She steps into her room behind me and gasps. The room isn't much smaller than mine, I made sure she has a king bed, plenty of storage, and her ensuite has a standalone tub so she can unwind whenever she likes. "Maverick. This is too much. I really. . .Honestly, I just need a bed," she laughs lightly.

"You deserve a space to escape, and I want you to be as

comfortable as possible here." She gives me a tight smile, shifting her weight back and forth letting me know she's uncomfortable, and I immediately feel as though maybe I overstepped. "Kodi, I'm sorry. I just. . .we've never had anyone stay here, and I wanted. . ."

Before I can continue my nervous ramble she cuts me off, "Hey, hey. It's okay. I've just never in my life had this much space to call my own. I mean, I was sleeping on a couch before you offered me this job, so I really do appreciate it. Tonight was just a little overwhelming, I'm out of energy and well,thank you, seriously." Just the confirmation that she appreciates the effort I've made is enough to calm my nerves about the situation.

To be truthful, I haven't had a woman in my home since Arabella's mother left in the middle of the night without a word. Having Kodi stay here, although we're not involved, still makes me nervous for Arabella's heart, and truthfully, mine too. If Kodi ever decides to move onto a different job, I get transferred back to the team in Carolina, or I meet someone being a few of the possibilities that could leave Bella and I brokenhearted. That's not including the ways that I refuse to give any thought to how beautiful she looks in the dim lamp light checking out the books on the shelves I had installed, or the way her curves call for me to grab them in the leggings that I crave to slide down her legs.

"I love to read, I can't wait to arrange my personal collection on these," Kodi says as she turns to me and gives me a shy smile and runs a hand along the shelves.

"What do you read?" I swear she turns a little pink, but

maybe I'm imagining it.

"Oh, just uh… romance mostly." I wonder if she reads monster romance, or if she's into fantasies or classics like Pride and Prejudice. Or, if she's into the ones that Grace refers to as her spicy books. I didn't need to know my little sister reads spicy books, but she subjected me to that information against my will.

"Well, I will leave you with your romance books and your space. My room is just a little further down the hall if you need anything at all. The guys will probably hang out a little longer, so if they get too loud, just text me, and I'll shut them up. Goodnight, Kodi."

"Goodnight, Maverick. Thank you again."

I head towards the theater, where the guys normally gather while I put Arabella to bed. A giant screen built into the wall sits on the far wall, a big black sectional takes up a majority of the floor space, and a small mini bar, snack pantry, and popcorn machine line the back wall. Sure enough, they have the Nintendo on. Dom is spread out on the floor, a pillow tucked under his chin near Nik's feet with snacks while Nik is typing on his phone with a scowl. Collins and Tatum seem to be in the middle of a very intense round of Mario Kart.

"Dude, throw another shell at me and see what happens!" Collins growls through gritted teeth. Tate responds with only a laugh.

I opt to plop down next to Nik, "You okay dude?"

He smooths his face out so quickly the grimace is barely noticeable. "Yeah bro, you know Romy. Every couple months she begs me to take her back."

I scowl, and Dom pops his head up, "I still don't understand what you saw in her man. You're so much better than that." I never met Nik's ex-wife, they were divorced before I moved here. They've all been playing together for years, and when I got traded to Tampa, they kind of forced their friendship on me when they noticed I wasn't hitting the bars after games. When they learned I had Bella, they began the family dinners so that they could get to know her and I, and I'm grateful for their companionship. Collins and Tatum mumble their agreement with Dom and Nik clenches his fist at his side. Dom notices and decides to quickly change the topic, "So anyway, Mav, how did you find Kodi?"

Before I can say anything Tatum basically yells, "He ran into her in the ice cream aisle while chasing after Arabella. She introduced herself as KJ at the time. While we were looking at potential nanny candidates, I found a resume for a Kodi that I felt Maverick would appreciate interviewing because of her experience. Then, KJ showed up for her interview and KJ was actually Kodi then they figured out an arrangement, and now she lives here."

"Well, isn't that an interesting little coincidence?" Collins grins.

"You know if she's single?" Dom waggles his eyebrows at me, and now I'm the one clenching my fists.

"Don't you even think about getting near her, Dominic," I attempt to keep my facial expression neutral because even a slight change in expression will have them busting my balls about Kodi.

Dom is basically vibrating with excitement, "Oh dude,

you two are totally going to—" *Thwack*. "Owwwwww," Dom whines looking at Nik with disdain.

"Be respectful, Dom. Yes, she's gorgeous, and yes, they will probably get to know each other better. But you don't have to take it that far." Dom averts his eyes and quickly apologizes. If it was anyone but Nik, Dom would have continued on just to poke buttons, but Nik is the oldest of the group so we all respect him.

After that, the conversation turns back to the upcoming start of the season. We're all excited and ready, but my thoughts are elsewhere. Leaving Bella with an essential stranger, spending time alone with said stranger; the fear of leaving my Dad in Florida for the first time since Ma passed, and how he will cope with not caring for Bella while I'm gone. How the hell am I going to balance all of these things? I wish Ma could be here to watch Arabella grow, give me advice on how to handle my growing attraction to Kodi, and to watch me play my first season with a new team.

"Earth to Mav," Tatum is looking right at me waiting for a response I don't have.

"Sorry man. What did you say?" He seems thrown off by my lack of awareness, and as my best friend, I know he's going to bring this up when all the guys aren't here.

"I said, I think we're all going to head out. It's getting late and we know Arabella will have you up bright and early."

I sigh. "Right, yeah. No problem. Thanks for coming over."

The guys help me pack everything up, put away snacks, and clean dirty dishes. They all leave with a chorus of 'good lucks'. On autopilot, I set the security alarm before retreating into the darkened house.

It's when I'm alone, under the stream of the shower, that I come to grips with it. *Man, am I fucked*. Stepping out of the shower and drying off, I head towards my bed, pulling my covers back and laying down, making sure the sound on the app connected to the camera in Bella's room is loud enough that it will wake me up. I will myself to sleep, hoping that I can control myself for all of our sakes.

CHAPTER 13

How Do You Take It?

Maverick

The next morning, I turn over looking at my phone to see it's 10 a.m.

There's no way I woke up that late. There's no way Bella let me sleep in this late.

Throwing myself out of the bed, pulling on my sweats, I rush down the hallway and hear Bella's soft giggles, but not from her room. Following the sound, I round the corner into the living room where Bella and Kodi are sitting on the floor and the music of Moana plays softly in the background. My heart does a little stutter, a weird feeling of calm and maybe hope, hope I shouldn't have, seeing how comfortable Bella is with Kodi already.

"Morning, Maverick," Kodi is smiling at me from the floor, Bellas arms wrapped around her neck. "I hope you don't mind, I heard her stirring when I got up and figured we could let you sleep in." Giving me a small smile.

"Not a problem at all. I honestly can't tell you when the

last time I slept in on a Saturday was."

"There's coffee and pancakes in the kitchen. We even added extra chocolate chips in them, didn't we, Bella?" My daughter looks up to Kodi then to me nodding enthusiastically.

"Ooo, my favorite! Do you need more coffee?" I ask.

"Actually, that'd be great. Thank you!" She hands over her empty mug.

"How do you take it?" Oh shit. She's turning red. Maybe that came out wrong. It definitely came out wrong. Trying to alleviate the awkwardness, "Cream, sugar, black?"

"Cream and sugar are good." She's not looking at me. Fuck. I really need to filter my thoughts. I rush into the kitchen, plating my pancakes, preparing our coffees then head back into the living room. I sit on the opposite end of the couch, handing Kodi her coffee, she smiles in return.

"So what's on the agenda for today?" Honestly, I haven't thought that far ahead. Saturdays are usually just Bella and I. Sometimes we just hang out in the house, other times we go out for lunch, and other times we head over to the aquarium or zoo.

"Let's get you more acquainted with Bella's routine and go over the travel schedule. The beginning of the season is probably going to be pretty hectic, so it might be better to keep y'all home, but we have a game in about a month in North Carolina against my home state and original team. That would probably be a good one to go to. Bella hasn't really been to many games, but I think she's about the age where she might enjoy it."

"Oh, I've always wanted to visit there. Were you born

in North Carolina?" Curiosity and excitement swim in her expression.

"Born and raised. I was lucky I got drafted to play for them, most people don't get contracted in their home states."

"Oh, yeah." She fiddles with a piece of lint on the couch. "Honestly I don't know much about hockey. Or any sport really. Maybe I can start watching your games on TV to learn and you could teach me about the game."

"Wait a minute. You've never watched a hockey game in your life?"

"I didn't say that," she laughs. "I've just fallen asleep during almost every sports game I've ever watched."

Throwing myself back on the couch, I cry, "I'm hurt!"

We are both laughing now, Bella joining us, even though I'm sure she has no idea what's going on. I scoop her up as she giggles, holding her close to my chest, relishing her arms wrapped around my neck.

"Alright, Bella, what do you want to do until lunch? We can go swimming, we can play, or we can color?"

"The park!" she squeals.

"Baby, it's way too hot for the park today."

"PARK!" her squeal sounding more frustrated than before.

"I know you love the park Bella, but it's too hot for that. We can swim, we can play with your toys, or we can color."

"Daddy, park please." Her little eyes looking into mine, beginning to fill with tears."I want to swing."

"How am I supposed to say no to that face? We can go, but not for long, and you have to drink your water," I tell her, and her tear filled eyes immediately brighten as her smile expands. I turn to Kodi, "You can stay here and when we get back I'll show you how we do her lunch and nap routine. I won't subject you to the heat of Florida today."

"Sounds good. I'll keep unpacking," Kodi says, "Y'all have fun!"

I take Bella and head to the car, getting her and Floppy buckled into her carseat before making the short drive to the park.

"Alright ,little lady, let's go play." Bella's little body wiggles in excitement as I get her unbuckled and set on the ground beside me. "Hand please." She eagerly grabs my thumb with her little hand, attempting to drag me towards the playground. The fact that she thinks she can drag my body behind hers makes me chuckle, and I play into it, pretending to trip over my own feet as she pulls me forward. Once we are inside the gated area, Bella takes off on the rubber turf.

"Slide!" she yells, running up the playground and giggling as she comes down the bright blue plastic. I stand to the side of the playground watching my little girl run laps, go down the slide, climb up the playground, over and over again.

"Daddy, let's swing please!" Bella and her little pink cheeks come up, patting me on the leg.

"Yes, but water first." She takes her pink princess water bottle, gulps some down, hands her bottle back, and then once again, takes off towards the swings. I follow closely behind her, lifting her into the bucket swing and beginning to push her.

"Higher, Daddy, higher." I put a little more of my weight

behind the next push.

"Five minutes Bella and then we are going to head home for lunch." And in an instant my sweet and happy little girl has dissolved into tears and kicking feet. I slow the swing to a stop, attempting to get Bella's attention by placing my hands on her knees. "Bella, hey. Remember we were going to swing and then go home for lunch. But, if you're kicking and screaming we can't enjoy our last few minutes at the park."

"No home, Daddy."

"We have four more minutes then home, okay?" She nods, wiping at her eyes, and we enjoy our last four minutes before heading home for lunch.

"How was the park?" Kodi asks as I get Bella settled in her tower at the counter, while I grab the ingredients to fix her a peanut butter and jelly sandwich. She instinctively grabs Bella's water bottle, refilling it with fresh, cold water before placing it in front of her with a bowl of berries.

"Thanks for doing that. She had a blast, but it is too hot to be outside like that right now."

"I figured she might need a snack when you got back. I'm waiting for the fall weather to kick in."

I place Bella's sandwich in front of her and swiftly clean up. She scarfs it down, clearly hungry from her adventure at the park before she begins to yawn.

"Tired Bella?" Kodi asks, Bella gives her a small nod. "Does nap time look like bedtime?"

"Pretty much, but I typically just do one book," I say

before picking her up and leading the way to her room. As soon as her head hits the pillow, her eyes close, and we exit the room.

I should have left ten minutes ago, but I couldn't drag myself out of bed. I'm exiting my room, towards the kitchen, to grab my protein shake before heading to practice, when I swear I hear tiny cries coming from Bella's room. I stop short of Kodi's room, thinking Bella may just be whining in her sleep, and when they calm down, I go to take a step when Kodi's door swings open and her smaller frame bounces off of mine. I reach out to steady her and rather than the soft feel of clothes, I'm met with the texture of terry cloth. She definitely is only in a towel, and the image I'm greeted with when I let her go and take her in has my jaw tightening and regretting my decision to wear sweats to the arena. Her dark black hair is dripping water onto the wood floors, her towel exposing her long legs and the swells of her breasts, her green eyes wide as she jumps back with a panicked squeal.

"Holy fuck, you scared the shit out of me. I thought you were gone already," she gasps, gripping her towel a little tighter to her body.

"I was on my way out when she started whining, so I was waiting to see if I needed to go in and get her calm before I head out." My eyes refuse to leave hers, seeing her wrapped in a towel was a vision I never thought I was going to get. Ever.

"Ugh, I'm sorry. I heard her whimpering while I was in

the shower, clearly. I just wanted to get her calm, hopefully back to sleep, and well, now we're here." She gestures to the puddle pooling at her feet. "I'll uh, get that cleaned up."

"Yep, if you wouldn't mind." I let myself do one more sweep of Kodi standing in my hall, dripping wet, gritting my teeth to avoid surging forward and ripping the towel away from her body just to see what hides beneath. "I really gotta get going, text or call if anything comes up. I should be home a little earlier today." Then, swiftly turning around, I decide I'll just grab a smoothie on my way into work.

CHAPTER 14
Fwoppy House

Maverick

I leave tomorrow for our first official game of the season, leaving Kodi and Arabella for their first full weekend alone, so we decide to spend our Thursday at the aquarium. We've finally got Arabella secured in her stroller, much to her disagreement, and we are walking through the doors of the aquarium. Both of the girls look adorable; they've got matching space buns, Arabella insisted on putting on a band T-shirt and her black high-top converse "just like Kodi", but instead of ripped jeans, she's wearing cotton shorts so she's comfortable.

We wander through the exhibits, making stops at all of Bella's favorite animals, spending almost an hour at the "fwoppy house" as Bella calls it. Kodi seems just as intrigued by these creatures as Bella. Kodi is sitting cross-legged next to Arabella while I stand back with the stroller letting them watch the stingrays glide through the water so elegantly alongside an array of colorful fish, sharks and other sea creatures. Against my better judgment, I snap a quick photo of the girls, their dark shadows against the huge enclosure. This is the type of photo I would love to make my phone background. For just a moment, I let myself imagine every weekend like this, except Kodi is mine, not just as my friend and caregiver for Bella, but mine to hold and care for, to love.

"Excuse me, Mr. Maverick," a small voice says from beside me, breaking my derailed train of thought. I find a little boy about eight years old looking up at me and wearing my jersey.

I lean down, "How can I help you little man?"

"Well, uh, my name's Hunter, and I want to be a hockey player like you when I grow up!" He is beaming now, excitement filling his eyes.

"I would love to watch you on the ice one day buddy." Behind Hunter's head, I see Kodi and Bella headed back in my direction hand in hand. "Why don't we take a picture? I think your Mom is waiting for you." *And I've got two pretty girls that I owe lunch.*

Hunter nods his head enthusiastically while Kodi gets Bella situated in her stroller. We snap a few photos and bother an aquarium team member for a sharpie so I can sign his jersey and start heading towards the exit.

"Are you hungry?" I ask Kodi who is walking next to me, fiddling with that hair tie on her wrist again.

"Yeah, actually, want to go eat by the water?"

"Yes, I know just the place, and we can walk from here.'"

Twenty minutes later, we are seated at a table by the water, Bella knocked out in the stroller parked next to our table. We order water and stuffed mushrooms when the waitress comes by.

"One question," Kodi states.

"One answer." My lips quirking up into a grin.

"Do you ever think about where you would be if you weren't in this moment?"

"Like if I wasn't a hockey player single-parenting a toddler? Sometimes."

"What does that moment look like to you?"

"I think I would probably still be in North Carolina, maybe married with a big piece of land. Probably working a corporate desk job."

"I could definitely see that. I can't imagine athletes, who seem to be constantly going, able to sit behind a desk all day though."

"I actually have a degree in business. My dad made sure I picked a degree that I could use if hockey didn't pan out. What about you?" I can't help but want to know more about what hides behind those green eyes. I find myself leaning into the table a little more, as if that will help me understand her better.

"Hmmm…" She's absentmindedly moving her straw in circles in her glass. "I'd probably be married too and unhappy about it." A disbelieving laugh leaves her lips. "Hindsight is twenty-twenty."

"That's right. Do you have any siblings?" The urge to question her further is right on the tip of my tongue, but I know I shouldn't push her to share more than she wants to.

"Ha, that's complicated, but I'd rather not talk about it."

"I get it. I have just one sister and brother-in-law. They live in California, no kids yet though." I make a mental note to call Grace when I have a free minute to check in on her.

Our waitress stops by to grab our order. I place mine, ordering a burger and fries that I know our nutritionist would be yelling at me for, but Kodi seems to be deep in thought. Her green eyes almost reflect the color of the river she's looking over, her loose hairs flying in the wind. The waitress coughs, dragging Kodi's attention back to the table.

"Just a burger, extra pickles and fries please." She smiles at the waitress who scurries away.

"If you could visit anywhere in the world, where would it be Kodi?"

"Europe. I want to experience the culture, the food, the people, the sights."

"Anywhere specific?"

"Italy or maybe Ireland. To be honest, just traveling around all of Europe would be ideal."

"Amsterdam is underrated, it's quaint and beautiful. Ma and I went there when I graduated high school." Ma, man I miss her. I think she would love Kodi, I can feel her encouraging me to get to know her better. Like a soft, uplifting hand on my shoulder.

"That sounds like a really fun bonding trip. Is there anywhere you haven't been yet?"

"It was, we had some. . .interesting experiences there. I would love to visit Japan, the culture seems intriguing, and there are some beautiful sights to see."

"What kind of experiences? Japan seems beautiful too,

especially when the cherry blossoms are vibrant and pink."

"Well, one night we were trying to find a pub to grab a beer and hear some live music. The local we asked for directions must have heard *club* and sent us into the red-light district. You can imagine what a shock that was. We decided at that moment to pay for our phone service so we could use google." A smile breaks across Kodi's face, lighting up the rest of her features. Rosy pink cheeks lifting, green eyes squinted, her head thrown back as she laughs, the sweet sound like a melody in my ears. One that I could easily see myself getting addicted to.

"That sounds crazy but like so much fun. I don't have any stories like that."

"Really?"

"No, it was just my mom and I. She did her best, but we couldn't afford to travel like that. And recently I was in a relationship for a while where it was never on my radar to adventure, but it turned out that's something he always wanted." She rolls her eyes.

"Oof. That's fucked."

"You're telling me. Everything happens for a reason though. I don't think I would've ended up here if that relationship didn't end."

"So, where have you traveled to?"

"My mom and I have done some smaller trips around Florida, Georgia, Tennessee, and New York City. That one was especially fun, my mom saved up for months to afford it and we had the best time. The pizza was just as good as they say it is." She smiles as she recalls that memory with her

Mom.

"Deep dish or pan? This could make or break your employment," I ask, invoking a fake seriousness into my voice that makes her smile widen.

"Pan, deep is too soupy for me."

"Good answer." I grin back at her.

"Do you have any other crazy travel stories with your mom?" she asks me.

"No, not really. We always did one big family trip a year, but that was the only time Ma and I travelled with just the two of us." I would've loved to take mom on her dream trip, which also just so happened to be Japan when the cherry blossoms were in bloom.

"Do you want to give Bella memories like that with you?"

"I do. I haven't done much traveling with her since she's so young, but I think once the season is over, I want to do a small trip, just her and I. Maybe Disney World or a cabin in the mountains."

"Oh, you should do the mountains. I'm definitely a mountain and not a beach girl."

"Yet you stayed in Florida your whole life?" I question.

"Like I said, relationship and family. Now I think I'm just comfortable here."

At this moment, our waitress drops our food off. We eat our meals in silence until Arabella wakes up and insists that Kodi shares her fries with her, which she does willingly. Once the bill is paid, we head back to the house so I can get ready for my trip.

CHAPTER 15

God, I'm In Trouble.

Kodi

The house is quiet, soft music flows from my speaker. Bella is down for the night, and Maverick escaped to his room to pack leaving me to entertain myself.

I'm snuggled up with my e-reader to finish the wolf-shifter, second chance romance novel I've been reading before I call it a night. It's fast-paced, fun, and I think I'm in love with Artemis just as much as Jay is. My phone pings from my nightstand and I see I've got a message from Sin in our group chat.

> **SIN**
> How was your aquarium trip with Daddy Mav?

> **ME**
> Her name is Bella, and don't call him that. It's weird.

SHOT TO THE HART

DARCY

> Well, Sin isn't wrong. Mav is a daddy and a DADDY. *eggplant emoji*

HARLEY

> Come on Ko. You know it's going to happen. We can all stop pretending you don't have the hots for your boss.

ME

> I don't have the hots for my boss. *eye roll emoji*

3 dislikes immediately roll through the chat

ME

> But the aquarium trip was actually pretty nice. We grabbed lunch by the river. Mav and I got to know each other a little better.

ME

> No, I will not be divulging details.

SIN

> Respect but also annoying.

HARLEY

> Wait...Did you just call him Mav?

ME

Um...Yeah?

DARCY

Oh, they are totally going to bone. She's using his nickname.

ME

Bitch what? All the guys call him Mav, why can't I?

SIN

Because babes, you're his employee. They're his friends.

ME

Alright, well on that note, I am going back to my book and ignoring you weirdos. Will try to update y'all throughout the weekend. Love ya *red heart emoji*

DARCY

Night babes. Kisses *lips emoji*

HARLEY

Sweet dreams *sleep emoji*

SIN

Love you to the moon and back *moon emoji*

With that, I set my phone back down and pad to my door,

getting ready to turn my bedroom light off, when there's a soft but sure knock. I figured Mav would be asleep by now but I guess I was wrong. I look down at myself realizing I am most definitely underdressed because I was not expecting company. I should probably put on pants, but against my better judgment I decide not to. My shirt is huge, I don't think he'll notice so I pull the door open.

"Hey, Mav." I stop in my tracks, the man is shirtless, in low-slung gray sweats and his hair is dripping wet—the deep V of his stomach pointing somewhere that I am suddenly very curious about. I resist the urge to squirm as he eyes me, briefly lingering on my exposed legs before bringing his gaze back to mine. He smells like citrus and rain. My room feels ten degrees hotter, and my heart has kicked up a notch. Doing my best to keep my tone casual, I ask, "How can I help ya?"

"Hi, Darlin'. Just wanted to let you know I will be out of the house by four a.m. I wanted to check in, see if you needed anything, and make sure your phone was still connected to the camera in Bella's room." Darlin'. That's new, and honestly I'm not mad about it.

"Nope, I think we're all good. When will you be back?" I ask.

"Late Sunday. Don't wait up." He throws me a wink, teasing evident in his tone.

"Wasn't planning on it, Big Guy." I pull my bottom lip into my mouth rocking back and forth. My mouth is very dry, that wink has my knees wobbling beneath me. *God, I'm in trouble.*

Next thing I know, a gentle hand is lifting my gaze to

his, my breaths are coming in faster with our proximity. "I'm serious Kodi. If you need anything at all, you call me. Understand?" I might combust if I have to maintain eye contact with him any longer. Those baby blues could knock a grown woman out, and I'm feeling pretty close.

"I. . .Uh. Yeah, I'll call you if I need anything at all. Got it." His hand has fallen back to his side and he's taken a step back, his chest rising and falling at a similar pace to mine.

"Goodnight, Darlin'." He's smiling and turning towards his room.

"Night Mav. Sweet dreams," I whisper yell at him, watching him walk down the hallway hoping he'll turn around. When he does turn back, he flashes me another one of those cocky smirks, and I feel my cheeks flush. Slowly closing the door, I wonder if his mind was in a similar place to mine. The thought keeps me up most of the night, overanalyzing every interaction I've had with Mav recently.

Early the next morning, Bella's sweet little voice comes through my phone. She's chatting about who knows what, but I'm glad she woke up in a good mood. Dragging myself out of bed and pulling on a pair of leggings, I make my way down the hall to her room. Heading over to her bed, I scoop her up, get her diaper changed, and decide that today is going to be a pajama day.

"Alright Bella, wanna be lazy today?" I ask as I plop her into her kitchen tower, slowly pouring a cup of coffee and setting it into the microwave to heat it up. It's evident it's been sitting since Maverick left this morning.

"Simba. Watch Simba!" she says excitedly. She hasn't

quite grasped the concept that the movie is called Lion King. I love the moments when little ones are still experiencing the world for the first time, where they don't quite grasp reality and live in a state of bliss. Where movies are known as the characters and everything is exciting.

"You want to watch Lion King?"

"Yeah, Simba!"

"Okay," I can't help but chuckle at her, "do you want oatmeal or toast and eggs for breakfast?"

"Oatmeals with rasp-erries," the b in raspberries gets lost on her little tongue.

"Coming right up." While I make her oatmeal, I turn on the playlist Maverick shared with me called "Bella's Jams" and hand Bella a few of her books to flip through while she waits. She devours her oatmeal, and once I get her cleaned up we head into the living room for our movie marathon. Bella cuddles up to my side with Floppy, and once the movie starts, I pull out my phone to make sure that Maverick hasn't texted, but I do have messages from Mom and of course Andy.

> **MOM**
> How's the new job?

> **ME**
> Just getting settled in. First weekend alone with the little lady.

> **MOM**
> It's going okay so far?

ME

Great, I'm really happy here.

MOM

Good, I love you sweetie.

ME

Love you too.

I tap over to see what Andrew wants, knowing it's probably him asking me to let him back into my life. Which is absolutely not happening.

ANDREW

KJ, talk to me. You can't possibly still be mad at me.

ME

You've got to be fucking kidding me with this shit. I'm not mad at you, but I'm not forgiving you. Go suck up to Lyla.

ANDREW

She left because she thinks I'm still stuck on you.

ME

Sounds like a you problem. Bye.

My phone buzzes a few more times, but I choose to ignore him and focus on the movie of my childhood. Halfway through Lion King, Bella has dozed off and I can feel my eyes getting heavy, so I let them fall closed.

CHAPTER 16
Dad Stuff

Maverick

Coming off of a win means that Coach gave us a day off to spend time with our families before we leave again. So I've decided to give Kodi a break and spend the day with Bella since I am leaving again for Minnesota at the end of this week. When I let her know she wouldn't have to work today via text, she told me she was going right back to sleep. My phone pings with a notification from the group chat.

NIK
What's everyone up to today?

DOM
Gym. Tan. Laundry.

TATUM
Bro. You didn't just reference Jersey Shore.

DOM

I did. And I don't regret it one bit.

I take this opportunity to send a photo of Bella and her barbies spread across the living room floor.

ME

Dad stuff. Probably also laundry.

TATE

Sometimes she makes me wonder if I don't actually want kids.

COLLINS

Literally nothing. Being around you guys all weekend is exhausting.

NIK

Ouch bro.

COLLINS

I will not apologize for it.

ME

The weather's nice. Y'all want to come over, we can grill and take Bella swimming?

A resounding "yes" rings throughout the group chat just

as Kodi enters the living room.

"Hey," she grumbles, looking a little worse for wear.

"You feeling okay?" I know not to tell a woman she doesn't look good because it never ends well.

A noise similar to a snarl comes from her direction. "Ugh, yeah. Just lady stuff. I wanted to grab coffee and a snack then go back to my hole."

"Do you need anything? Do you mind if the guys come hang out? We were going to take this little lady swimming and do a little BBQ since it's nice out. You're more than welcome to join us."

She laughs, "Maverick. It's your house, you don't need my permission to invite people over. As fun as that sounds, I may need a raincheck. And I don't need anything. Thank you though."

I give her a smile as she exits the room. Pulling out my phone, I place a grocery drop off order for the things I noticed Kodi had scrawled on the notepad in the kitchen, as well as some stuff for later. I throw in a few womens products, snacks, and drinks to help her stay hydrated; all things that a quick google search says most women crave or need during this time of the month.

An hour later, the guys are all outside with Bella and the grocery order is dropped off, so I head to the front door to receive the items. I organize them in the kitchen, putting all the items I got for Kodi in a separate bag.

I head towards her room, but her door is closed. I knock softly, bouncing back and forth between my feet waiting for her to answer. After a minute of waiting, I decide to leave the bag at her door and type out a quick text to let her know I left it there.

As I turn away, the door creeps open and a groggy Kodi is shooting daggers at me.

Oh shit, what did I do wrong?

CHAPTER 17

BECAUSE FEELINGS AND NICE GESTURES AND HUGS.

Kodi

Oh my God. My body is trying to take me out. The hot bath didn't help. The meds aren't helping. Staying hydrated isn't helping. And to make things better, now someone is knocking on my bedroom door.

Groaning, I pull myself out of bed and gingerly make my way to the door. Opening it, I notice a bag of groceries sitting on the floor and Maverick standing there looking like he got caught with his hand in the cookie jar.

"Um, what's up?" Not sure how to approach whatever this is.

"Well. . .uh. . .I figured you could use some stuff and I had to order groceries anyways. There's some meds and snacks and lady products you might need in there. I just wanted to make sure you had everything you needed. The house isn't really stocked for female company."

I think my eyes are tearing up a little bit, and my heart stutters at this gesture. Whenever this time of the month rolled around, Andy would leave me to fend for myself. He didn't feel the need to care for or check on me, using it as an excuse to give me "alone time" and sit in his gaming room, paying me no mind. That should have been a sign that he didn't care as much as he led me to believe, but I was blinded by his empty promises.

Without thinking, I hesitantly step towards Maverick and wrap my arms around his waist, pulling him in for a hug while letting a sniffle slip out and murmuring into his chest, "Thank you, Mav. I didn't think I needed this, but it was so kind and I appreciate you looking out for me."

He's rubbing small circles on my back, the gesture feels more intimate than it should, but I haven't been embraced like this since my breakup, so I decide to soak it in. Even though I know that I shouldn't have my boss's arms wrapped around my body like this. "You're welcome, Darlin'. I should probably get back outside, but text me if you need anything. Try to get some rest."

Tentatively, I back away from Mav, giving him a pained smile. We both lean down to grab the bag of items he bought me at the same time, knocking our heads.

"Oh, fuck," he groans, "I'm sorry, I was just trying to help."

"Owwwww," I whine because more pain on top of the tiny soldiers waging war on my uterus is just what I needed today. "Nope, it's okay. I'm just going to head back to bed. Thanks again," I respond, taking the bag from his hand and heading back into my room as he walks away.

Dumping the contents out on my bed, I find about ten different varieties of tampons and pads, chocolates (caramel, nuts, dark, white), a red-and-blue Gatorade, three different types of pain meds, and the best part, a heating pad. That immediately gets unboxed, and then I snap a picture of the items and send it directly to Darcy.

ME
I shouldn't read into this too much right?

DARCY
OMG! Did he get all of that for you?

ME
Yes, all I did was mention the tiny knives stabbing me earlier this morning.

DARCY
Well, that was sweet of him.

ME
I know and it makes me want to throw up.

SHOT TO THE HART

DARCY

Uhhhh why?

ME

BECAUSE FEELINGS AND NICE GESTURES AND HUGS.

DARCY

Those all sound like good things?

ME

Ugh. You don't get it.

DARCY

Apparently I don't. Care to explain?

ME

No! As my best friend, you're supposed to just read my mind when I can't explain.

DARCY

You are so dramatic. It'll be fine, he's just being nice. That's all.

ME

> Yeah right! I'm going back to sleep. Love ya.

My phone pings one last time, but I choose to ignore it and curl into my heating pad, letting the quiet and dim lighting put me to sleep.

CHAPTER 18

Horngry

Maverick

Once I'm back outside, I realize by the glances coming my way that I was gone way longer than I intended to be. I scowl at Dom who has a shit-eating grin on his face. "Don't say a fucking word Dominic."

"Fine. No words. But how about this?" He waggles his eyebrows at me before jumping backwards into the pool. I continue to scowl in his direction, even though he's now distracted by Bella holding onto his neck for dear life.

I join Nik by the grill, the smell of charcoal and hot dogs assaulting my nostrils. "How is she?" he asks, genuinely concerned. I didn't divulge with the guys why Kodi wouldn't be joining us, just that she wasn't feeling well today.

"She's going through it, dude."

He chuckles. "Just steer clear bro. Women have two modes when their bodies are raging war on them. Anger and horngry."

I chortle at that. "Horngry?"

"Yeah man, horny as hell but in a hangry way. It can be hot in the right situation," he states matter of factly.

I decide that I don't want to know what he means by that statement and join everyone else in the pool. Dominic and I stand on either end of the shallow side of the pool letting Bella, wearing her pink two-in-one flotation device, practice her swimming back and forth between us until she finally gets worn out and the hot dogs are ready to eat.

Bella was exhausted by the time everyone left, so I got her bathed and down for the night before showering myself. I then head to the kitchen to make Kodi a plate to drop off at her room on my way to bed. However, when I enter the kitchen I hear the television quietly playing in the living room and find Kodi sitting on the couch, a small plate sitting in her lap.

"Hey, mind if I join you?"

"Jesus, Mav. You scared the shit out of me," she gasps, hand clutched to her chest, "You watch *Big Bang Theory*?"

"I can't say that I have."

"No way! Okay, well we are going to start over from the very beginning because you have to watch from the beginning."

"Sounds like we need snacks. Popcorn? M&M's?" I ask her. I wonder if she's a salty or sweet kind of woman.

"M&M's in the popcorn?" she questions back, wiggling her eyebrows at me.

It's so damn cute.

"I like your thinking Darlin'. Be right back." I wait two minutes for the popcorn to finish before adding in a hefty scoop of the chocolate candies, gently mixing them in so they don't smoosh, and grab two beers before heading back into the living room. "Snacks and beverages have arrived."

Kodi immediately presses play on episode one and starts snacking, bopping her head along to the beat of the theme song.

"Okay, so all the guys are socially awkward scientists that end up living across the hall from a mess of a pretty girl, and they don't know what to do with themselves?" I ask about halfway through the first episode.

"No, just Sheldon and Leonard live across the hallway. Wolowitz and Koothrappali might as well live there but don't."

"Hmm. . .okay. Hand those snacks over here," I tell her, sipping on my beer. Instead of handing the bowl over, she moves close enough that I can reach, but I'm not touching her. I find myself itching to put my arm around her shoulder and pull her into me just to feel her body against mine again.

When the first episode is over, she turns to me, "So, what did you think?"

"Penny and Leonard have to end up together right?"

"You'll have to watch and find out." She smiles mischievously at me.

"Well don't keep me waiting, start episode two."

Ever since the guys grill-out last weekend, Kodi and I have found ourselves in this exact place after Bella goes to sleep, watching a few episodes of *Big Bang Theory*. I'm finding myself wanting to stay up with her later each night. She's pragmatic and her eyes crinkle at the sides when she gets really excited. Her laugh brightens any room. Tonight was no different, we moved out to the patio after watching an episode of "our show" since it's not unbearably hot, drinking beers and watching the stars in the sky.

"Can I ask you a personal question?" Kodi asks, suddenly breaking the tranquil feeling of the night. Trepidation creeps up my spine, I look into her eyes and she seems nervous. I nod in her direction, urging her to continue. "You don't have to answer this question, but you're handsome and young, so I am just a little confused. . .I guess?"

My lips tilt up in a sly half smile. "You think I'm handsome?"

"Well, duh. Anyone with eyes would think you're handsome. Don't let it get to your head, Big Guy," she continues. "I've just been wondering where Bella's mom is?"

Uneasiness begins to take over, I fiddle with the lip of my beer bottle for a moment, contemplating if I want to share this story. "Wow, hard hitting questions then. I've honestly never really talked to anyone about this except my parents and the guys."

"I know it might be a tough subject, but if this is something that could affect my ability to care for Bella, I think I'd like to know what I'm getting myself into. Like is her mom going to show up and call me a homewrecker one day without knowing that I'm just the nanny?" Kodi rushes out. I gave up thinking Lily would randomly show up after Bella's second birthday, another unanswered text, and another stack of paperwork that never showed up signed.

I can't help but laugh. "Yeah, I doubt that will be a problem. I honestly don't know where she is. When I was still on the team in Carolina, I was young and would rarely mess around with the bunnies. But one night after a really bad loss, Lily approached me, and I thought that going home with someone would make me feel better, and apparently a terrible pull-out game later, I'm getting a text from Lily of a photo with two pink lines. My parents raised me to be responsible, my dad took care of our family growing up and instilled those same values into me. We met up and discussed what our options were then she signed a bunch of paperwork with Carolina legal team, basically stating that if she ever left our relationship she wouldn't be able to just come and take Bella or ask for money. She didn't want to get rid of the baby, and while I wasn't ready to be a Dad, I felt like it was my responsibility to take care of both of them. I got her pregnant after all."

My throat is starting to clog a little, so I give myself a break. Kodi reaches for my hand reassuringly, letting me know she is here when I'm ready to continue. As her boss, I shouldn't be seeking comfort from her but her soothing touch is something I need as I continue to speak, "I moved her into my place, we dated, but there was never really any love there except for the life we created together. When Bella was about two months old, I woke up in the middle of the night to her cries, which was weird because Lily usually took night duty. I felt for Lily beside me in bed, but she wasn't there, so I got up and went over to the bassinet. After I got

Bella calm, I searched all over the house but couldn't find her. Then I discovered all of her stuff was gone and she wouldn't answer her phone. I haven't heard from her since. She doesn't engage with contact from the legal team and has never sent the parental rights paperwork back."

Kodi's grasp on my hand tightens a little and when I look into her eyes, she's tearing up. Through a shaky breath she says, "Oh Mav. I'm so sorry." I don't think she realizes she's doing it, but her thumb is rubbing little circles in a soothing manner while she speaks and it's keeping me grounded in this moment with her. Another thing I've learned about Kodi is that she's incredibly empathetic towards everyone who crosses her path, and I admire that about her. "Have you always done this alone? Don't you need a break from time to time?"

Here we go. I don't know if I'm ready to share this part of my past either. She's asking me to be even more vulnerable. Talking about Ma though, that is something I haven't done with anyone except my family and Tatum. Even the guys haven't heard the full story, they only know that we lost her.

I want to get the words out, but she doesn't have a child, she might not understand why I don't give myself that break. My mouth is getting dryer by the second, my eyes are definitely watering. She isn't rushing me, just waiting and giving me the time I very clearly need, still rubbing small circles on top of my hand. Taking a deep breath, finally ready enough to speak, "As soon as Lily left, my family stepped up. My Dad, Ma, sister. They all took turns staying in the guest room on late nights or early mornings. My Ma, she was the one who was basically with Bella around the clock when I couldn't be.

She did everything she could to make sure that my little girl knew she was loved when I wasn't able to be around."

I glance up into the dark sky heaving a breath. "But one day, about ten months ago, she got sick. She couldn't get out of bed, couldn't lift Bella. It came out of nowhere and her health declined rapidly. Then three months later, the cancer won. It hit my family hard. My Dad tries to help, but he's still grieving and he's older than Ma was. He's also decided that he wants to take a step back and focus on himself. My sister and her husband live thousands of miles away. The timing, although unfortunate, worked out in our favor, because we were in off season and I was home more, but with things picking up again that's when we decided we needed help. And then you came along." I try my best to smile at her, but I know it's wobbly.

Kodi gives me a reassuring smile back, taking her hand off of mine, and I find myself immediately missing the touch, wanting to pull it back and hold hers in my lap. "Well, I really appreciate you sharing all of that with me. I know it couldn't have been easy, and I'm grateful and happy that I get to be a part of Bella's life and yours too."

"Thank you for giving me the space and the time to tell you about it."

"Of course, any deep-seated questions for me Mr. Hart?"

"Not really deep seated, more like curiosity getting the better of me." I think for a moment. "You said it was just you and your mom?"

"That would be correct." She takes a swig of her beer waiting for me to continue.

"Where's your dad?"

"Probably galivanting Europe or some other country with Janice and my half siblings. I'd have to care enough to check in on him via social media to know for sure. Since that's the only way he cares to let me into his life." She shrugs and while she says she doesn't care, I can see the wheels turning.

"If you don't care, why did you add him back?"

"Sheesh, what are you, my therapist?" She chuckles attempting to break the tension, "I don't know honestly. I was eighteen and thinking maybe that he finally wanted to get to know me. I hoped for ten years that he would come back, and when he finally did, I saw I had two half-siblings I don't know anything about. When I messaged him to ask 'why now', I didn't get a response."

I find myself irrationally angry with a man I've never met for abandoning her when she was so young. "Well he missed out and doesn't deserve to know you now."

"I know." We sit in silence for a few more moments before I decide to ask her one more question before I know we need to head in for the night.

"Darlin'. One question."

"One answer." She smiles at me from her seat across the small, lit fire pit.

"If you could have any animal as a pet, what would you choose and why?" I'm hoping this question has the desired outcome. When she starts giggling uncontrollably, head thrown back, eyes crinkling in the corner, the sound higher pitched than normal, I know that it did. I also have the fleeting thought that I love the sound of her happiness, "You alright over there?"

"I'm-oh my God." She swipes under eyes, "We were just talking about our abandonment issues and you asked me what animal I would have as a pet."

"You're right, I did. I wanted to see you smile. Now answer the question, I'm ready."

"Okay I would choose a penguin. A puffer to be specific. I'd have to move to Antarctica or something, but I find them fascinating, and they are also a little stupid so I think that they could provide great entertainment. I also love that they mate for life and bring shiny pebbles to impress the females."

"Interesting, I could see you with a penguin laying in your lap. I would choose a tiger. They are just majestic and loyal, but also if you've ever seen a video of them playing with their enrichment activities, it seems like they could be fun."

"Interesting, I don't think I trust those teeth."

"That's why it's a hypothetical question. We can take away all of the bad features of the animals and focus on the good ones. We better head in, Bella will have you up in a few hours." I get up, offering my hand to Kodi, the warmth still there from where she was comforting me not too long ago.

We walk through the house in silence, side by side, before reaching Kodi's door. My mind and my body are warring with each other; I want to stop her from going into her room, feel my lips on hers, but doing that could lead us down a path I'm scared to visit, so I won't kiss her. . .Yet. Before I can give myself time to question my decision anymore, I step into her and when she sucks in a breath but doesn't retreat, I find myself placing my hand on her cheek and placing my forehead against hers, my thumb gently caressing. Her eyes are wide, but she makes no effort to move away from me, almost holding her breath to see what will happen next.

"Goodnight, Kodi. Thanks again for tonight," I whisper before gently kissing her cheek and retreating to my room.

"Um. . .goodnight, Mav."

CHAPTER 19

Sleepover

Kodi

The Manta Rays are off for another two-week stretch after playing Minnesota here the other day and Maverick was out of the house before Bella and I were even awake this morning. I keep thinking back to the way his eyes kept traveling to my lips, but then he didn't follow through. I'm simultaneously grateful and infuriated at the fact that he didn't kiss me. I'm waiting for Bella to wake up, so I text the girls.

ME
I think that Maverick wanted to kiss me last night and I don't know how to feel about it.

HARLEY
He what?

ME

You read that right. Well I'm not 100% sure, but it definitely seemed like it. And then he didn't.

SIN

Uh. . .why not?

ME

Do I look like Maverick? I don't know. What's worse is I think I would have let him.

DARCY

You would have?

ME

Ugh, yes.

SIN

This is getting interesting.

ME

You guys are no help!

DARCY

There is literally nothing we can do to help you.

My phone buzzes two more times. One message from Andy and one from Maverick. Hoping that Mavericks' message will soothe the irritation from Andy's, I open the message from my ex first.

> **ANDY**
> KJ, why did I hear from the barista that you aren't working at Wake, Bake, Repeat anymore?

The audacity of this man to think that I owe him an update on my life.

> **ME**
> Because my life is no longer yours to keep track of.

I wait for a retort but it seems that was enough to shut him up for now.

> **MAVERICK**
> Hey, sorry I didn't say bye this morning, didn't want to wake you. Last night was nice, thanks for the chat.

So we still aren't addressing the not-kiss from last night, which is perfectly fine because I don't know what to say.

> **ME**
> Anytime, thanks for asking me silly questions to change the topic when I don't want to talk.

MAVERICK

Anytime. Send updates.

ME

Of course. Talk later.

I hear Bella stirring through the speaker of my phone and head in to get her up and ready for the day. Peeking into her room, I see that she's already up and moving around, "Good morning, Bella."

"Good morning, Kodi!"

"We have tumble class today."

"I like tumble class!"

"I'm excited to watch you." I smile at her. "Flips and jumping need so much energy, so what do we always do first?"

"Eggs." We get her pull-up changed after an attempt at sitting on the potty and put on her leopard-print, neon gymnastics leotard before heading to the kitchen.

"What else should we have with our eggs?"

"Hmmmm... toast." I get busy with breakfast and coffee while she has a dance party in the living room with Floppy.

"Those are some cool moves Bella!"

"Watch this!" I don't know what to call the move that follows, almost like a baby bird learning to fly combined with a fish out of water, but she's having fun and that's all that matters.

"Whoa, that was so cool. Breakfast is ready, so please come here once this song is done, but we can leave the music playing." She continues dancing for another minute before coming and letting me place her in her tower. We eat breakfast together and then get loaded into the Bronco to head to tumbling class.

I pull up to a brick building labeled Tara's Tumbles and hop out, grabbing Bella and heading to the reception desk. This is the first class I'm taking her to by myself, but I've observed a few with Maverick present. Approaching the desk, there's a very bored teenager playing on her phone, "Hi, Araballa Hart. She does the toddler tumbling at nine-thirty."

The teenager looks up at me, clicks something on her computer and then says,"Go ahead."

We walk down the hall, past the larger gym filled with blue mats, trampolines, and other assorted equipment, and enter a smaller room that's filled with rainbow mats, varied sized squares, trapeze beams that basically touch the ground, and a smaller trampoline. I set Bella down and Cara, her teacher, approaches us,"Hey, Bella. Kodi right?"

"Yes, Kodi. Nice to see you again."

"Glad you guys made it! You know where to sit. I'll wave the parents into the room once class is over to collect the little ones."

"Sounds good. Have fun Bella." I crouch down and give her a little squeeze before she runs off to play with the other kids. I exit the room and take a seat on a black plastic chair close to the door. I make sure to sit where I can still see through the glass paneling that allows us to watch class and pull up my e-reader. I fell in love with one of the side characters in my wolf-shifter romance, but the author hasn't released the second book. Curiosity got the best of me, so I picked up a hockey romance, then another, and now I'm on my sixth one in the past few weeks. This one follows a reformed playboy who wants the girl that clearly wants nothing to do with him. I start reading, peeking up and watching Bella twirl around the room or attempt to do flips every once in a while then the next thing I know her class is over. The male character was just about to get on his knees and beg the female for a chance. I know what I'm doing once Bella is asleep tonight. I think I've found my new addiction, hockey romances are like candy that I can't stop eating.

I've got Bella in her carseat when my phone starts ringing with a Facetime call from Maverick.

"Hey, hey! Bella look who it is." I turn in my seat holding my phone so Bella can see Mavericks face.

"Daddy!"

"Hey little lady. How was tumbling?"

"Fun. I did jumps. And flips." Bella jumps into a toddler rant about tumbling class and Maverick chuckles at her, letting her get it all out.

"Wow, that sounds like so much fun. I've gotta go skate, but I love you."

"Bye Daddy! I love you!"

"Bye Kodi." Mav's deep timbre sends a shiver down my spine before he ends the call.

※

When the Sunday before Maverick gets back rolls around, I decide to take Bella to the aquarium. Afterwards, we grab lunch with Sin, Harley, and Darcy. We snapped a selfie that included Bella, and once I got her down for bed, I decided to send it to Mav, even though he might not see it since he's probably sleeping or celebrating. Watching the game, I had no idea what was happening, but I could tell they were fighting for their win. I set my phone down, but it pings almost immediately.

> **ME**
> Bella got to have a gals lunch today and had the best time. *picture attachment*

> **MAVERICK**
> Aw, look at my lil' lady. Looks like she's made herself 3 more best friends.

> **ME**
> She had so much fun, she introduced them all to Fwoppy, it was fucking adorable. She definitely was worn out after spending most of the day out, and gave me a little bit of a hard time going to bed, but I think she was overtired. A few extra snuggles and she was knocked out.

> **MAVERICK**
> I'm sorry she gave you a hard time. I miss her so much.

Feeling a little emboldened hiding behind my phone screen. I quickly type and send a message before I can second guess it.

> **ME**
> What about me? *winky face emoji*

Three little dots appear then disappear then appear again.

> **MAVERICK**
> Well, of course, you too. *smiley face emoji*

Wait... Is he serious? I mean there's definitely energy with Maverick. I can't quite figure out what kind but this energy kicks butterflies up in my stomach.

> **ME**
> Be serious.

> **MAVERICK**
> I am. We've developed a friendship and a routine, and I miss it.

> **MAVERICK**
> ...And you.

Remembering that I forgot to congratulate him on his win, I add that into my response.

SHOT TO THE HART

ME

> We miss you too, Big Guy. I should probably head to bed. Good game tonight! I still had no idea what was going on, and you move so fast, but I think I may understand it a little better now. Have fun tonight and we will see you Tuesday morning.

MAVERICK

> Thanks Kodi. I'm glad you watched the game. Goodnight!

Right after I read that text, soft cries flow through the monitor app on my phone. I look at the camera feed and see Bella sitting upright, her cries getting louder. Floppy has been thrown out of her bed and she looks disheveled.

Rushing down to her room, the tears streaking down Bella's face break my heart. I find myself wondering what could have scared her this much that she's almost inconsolable. Pulling her into my arms, I find myself swaying back and forth with her in my arms, gently humming in the same way I remember Maverick doing that day during my interview. It seems to help her calm down some, at least to the point that she's no longer sobbing and I can sit in the rocker with her in my arms. Yawning, I look over to her sound machine to see that I've been holding her for almost thirty minutes, and when I look down at her face, those sweet, blue eyes while they look exhausted, are still wide open.

I sit on the rocker for another ten minutes before I give

up, grabbing Floppy and carrying her down the hall and into my room. I turn on soft music on my phone, grabbing all of my spare pillows, setting them carefully around the perimeter of the bed before sliding in and snuggling Bella into my side. Eventually her breathing evens out, but moving her to her room is a risk I can't take if I want to sleep tonight, so I let myself drift off with her.

CHAPTER 20

Goosebumps

Maverick

The arena is loud and filled with people wearing white and light blue in contrast to our maroon-and-black jerseys.

Standing in the tunnel waiting to skate out, I take a steadying breath, ready to help bring home a win for the team. I wonder if Kodi is watching the game tonight, she said she wanted to learn more about the sport I play. I even got my dad a seat with Tatum and a couple of the other families who came to support the team. The music and the cheers grow louder, and Nik, our captain and goalie, leads us out onto the ice taking his place in front of the net while the rest of us get into position for the puck drop.

The puck hits the ice with a thud and I immediately take possession of it, trying to push it to the opposing side of the rink. I barely make it five feet before I'm checked into the boards and California's defense takes the puck, beelining for Nik and the goal. Our fans lose it, banging on the plexiglass and yelling for the ref to call it, but he doesn't. Dominic screams in rage at the ref, getting himself put in the box for two minutes, meaning one less person is defending Nik and the net, which pisses me off more than being checked into the board. Collins had to fight to keep the puck and speed with it down the ice because the defense is trying to keep a gap between us. We were passing the puck back and forth more times than I can count even with that barrier. Nik did everything in his power to keep the puck out of our net, only letting one get by him while Dom was in the box, which he kicked himself for as he watched it happen.

We won. Barely. After making sure my Dad got back to the hotel, we are now sitting in an overcrowded bar, beer and buffalo wings spread about the table. Women, presumably puck bunnies, trying to grab our attention from across the bar. "Ya'll celebrating in more than one way tonight?" I direct towards both Dom and Nik, knowing they typically will bring a puck bunny back to the hotel if they are still riding the high of a close win.

"Not tonight," Nik says with a scowl.

At the same time Dom says, "Maybe. We will see what the night brings. How's the hot nanny doing so far?"

"I bet that it's hard to focus when you've got a distraction sleeping in the room next to you. I know it would be if it were me," Tatum chimes in.

"She has a name and she's not a distraction. They seem to be doing fine," I retort with clenched teeth and balled fists. Aggravation at him calling her hot roiling under my skin. My phone vibrates against the table. I checked in with Kodi after the game, but she didn't respond when I told her that I did miss her, just as I missed Bella.

> **ME**
> We miss you too, Big Guy. I should probably head to bed. Good game tonight! I still had no idea what was going on and you move so fast but I think I may understand a little better now. Have fun tonight and we will see you Tuesday morning.

"Why are you smiling at your phone like that? Stop, it's creepy," Collins says as if I've personally offended him, which maybe I have, it's hard to tell with him, but I wipe whatever look I had off my face.

"Nothing man," I say as I clear my throat and quickly text her a response.

> **ME**
> Thanks Kodi. I'm glad you watched the game. Goodnight!

"You're so lying. She texted you didn't she?" Dom asks.

"Just told me it was a good game and Bella said goodnight."

It's nice to have someone that isn't my family or the guys acknowledge my efforts in the game. I haven't had that happen since the night Lily and I met. I'm ready to get back home to Bella, and honestly Kodi, too. They make me smile every day and she cares about me too, not just Bella. Her friendship has been something I didn't know I needed, and her care for Bella has been a blessing.

It's close to three in the morning when I finally park my car at home after making sure Dad got back to his house. Sunday night after our win was the first time in a long time that I've seen my Dad genuinely smile. I'm so glad I got him to join me this weekend.

I'm exhausted and trying to sneak through the hall without being too loud. I notice that Kodi's door is cracked, which is weird considering she normally sleeps with it closed. Craning my head back, I notice that Bella's door is open too. That's odd. I enter Bella's room and she isn't in her bed which causes my heart to race a little quicker, my palms beginning to sweat.

Slowly, and as quietly but as quickly as possible, I push Kodi's bedroom door open. The sight that greets me, illuminated by the soft moonlight, knocks the wind out of my chest. Snuggled up in the middle of the bed are Kodi and my daughter. Arabella in her princess nightgown has her little hand resting on Kodi's cheek and her face nuzzled in Kodi's chest. Kodi is wearing a big tee shirt and short loose shorts, not covered in a blanket, and doesn't even have a pillow under her head. It looks like she created a barrier between the edges of the bed and my daughter's small body.

Creeping closer, I decide I should move Arabella to her room and let Kodi get comfortable. I lean down near where she lays and gently run a finger along her bare arm trying to wake her without frightening her. She stirs and makes a small noise but doesn't wake. Trying again I whisper, "Kodi," and goosebumps erupt along her skin. I take a moment to take a closer look at her tattoos, they aren't particularly cohesive and I wonder if any of them have meaning. She has a penguin tattooed along her forearm, a tiny cherub sits beside the melted smiley face that I noticed when she came in for her interview. I wonder if there are any hidden beneath her clothes.

I finally give her a little shake and say, "Kodi, Darlin' wake up for me." This is what I've always hoped for and I suddenly wish I could do this every time I get home from a weekend away.

That last attempt wakes Kodi up, she's squinting at me in the dark and whispers, "Mav?"

"Hi, gorgeous." Grabbing a pillow from the edge of the bed, I whisper back, "I'm gonna take Arabella to her room and then head to bed. Let me put this under your head and you go back to sleep."

I can see her soft smile as she adjusts the pillow I've just laid under her head, kissing Bella on the top of her head and then unwrapping her tiny body as carefully as possible, to avoid waking her up, from where it's wrapped around hers. "Thanks, Big Guy. See you in the morning."

I walk around the bed, carefully and quietly lift my daughter and get Bella settled into her bed with a quick kiss and a whispered, "I love you."

As I pass back by Kodi's room, I take one more peek in and see she's fast asleep but still not covered by a blanket. I quietly step further into the room and find myself leaning closer., Her dark hair is fanned over her pillow in all different directions, her lips slightly parted as tiny snores escape, and the moonlight coming in from the window highlights the curves of her body. She doesn't stir and I don't know what comes over me, but after pulling her blanket over her body I lean down, tenderly placing a kiss on her forehead. Leaving her room, I close her door then head to my room for some much needed rest.

CHAPTER 21

Teach Me

Maverick

We leave for our game against Charlotte in two weeks, and since the girls are asleep I decide to watch some tapes to prepare to go against my home team. Sitting in the theater room with my coffee watching Dom and I race down the ice, I hear the door click open behind me. Turning around, I find Kodi in those black yoga shorts that have me trailing her legs with my eyes and a baggy T-shirt, a glass of water in her hand. Her face groggy like she just woke up, her messy bun is falling to one side.

"Hey. Did I wake you?" I ask her.

"No, I just woke up and couldn't get back to sleep. Whatcha doing?" She comes closer, plopping herself down beside me. I reach around her to grab the remote, leaning into her a little more than necessary just to feel our bodies connect for a brief moment. I hear her take in a quick breath, holding it until I've removed myself from her space, but I leave our arms touching as I lean back into the couch.

"Watching tape, gotta get ready for the game in Charlotte."

"Oh, that sounds. . ." she trails off.

"Sounds *what*, Darlin'?" I look over to her, raising a brow and waiting to see how she's going to insult my career.

She lifts her chin and giggles, "Like the perfect nap time."

I roll my eyes at her. "Come on. I'll teach you a thing or two. And trust me, it's so much more intense being there watching it happen."

I click play and watch Collins and I pass the puck to each other, Dom protecting Nik and our net. "Okay, see here. Collins is a right winger. His job is to help me, the center, get down the ice with the puck as fast as possible and score goals if I can't. But the defenseman also help me get down the ice, they just don't want to leave Nik and the net wide open for too long."

"Holy shit. You guys are moving so quickly," she mutters as Collins passes the puck and I shoot it right past the goalies head. She's sitting a little more upright now, paying special attention to the screen as we move flawlessly about it.

"So Nik is the goalie, that's pretty self explanatory. What does Dom do?" she asks, keeping her eyes glued to the screen.

"Dom is a defenseman. He gets to be a little more aggressive than the rest of us," I explain.

"Oh, I bet he loves that." She chuckles. "You know, this doesn't seem as complicated as I thought it was going to be."

I blow out a breath. "It's definitely easier to watch."

"Oh, trust me, I would never try to do what you guys do. I can't even skate."

"Well you work for a hockey player now, that is just

unacceptable." I laugh, bumping her with my shoulder.

"Some of us were not born with natural athletic ability dude." The sweet sarcasm so easily rolls off her tongue when it's just us. She's looking at me now, our faces inches apart, my gaze darting to those full, pink lips then back to her eyes. I pull back first, she blinks away her disappointment so fast I could have missed it if I wasn't so entranced by her.

"I'm serious Ko, we gotta change this. Can I teach you?" I ask nudging her with my shoulder.

"Fine, you can teach me, but you keep me upright. I will not let myself fall on my ass in front of a rink full of people." She crosses her arms in front of her chest with a huff.

"We can make that happen, Darlin'."

Since we have a week before Charlotte and it's starting to cool down, Kodi and I have both invited our friends over for a dip night and smores over the fire pit. Bella has already hung out with Kodi's friends and I haven't gotten to meet them yet, so this felt like a good opportunity to get to know them.

Kodi flits around the kitchen finishing her buffalo chicken dip while Bella runs around out back with Dom who is early to everything. I'm working on booking the room for Charlotte that Bella and Kodi will be staying in. I've already asked Hudson, our travel agent, to call the hotel tomorrow and make sure that Kodi and Bella's room is near mine.

"Hey Ko." She stops buzzing about, turning towards me. She has some hairs falling in her face and buffalo sauce on her forehead somehow.

"What's up?" Her brow furrowed in confusion.

I chuckle while moving the hair behind her ear then gently rubbing the sauce off her forehead with a kitchen towel, "Are you okay with the king bed in your hotel room for Charlotte?"

"I mean, anything works."

"Okay, I'm going to have Hudson book it." I shoot him a quick text to remind him to book Kodi's room under her name, near mine, and that it has a king bed, regardless of upcharges.

"Alright, and when are we flying out again?" She continues mixing her dip before plopping it into a pan and sliding it into the oven.

"Thursday morning on a private plane." She doesn't get a chance to say anything because the front door rings and I open it to Tatum, Collins and Nik all holding trays. "You can drop those in the kitchen, just don't get in Kodi's way and maybe see if she needs help."

A small, blue SUV pulls into the driveway before I've closed the door and three women who I recognize from the aquarium photo last time I was out of town, hop out of the car carrying dishes and meander up the driveway. Before I've had a chance to appear, Kodi is sliding past me and being pulled into a hug by all three girls.

"Maverick, this is Darcy, my best friend who we definitely need to keep away from Tatum." The blonde slaps Kodi playfully. "Sinclair or Sin, the real trouble." The redhead rolls her eyes at this description. "And Harley, she gives the wisest advice that she can't follow herself." The brunette nods in agreement, shrugging her shoulders.

"Well, come on in. I can show you where to drop those off and then introduce you to some of my teammates." I smile at them before turning on my heel and leading them to the kitchen. As we walk past the living room, the guys all lift their heads and take in the women, nodding slightly before turning back to their puzzle they've been dragged into helping Bella complete.

"Let me take care of these, you go introduce everyone." I tell Kodi as I begin unwrapping the dips and organizing spoons while she guides the girls into the living room.

"So, Tatum, Collins, Dom, Nik, meet my best friends Darcy, Harley, and Sin." I can see Kodi pointing at each person as she introduces them and then she goes, " And you all know Bella."

"Alright ya'll ready to eat?" I holler for them to come and make their plates. Collins carries Bella on his hip into the kitchen as everyone else follows making small talk.

"What's she eating?" He asks me as he picks up two plates.

"I'll make her a plate dude, don't worry about it. Thanks though." He sets one back down but continues his hold on Bella, snuggling her into him.

"I want to sit next to her tonight, Dom is such a niece hog." It's true, Dom has declared on multiple occasions that he always gets a seat beside Bella.

"She's all yours Collins. Just get your plate and get y'all seated before he makes it in there. I'll bring you some water I assume?"

"Correct, thanks." He moves on, and I stand to the side until everyone has made it through the kitchen and taken their seats. Kodi is last and I join her when I hear Dom go, "Ah, what the heck man? That's my spot."

"Dom, other people can eat next to Bella," Collins chides, and I look up to see a giant grin on his face.

"Fine." I watch him plop down between Darcy and Nik.

"Seems like everyone is getting along." Kodi smiles as she continues sampling the different dips with a tortilla chip then places it on her plate.

"I'm glad, your friends are more than welcome here anytime Kodi."

"Thanks Mav." We join the others at the dinner table; there just happens to be two seats sitting together. and if I know my friends, that was intentional.

"So how do you all know each other?" Nik asks the women at the table.

"Been friends since high school," Sin answers.

"Inseparable ever since." Harley shrugs.

"How long have y'all played with each other?" Darcy asks.

"Nik has been with Tampa the longest, eight years I think. Dominic and Collins got signed at the same time. Then Maverick came along around two years ago. I'm just their personal assistant and chaos wrangler," Tatum answers, pulling a giggle out of the girls at his chaos comment.

"Yep Nik is our old man." Dom elbows Nik but his expression doesn't change, it rarely does.

"This artichoke dip is delicious," Kodi says from beside me, "I'm going to need everyone to share their recipes please."

We finish our dips and the girls head into the kitchen to help Kodi clean up and catch up while I take Bella to do her bath and get her into bed. Meanwhile, the guys head out to the patio with their beers and the s'mores supplies.

Once I've got Bella down, I join everyone else on the patio. The girls are snuggled up on one couch, while Nik is in one chair and Tatum is in the other, leaving me to plop down onto the other couch with Collins and Dom. Dom hands me a beer and I nod in thanks before cracking it open.

"Have you all been to that new club, Lockout?" Dom asks the girls, and Darcy gives Kodi a look that I can't decipher, but it makes her cheeks flame with color.

"We have! It was so much fun but so crowded. Apparently the hockey teams were there on opening night celebrating a win. None of us except Harley really keeps up with sports," Sinclair says.

"Yep! We were all there, celebrating kicking the Titans' asses," Collins says with a grin.

"Crazy how we've all ended up here now," Darcy adds in.

"Crazy," Kodi mumbles, chugging down the rest of her beer.

"Well anyways, like a week after the game, it's my birthday. The big two-five. You all should come out with us, we will get the VIP area and I'll obviously have to buy a few bottles to help us celebrate," Dom says excitedly, hoping that he can spend more time with Kodi's friends.

"I'll have to talk to my Dad and see if he can take Bella for the night so I can join," I say, knowing my Dad will probably be ecstatic to spend the weekend with Bella.

"That sounds fun, right Ko?" Sin elbows Kodi and she grimaces.

"Um. . .duh. Count us in." Kodi smiles at Dom.

CHAPTER 22

Pickle Sandwich

Maverick

The air in Charlotte is crisp and cold this time of year, the leaves are an array of oranges, reds and browns. It's absolutely breathtaking, and I can't believe I get to share it with Kodi and Bella.

She hasn't been on a plane since we moved down to Florida and I wasn't sure how she was going to react. She did really well, refusing to sit on my lap, choosing Kodi's to watch her princess movies and play with her dolls.

"So, I have a few hours once we land and was thinking we could send our bags to the hotel, pick up some food, and then have a picnic in Freedom Park before I take y'all back to the hotel to get ready for the game while I head to practice. It's gorgeous and the weather is perfect."

"Oh, that sounds really nice actually." Kodi looks up at me from her book. "What kind of food?"

"There's a locally owned sandwich shop that I used to frequent, Barb's Sandwich Co., figured we could swing in there. You should ask Kenny, the owner, how Barb's came to be, it's a lovely story."

"I definitely will." The pilot makes the announcement that we will begin our descent shortly. Both of them are bundled up as we step off of the plane that I chartered so that Bella could be with me.

"Welcome to Charlotte," I tell Kodi as our car pulls up, opening the door and getting Bella's car seat settled in. After running to throw our bags, the stroller, and the playpen in the back, Kodi slides in and I follow behind, directing our driver for the weekend, Trent, to drop us at Barb's.

"Oh, Mr. Hot Shot decided we are worthy of his presence," Kenny jokes as we step into the small sandwich shop. "I'm kidding, bring it in, kid." I hug the older man, noting how his wrinkles have become more prominent since I've seen him last and he walks with a sort of hobble.

"Kenny, this is Kodi, Bella's nanny." Kodi smiles shyly towards him as she pushes Bella's stroller further into the shop.

"Welcome to Barb's. I think I have the perfect sandwich for you. You like turkey?"

"I do. I heard that you have a fun getting-started story that I need to hear Kenny." Kodi beams at him.

"That I do." He smiles fondly before continuing, "My Barb, may she rest in peace, birthed me three wonderful children; however, with her first pregnancy she had the oddest pregnancy craving. All she wanted was a turkey sandwich but to use the pickles as bread, but obviously pregnant women are told to stay away from deli meat. Rather than turkey, we used egg salad, and I was making two to three of those bad boys a day for weeks. Eventually, we were giving them to our friends and family who always said they would buy those in a store. So, I saved from my corporate America job and dreamed up Barb's Sandwich Co. The star of the show, of course, being Barb's pickle bread sandwich, and the people ate it up."

"Oh, I love that. Let me guess, I'm about to have a Barb's pickle bread sandwich?" Kodi asks.

"Both of you are and a PB&J for the little one," Kenny says, still working on our sandwiches, "To go?"

"Yep, going to have a little picnic in Freedom Park before I head to the arena," I state, taking in how the shop has changed. It really hasn't, aside from a few new photos on the walls and some small round tables that look fairly new compared to the red plastic ones that used to be in here.

"Here ya go, these are on the house. It's always good to see you, and good luck tonight Maverick. Enjoy your sandwiches." Kenny smiles at us, sliding the sandwiches and three water bottles over the glass casing. I leave a fifty dollar bill in the tip jar after Kenny turns his back rather than arguing over paying the bill. We exit the shop, a small bell dinging above our heads as the door closes behind us and begin our short walk over to Freedom Park.

"He was nice," Kodi speaks as she takes in our surroundings, the occasional small boutique or local eatery. We aren't deep in the downtown area so this environment is quiet and calming compared to the hustle and bustle of the city that we will experience later today when we head to the arena for the game.

"Yeah Barb's has been around since I was a teen. I always like to stop in when I'm in town. Let's go in through that entrance." I gesture towards an archway across the street from us.

Entering the park, we are greeted by a large lake surrounded by trees that have switched from vibrant greens to muted oranges, yellows, and browns. A brick bridge goes over the expanse of the lake. There's a playground to the right that I'm sure Bella will want to run around on. People are spread out over the area, eating lunch, throwing tennis balls for their dogs, reading books, chasing their kids, and taking walks.

"Wow, this is beautiful," Kodi says, "Let's sit under that tree!" She gestures to a tree that overlooks the lake, has a park bench under it but isn't too close to the water and far enough from the playground that we can feed Bella before we lose her to the playground.

I park Bella where she can see the ducks swimming in the lake, but I can still see her face and put her sandwich and water bottle on her stroller tray. "Eat up little lady, then we can go play."

Kodi passes me my sandwich and I send a quick picture of it to Grace and my Dad before we eat in silence for a few moments, watching the water ripple and the people go by.

> **GRACE**
> Lucky bastard. I miss Barbs.

> **DAD**
> Grace Lynn, watch your language. How's Kenny?

ME

Yeah Grace, watch your language. Kenny is doing great. Brought Bella to Freedom Park too.

I attach a picture of Bella with the scenery in the background.

GRACE

She's so big. I miss her.

ME

You guys can come visit her anytime. I hope, if anything, you make it down when I'm in the cup.

GRACE

We wouldn't miss it for the world.

DAD

Look at my grandbaby. So cute. Miss and love you all.

ME

Love you both.

GRACE

Love and miss you.

"This is delicious, I would've never thought to do this myself," Kodi says through a mouthful of sandwich.

"Pretty genius, right?" I chuckle.

"Why did you leave Charlotte? You seem really at peace here."

"Daddy, help," Bella whines from her stroller, "No crust."

She ate half of the sandwich with its crust but has apparently decided the crust is no longer a feasible option for her. I take the time to remove the crust off the other half and place it back down in front of her.

"And now we say what Bella?" I look to my daughter, waiting for those two little words that I know for a fact I ingrained into her.

"Thank you Daddy." Bella smiles coyly before diving back into her sandwich.

"Well when the NHL drafts you, you can say no to a trade from another team, but you may not get picked up by another team, and I didn't want to lose my livelihood. So, when Tampa decided they wanted me and offered me more, I took the opportunity," I answer Kodi's question from before.

"Hmm. . .interesting. If they wanted you back, do you think you'd come back?"

"Truthfully, I don't know. Tampa has felt like home for two years now, we are all happy and we've found a really good group of friends who I now consider family. I don't think I'd want to lose that."

"That's fair, I think if I were you I'd feel the same way."

"Kodi, swings please!" Bella grins at us, her face is covered in peanut butter and jelly causing Kodi and I to chuckle at the sight. I grab the wipes from the diaper bag and clean her face up while she thrashes her head back and forth.

"Can Daddy push you on the swings?" I ask her.

"No, Kodi!"

"I don't mind really." Kodi looks at Bella with adoration in her eyes.

"Okay fine, you two go, I'll throw this trash out and then meet you over there. We only have about twenty minutes before we need to head out," I say before Kodi is chasing Bella towards the playground, both of them laughing wildly. Kodi looks back at me as she follows, my heart seizing in my chest at how beautiful she looks at this moment. Her curls wild from the wind, bright smile on display as the sun creates a frame behind her head. Then I look at Bella whose little legs are moving as fast as they can, her little space buns bouncing as she runs, and I can't help but think that this is exactly where I'm supposed to be in life right now.

The fact that Kodi has only been around for a few weeks and Bella is so enamored with her, scares the shit out of me. The thing that scares me more is the possibility that Kodi might leave one day, leaving mine and Bella's hearts in pieces.

CHAPTER 23

The Hotel Fiasco

Maverick

"Let's get you guys to the hotel and then I have to head to the arena," I tell Kodi as we exit the park and head to the car I called for us.

We ride the short distance in silence. Pulling up to the hotel, I grab our belongings, and Kodi follows holding Bella as we walk up to the concierge. "Mr. and Ms. Hart." She smiles at me then Kodi, who has turned the cutest shade of pink at the inference she's my wife.

"Mr. Hart and Ms. Roscoe. There should be a room for each of us," I correct.

"Oh. I'm so sorry. Let me just get you guys checked in. Alright, room three hundred and seventy-six for Mr. Hart and room three hundred and sixty-four for Ms. Roscoe. Just take those elevators by the bathrooms up to the third floor." She hands me two room keys.

"Thank you Wendy." I smile. peeking at her nametag,

taking the keys from her hands before walking beside Kodi towards the elevators. Once the doors have closed, I speak, "I'm sorry about that. I swear I told Hudson to put your name on the reservation too."

She shrugs, letting out a laugh, breathy and light, that is music to my ears. "It's okay. It's just funny. I guess I should get used to it. People seeing me with you and your daughter are probably going to make them assume things."

The doors open and we head to her room first. Opening the door, Kodi steps in first with Bella, but it immediately feels like we are stepping into a hair dryer.

"Oh no." She gasps, the room is humid and smells horrible, the floor squelching beneath Kodi's feet, and I wonder how long the air conditioning hasn't been working in this room that it's this damp and hot.

"I'll get this sorted. But for now, just come with me." I grab the suitcases and begin ushering Kodi towards my room. Stepping into my room is the exact opposite of Kodi's. Ice cold air breezes, the carpet is dry and the king bed sitting in the middle of my room looks fit for a King. I rush to the room phone, calling the front desk immediately.

"This is Wendy."

"Hey Wendy! This is Mr. Hart, you just checked us in, and well, Ms. Roscoe's room is not habitable. The floor is soaked and the air conditioning is definitely not working. Do you have another room you can put her in?"

"Oh, Mr. Hart. I am so sorry about that, but unfortunately

we are all booked up this weekend. I can offer the team a refund and bring a cot up for your companion." *Fuck..* There's no way that I'm making Kodi sleep on a cot. The thought of sleeping in the same bed as her has my blood heating up.

"Well, okay then. If anything changes, please call me."

"Of course, sir. Good luck tonight."

"Thanks Wendy." Setting the phone down and turning to Kodi who is playing around on her phone. "So I. . .uh, the hotel is booked up this weekend."

She nearly loses her phone, frantically grabbing it to keep it from hitting the floor and looking up to me with wide eyes. "Oh. . .Um, okay. We will figure it out."

"I'm so sorry to leave you like this, but I really have to get to the arena. Bella's new jersey will be getting dropped off about an hour and a half before the game starts." I know for a fact I have more to say to her, but my brain is so frazzled by the fact that we will definitely be sleeping in the same bed tonight. It is making every single thought I've had today leave my brain.

"Sounds good, Mav. Thank you. I'm excited to go to my first game.Good luck!"

Scooping Bella up, I give her a hug and kiss then set her down and head to the arena.

Once I'm in the Uber, I send her a quick message with the last bit of advice I had for tonight.

MAVERICK

> Hey Ko! I wanted to tell you a couple more things. I would try to get there thirty minutes prior to start time. You'll be in seats right behind our bench. Feel free to grab some snacks and a drink, and I would bring Floppy for her in case she gets tired. There will also be family passes with her jersey so that after the game you can come down to the tunnel and wait for me. We can order food once we get back to the hotel together. I don't want y'all walking in the dark by yourself after the game. Thanks again!

Then I pocket my phone, feeling my blood pumping in anticipation for this game and trying to figure out how we are going to handle one bed tonight.

CHAPTER 24
One Bed

Kodi

ME

ONE BED! We are now stuck with just one bed because my room was flooded and felt like the Amazon Rainforest as soon as we stepped into it.

SIN

spitting out water gif

SIN

Come again?

ME

You heard me! And they can't give us another room. Which means...

DARCY

> You're sleeping in a bed with your hot boss tonight.

I need to breathe. Everything is fine. In. *One. Two. Three.* Out. *One. Two. Three.*

ME

> Fuck. I am. OMG! What if I snore? Or he smells my morning breath? Or we accidentally cuddle?

HARLEY

> Accidentally cuddle???

DARCY

> Yes! You know how she moves closer to him in her sleep because there's warmth and they wake up with her head on his shoulder.

SIN

> If Bella wasn't sleeping in the same room, you guys would be in trouble...

Before I can respond, there's a knock on the door. Leaving Bella with her chicken nuggets and Bluey, I saunter over to the door assuming her jersey must be here. Opening the door, a young man in a Tampa Bay Manta Rays polo stands with

SHOT TO THE HART

a box.

"Hi, Ms. Roscoe. Mr. Hart asked me to deliver this to you and to say thanks again for bringing Bella to the game tonight."

"Well, thank you," I say, taking the box from him and closing the door behind him. I set the box down and open it pulling out not one, but two long-sleeved jerseys. A Bella sized one and. . .one for me? My heart flutters that Maverick would even think to send me a jersey as well. The red and black jerseys have Hart and the number twenty-one embroidered into the back. My phone is buzzing again.

HARLEY
You alive girl?

ME
Yeah, um sorry. We got jerseys dropped off for the game tonight.

SIN
We???

ME
He sent us both a jersey. . .I have to get ready, I'll talk to you soon. Let's grab brunch when I get back into town.
<3

DARCY

Yes please! Lots of love. Xoxo

SIN

I love mimosas. Kisses

HARLEY

I'm in. Hugs.

Stepping through security an hour later, it's already loud and the lights are bright above us. There are so many bodies waiting to get into this arena, all of them wearing jerseys or team beanies. The smell of beer and soft pretzels wafts to me. Bella is clinging to me tightly, her little hands scrunched in my jersey, her face pressed into my neck as I make my way to concessions to grab a water bottle and snack. "Bella, baby, do you want a pretzel or nachos?"

She finally looks up to me with a smile, "French fries."

I laugh at her excitement stepping up to the register. "One water bottle, french fries, and a soft pretzel please." Handing the credit card that Maverick got me to the young lady with a smile, she passes everything back over and I take a minute to get myself organized. Setting Bella down, I make sure she's got her hand on my leg and I can see her before setting the backpack down on the counter to put my card away, along with the water bottle. Looking at the pretzel and fries, I still don't know how I'm going to do this. I know there are people standing behind me but there's no way that Bella, the food, and I are all making it to our seats without dropping something.

"Wanna move out the way, sweetheart?" An older man who reeks of beer says from behind me.

"I'm good, but thanks. I'll be done here in just a moment. You can clearly see my hands are full," I throw back at him. Taking my time, wrapping the pretzel carefully in some napkins and sticking it in the smaller empty pocket of the backpack and finally being able to hold Bella and the fries, I walk away then smile at the same old man who I now see is wearing a North Carolina jersey, "Can't wait to watch my friends kick your ass."

Following the signs to our section, I make sure to make note of the bathroom and take my time down the steps so I don't end up falling down them. I flash my tickets at the same young man from earlier and give him a smile.

Stepping into our row, I realize how close we will be to the action of the game. My heart is racing and my palms are sweaty in anticipation of my first live game. I wonder if Maverick is a brute on the ice, he's such a gentle giant outside of here. I also realize that if we look to our right, the guys will pass right by us to enter the ice.

"Want to sit in your seat and have your fries?"

Bella nods against my neck, but as I go to set her down, I hear, "Darlin'!"

Looking towards what I've learned is the tunnel, I see Maverick in his gear, wet hair, and a huge smile on his face. Holy cow, if the gray sweatpants were hot, his hockey gear is smoldering. The pads adding to his muscular frame, his skates making him three inches taller, his wet hair dripping down his face once again. My spine is tingly and the sweaty palms and racing heart have kicked up a notch.

"Come here. Let me get a picture with my girls wearing my jersey." My. Girls. Oh my God. That was surely an accident, I'm sure he just meant my girl.

Stumbling over my feet, I make my way to the barrier that sits just above my waistline, handing Arabella over to Maverick so he can hold her for the picture. When I go to walk away, he wraps his arm around my shoulder, pulling me back and closer, and smiling in the direction of Dom who somehow ended up with my phone. I don't know when I handed that to him, but I did, I guess. Maverick whispers just for me, "You look great in my jersey."

I bet my cheeks are going to be bright red in these photos.

"Thanks." I smile, taking Bella back.

"One question," he asks. This little thing just between us sends butterflies rampant every time.

"One answer." I grin back at him.

"You're only going to cheer for me tonight, right?"

Smacking his chest playfully I say, "For you. . .and your team."

"Fine. That's acceptable. You guys comfortable in your seats? No one is bothering you right?"

At this moment, Nik appears in the tunnel entrance. "Hart, get your ass in here. We've got a game to win."

"We'll see you after the game. Good luck!" I rush him off.

"Thanks Kodi!"

"I'll score a goal for you, pretty girl!" Dom screams at me, making me laugh. Maverick on the other hand, if looks could kill, well. . .Dom would be dead.

We get settled and I get Bella's headphones on as the music begins to ramp up, letting us know the players are about to skate out. When they do head out, Mav makes one lap, stopping in front of Bella and I, pointing his stick at us. No not us, at her with a hand on his chest. I can't help but smile back at him.

The arena lights are back to full brightness as Mav and the North Carolina center step up to the line. The ref drops the puck and they spring into action. North Carolina gets possession, but the puck is swiftly stolen by Collins who attempts a pass to the left-winger, but it gets intercepted by number sixty-two on Carolina's side. The fans wait in anticipation to see if it will get past Dom and the other defenseman. Number eighty-three on Carolina shoves into Dom, knocking him backwards as he attempts to shoot a goal and misses. The Carolina fans boo and the Tampa fans scream at the ref to 'get his eyes checked' and to 'call a penalty' for allowing the shoving, but the ref ignores the screaming, letting the game continue as it was.

Throughout the next two periods, Collins and Mav pass the puck back and forth with elegance. At one point, Dom ended up in the penalty box for intentionally shoving number eighty-three; the coaches and rest of the team, along with a few fans, began losing their minds over this call after he let eighty-three get away with shoving. During this time, I couldn't keep my eyes off of Maverick as he carried the puck for a goal, barely relying on the left-winger. Nik has been defending the net with all he's got. Only letting two pucks past him the whole game, one of those times being when

Dom was in the box.

Bella is having the time of her life, squealing and cheering anytime one of her uncles or her Daddy skate by or are on the bench making silly faces at her. I can't help but join her. The energy is electric in this arena.

Standing with Bella on my hip, I watch in anticipation as, in the last minute of the game, Mav and Collins make their way down the ice passing the puck back and forth avoiding the Carolina team trying to block their flow with ease. Collins finds a pocket, quickly pushing the puck towards Mav who has an opening on the right side of the net. The timer counts down quickly and in the last five seconds, the puck reaches Mav and he slaps it into the net, bringing home the win. The arena erupts in cheers and boos, and Bella snuggles into me covering her headphones over her ears as the guys huddle around Mav and Collins bumping shoulders and whooping.

CHAPTER 25

My Girl

Maverick

"Huddle up guys!" Nik booms over the noise in the locker room, and we all come together. "Listen, we did great tonight. We need to keep this energy up if we want to make it to the playoffs and the championship. Keep up the good work. Go have fun tonight, but don't be stupid. I'll see some of you tonight and some of you back in Florida. Go get showered up fuckers, you stink."

We break and I rush to get clean and changed. "Someone's in a hurry." Nik sits beside me pulling his shoes on.

"Ready to get to my daughter, man. She's probably exhausted, she's never up this late."

"Not trying to get to that raven-haired angel out there?"

I side-eye him as I pick up my bag and shrug. Of course I saw Kodi, who wouldn't be able to keep their eyes off of her? She's absolutely stunning, and the way she looks wearing my jersey does something to my body that I can't acknowledge if I don't want to draw attention to my package in the locker room. "Don't know what you're talking about. . ."

"Come on Mav, we all saw you looking towards their seats after every goal."

"Yep to my daughter."

"And to Kodi." Dom sidles up, clasping a hand on Nik's shoulder. "Ready?"

"See you later guys. Have fun tonight," I say as I walk towards the door.

"Oh I will!" Nik calls after me as I make my way out of the room.

Spotting my girls, I rush over, pulling them both in for a hug then taking Bella, who snuggles deeper into my arms, her eyes closing immediately. "Thanks for being here. You guys hungry?"

"Yes, for sure. She may not eat. She threw back french fries like they were going out of style." I chuckle at this because potatoes are definitely Bella's favorite food group.

"Let's go. I know a place we can order from, but I think we should get Bella home." I place my free hand on Kodi's lower back guiding her through the hall and the waiting family members and friends.

"KJ, baby!" A booming and familiar voice says from behind us. Kodi's shoulders lift to her ears and she tries to keep walking, but I stop and turn to find Conrad Hoyer. Fucking hell, I hate this guy. He's a terrible winger and even worse man. When I played for Carolina, he was constantly sleeping with a new woman, leading them on until the next one took his attention. It's a miracle the guy doesn't have ten kids running around somewhere. He thought he was God's gift to hockey but could barely keep up with me on the ice.

"Conrad." She offers a soft smile while I shoot daggers at him.

"What are you doing here? Why wouldn't you tell me you were coming to a game?"

My blood is suddenly boiling and I need to know how he knows my girl. A sense of possessiveness washes over me, wondering why he thinks he has any sort of right to know Kodi was at the game and why he would even want to know. I roll my shoulders back involuntarily making myself look a little taller.

"And what was it about me leaving in a hurry and not texting you back that made you think I would be interested in a sure to be underwhelming round two?" she states. She's trying to maintain her composure, but she's fiddling with the end of her ponytail and her chest is rising and falling just a touch faster than normal. Dom and Nik are approaching, stopping when they see who we're talking to.

He steps closer and I immediately pull Kodi into my side. "You know that's not what happened girl. I'd love to redeem myself."

Before she can respond, I step in, letting my voice drop a cadence. "She's good, bro. Thanks, see you next time."

"It was nice to beat your ass instead of carrying it tonight," Dom tosses at Conrad. They played together in college before Conrad was drafted to Carolina and Dom to Tampa.

I turn us around to walk away, but Conrad grumbles just loud enough, "Fucking puck-bunnies."

Oh hell no.

I stop, handing Kodi my daughter, gently gripping her chin so she looks into my eyes and calmly letting her know, "Kodi, Darlin'. You and Bella meet me at the exit doors. I think Conrad and I need to have a little chat."

"Mav, really it's not—"

"Oh, it is. Please go, you guys don't need to see this, I won't be long." And I turn on my heels. Conrad is waiting for me with his chest puffed up, casually leaning against the wall, as if I'm worried about his stringbean ass. Perfect.

Nik and Dom lean against the other wall, watching and waiting.

I approach him quickly, grabbing him by his collar and pushing him further into the wall, seething. I can see the vein in my forearm popping with the pressure I'm putting into keeping him still. "If you ever look at her, speak to her, or say some stupid shit again, I will not hesitate to beat your ass."

"Yeah right, bro," Conrad says, his voice a little unsteady. I laugh, actually laugh, adding a little more pressure. Now he's squirming beneath my grip.

"I mean it Conrad. Stay. The. Fuck. Away." My jaw is starting to hurt from how my teeth are grinding against each other, waiting to see if he is going to keep pushing me. As if they knew I was losing my cool, Nik and Dom are at my side, attempting to pull me off of him.

"Maverick, he's not worth being benched and fined." Nik grunts at my struggle, still holding tightly to Conrad's collar.

"Come on man, let's get out of here. You've got two pretty girls waiting on you." Dom pulls harder now and I loosen my grip, taking a step back and shaking them off my shoulders.

I'm turning to walk away but Conrad grips my shoulder. "She wasn't even that good of a lay, but maybe when she's done with your crusty ass, she'll let me take her for another ride."

Before I know what's come over me, I turn and let my fist meet Conrad's nose. He groans in agony, blood trickling from his nostrils, "Fuck, fine. Jesus bro. I hope she's worth it."

"She is."

CHAPTER 26
Pizza And Banana Pudding

Kodi

Mav bursts through the door leading out of the arena clenching and unclenching his right fist, it's red and angry. Nik and Dom follow, giving me curt nods and scurrying off.

"Oh my God, Mav! Are you okay?" Trying not to be too loud, although Bella still has her noise canceling headphones on as she sleeps against my shoulder. The players exit is pretty barren of people aside from a few straggling security members.

"Yeah, Darlin'. I'm fantastic." He's smiling but I can feel the tension radiating off of him.

"I don't believe you. It really wasn't that big of a deal. Conrad isn't a good guy."

"That is an understatement, Kodi." His nostrils flaring in time with his escalated breathing.

"Listen, I don't know why you dislike him. I just wasn't expecting to see him, I didn't even know who he was when we met."

"And when was it that you met?"

"Does it really matter?" I huff, getting agitated that he even wants to talk about this.

"It does to me. I just punched the man in the nose for you Kodi!" He's pacing back and forth in front of me now.

"You. . ." Sucking in a breath. "You punched him in the nose?" It's kind of hot that he would do that, but I need to focus on the fact that he is pushing a conversation that I don't want to have.

"Yes, he deserved it."

"Why would you do that?"

"Because he clearly made you uncomfortable and was being a prick. He said some disrespectful things Kodi, and I'm not okay with that." His pacing has slowed and he's standing in front of me again as we speak.

"Oh my God, okay. You didn't need to punch him though. Let me guess, he called me a bunny and probably said something about him wanting another go? Because in less words, that's what he implied the first time I met him."

"He deserved way more than a punch in the face. I'm already going to be benched for that. Fuck." He runs his hands through his hair, realizing now the mistake that he made in punching a nobody like Conrad in the face over me.

"Jesus, Mav you can't do that again, they need you on the ice. Do you really want to know how we met?" I ask, looking down at my feet.

"It's too late, you deserve respect. But yes, I do want to know."

I spit it out before I can stop myself. "We met at Lockout

and we hooked up afterwards."

"You slept with him?" His arms crossed and lips pressed into a flat line.

"Yes, Maverick. I, a grown-ass woman, consciously made the decision to sleep with that man months ago when I was drunk and lonely." Lifting my chin in his direction. I can't believe he's doing this right now. After the day we've had, I'm starting to feel worn down. "I really cannot fathom why you are making such a big deal of this."

"What do you want me to say Kodi? Do you want me to tell you that fu—Conrad will never be worthy of your time? Do you want me to tell you that the thought of him touching you and hearing him call you 'baby' made my skin crawl?" I flinch at his admissions and the slight frustration in his voice. My hackles are rising, making me feel like I can't continue this conversation,and I turn, stalking down the street away from him with Bella still sleeping soundlessly against my shoulder.

"Kodi, wait! Come on!" His footsteps are quickening behind me and his hand gently grabs my free arm to turn me around. "I'm sorry, okay. I just really don't like that guy; he didn't deserve whatever time you gave to him, and when he spoke to you that way, it just really got under my skin."

"It's whatever, Maverick. It's not worth talking about. Can we just get back to the hotel and get food?" I beg. I need this topic to change. I don't even understand why he's so upset about it, it's not like we're together. Even then, it was forever ago, and I wouldn't go there again with Conrad.

He heaves a breath as if I'm the one who just went barbaric

back there. "Let's go, I'll order food to be delivered to the hotel. Do you want anything specific? There's a place around here that has really good pizza, or a place that has smoked brisket and banana pudding that is to die for."

"The pizza and the banana pudding both sound so good."

"Okay, I'll order both. What toppings?" He takes Bella from me and we begin our walk back to the hotel.

"No way! Those fees are going to be astronomical. Just the pizza is fine. Meat lovers is the best way to go."

"Kodi, trust me, the fees won't kill me. You'll regret not having this banana pudding, so I'm getting it."

"Fine, if I must enjoy the most-definitely delicious pudding, I will, but I'm going to grumble about the fees."

"Okay Ms. Frugal Franny." I slap his arm playfully and we both laugh now. Some of the tension easing.

We make it back up to the room in silence, Mav gets Bella set up in her playpen while I head to the bathroom to get changed. Opening my suitcase I realize I've fucked up, my sweatpants are nowhere to be found. "Shit," I mumble to myself. Mav's voice is now drifting through the door.

"Food's almost here. You about ready?"

"Uh, yeah. Just one minute." My voice definitely wavered there, the weight and exhaustion of today is hitting me hard. I feel my throat tightening and tears welling in my eyes.

"Kodi. What's wrong?"

"Nothing."

"No, Kodi, I can tell something is wrong. Open the door." I hear his forehead thunk against the door. "Please, or the fees that I have to pay to fix it will be nothing compared to the delivery ones. I don't want you crying in the bathroom if it's something I can fix or need to apologize for." If I wasn't so in my head, I probably would laugh. Sighing in resignation, I open the door, looking up to him with watery eyes and slumped shoulders.

"Whoa, hey what happened?"

"I'm just so tired, and you got upset with me, and I'm hungry, and I. . ." A whimper escapes my lips. "I can't find the sweatpants I was supposed to sleep in tonight." God damn it. This is the second time I've cried in front of him over something so silly.

Maverick pulls me into his arms, rubbing small circles on my back and I decide to let the tears freely fall. "Sweetheart, don't cry. I'm sorry that I misdirected my anger at Conrad towards you. You didn't deserve that and I won't let it happen again, I shouldn't have let it happen in the first place. You know, it's okay to feel worn down, you've had a long day. I appreciate you being there for every part of it and taking the challenges with grace. You can sleep in my sweats, and the food should be at the door right now." The tenderness in his voice isn't something I'm used to with a man. If this was Andy, I would be told I was acting 'ridiculous' and 'crying was unnecessary'.

I really don't know how I stayed with that man for so long.

"I didn't handle it with grace," I sniffle. He pulls back just enough to look into my eyes. His baby blues looking right into my soul.

"What do you mean?"

"I. . .I told an old man that I couldn't wait for my friends to kick his team's ass cause he was being a jerk about me trying to get organized before walking away from the register at the concessions stand." The laugh that erupts from Maverick is hearty and full. I've never heard him laugh like this. It gives me the same feeling that the sound of the ocean crashing into the sand at sunset gives. Something I want to experience over and over, and it pulls a watery laugh out of me.

"Oh, Darlin'. That is the best thing I've heard in a while. Let's eat." Maverick grabs our food and we eat in silence, sitting on opposite corners of the bed. The room is thrumming with an unsettling energy now as we edge closer to sleep.

After we eat, I excuse myself to the bathroom with the borrowed gray sweats, and when I come back Maverick has created a pillow boundary and placed himself as close to the edge of the bed as possible. I make my way over, lift the covers and slide in. Turning off the light, I turn inwards. I can't sleep with my face towards the outer edge of the bed, it freaks me out. Mav is facing inwards as well, and his eyes don't leave mine for a long moment. It feels like he is trying to read my mind or he's searching for some sign that he needs to sleep on the floor, but I won't give that to him. This is fine, everything is fine, even if my delicious boss is sleeping two feet away from me.

Clearing my throat, "Well, uh, goodnight, Maverick."

"Night, Kodi. Our flight leaves at ten, I've got an alarm set."

"Awesome."

Maverick begins to fidget, sighing and turning, trying to

get comfortable.

"Mav, I don't have cooties. Make yourself comfortable, you've got to be exhausted and sore."

"Uh yeah, I am. I just don't want to make you uncomfortable." It's criminal that I am sharing a bed with this man and he's not moving these pillows out of the way and pulling me into his arms to hold me as his breathing lulls me to sleep.

"We aren't cuddling, it's okay." *But I wish we were.* He moves around a little bit more before finding a spot where we aren't touching, but his body heat is sending warmth my way and I want to snuggle into it.

Mav's breathing eventually evens out, and that's when I finally let myself relax, drifting into my own sleep.

※

"We woke up face to face. His arm was slung over my waist! He scrambled out of the bed so fast, you'd think I had leprosy," I gripe. We got home from Carolina three days ago, and I snuck away for brunch with the girls after Maverick got home from practice today.

"Then what happened?" Sin takes a sip of her mimosa.

"He fell over and bonked his head on Bella's playpen, jostling her awake. It took him twenty minutes to calm her down, and we almost missed the flight back."

"Oh my God." Darcy chokes on her coffee. Harley pounds on her back until she gets it together.

"You guys, this is not funny. I don't know what to make of all this back and forth."

"Just let it happen naturally, babes. He might be dealing with some complicated emotions if he's got feelings for you and simultaneously doesn't want to cross the boss and employee boundary," Harley, ever the sympathetic friend adds.

"Why do you always have to be right?" We all laugh.

"So, you clearly are feeling conflicted too. What's going on in that pretty head of yours?" Darcy asks.

"Pfft, that's a loaded question. I guess for starters, I don't know what's going on inside his head, and I'd love to start there."

"Well we can't know that, but we can process your feelings." Harley offers.

"It's just that he's so kind and caring and he doesn't ever discredit my feelings. I mean he's constantly checking in, giving me breaks, and making sure I have everything I need. And the way he loves that little girl, you guys." Saying all of this out loud makes my feelings real which is absolutely terrifying.

"I can see the hearts in your eyes, it makes me want to puke," Sin states, throwing her mimosa back fully.

"Don't be bitter Sinclair." Darcy shoots a pointed look at Sin. "He seems like a great guy, Ko. Don't write him off just cause he's not ready to explore those feelings yet."

"UGH. I know. Why do men have to be men?" I sigh, throwing my head into my hands.

"When you find out, please do share the wealth." Darcy's voice is laced with sarcasm.

"What have the rest of you been up to?" I ask, feeling like we haven't gotten to really catch up in a while.

"Drowning in work instead of dick. To be quite honest, it is the most unfortunate of circumstances." Sin's statement has us all cackling.

"I mean aren't you off like three days a week, couldn't you go have fun then?" Darcy asks.

"I do, maybe once every three weeks, I've honestly been too exhausted."

"Have you considered taking a vacation?" Harley pipes in, "It's definitely important to give yourself a break when burnout hits."

"I'll take one when you take one, Ms. Graduate Student," Sin throws back at Harley.

"Touche'." Harley sighs. "I'd like to report that Benji has been on his best behavior."

"And he better stay on it," Darcy replies. "I had to stop seeing Leighton."

"What? Why? He seemed nice," I admonish.

"He was getting too clingy and I don't do clingy." That's true, Darcy's independence is one of the most important things to her, especially considering how over the top her socialite parents were in her upbringing. I can't blame her, but I've seen my best friend let go of some really awesome men because she's fearful of losing her independence.

"Fair enough, I have to get back. Mav has practice soon. Thank you guys for meeting me today. I needed it!"

Paying our bills, we all grab our things and head to the parking lot. Giving hugs and promising to do it again soon, I head home for Bella duty.

It feels like we just got back, but Maverick is already

leaving for another away game. He got home from practice and headed straight to pack for his flight in the morning. He wasn't even able to join us for dinner. I shouldn't be disappointed, it's not like we have to eat together or hang out. I enjoy the time I get to spend with Mav, I'm realizing every day I want to keep spending time with him. I want to hear him laugh and watch him snuggle his daughter, wishing I could feel that warmth and love from him.

While we continue to toe the edge of a cliff, at this point I think we are both fighting the inevitable. We skirt around the boss and employee boundary but never fully cross it, one of us pulling away or stopping the cord from snapping.

CHAPTER 27

You're An Idiot

Maverick

A few nights later, I walk in from practice and notice soft light illuminating from the living room. I don't get to play the next game because I punched Conrad in his smug face and paid a hefty fine. My body is sore from how hard Coach pushed me because even though I'm benched, I still practice. Coach was pissed, and I'm wondering if punching him was the right move. Peeking my head around the corner, I notice a rosy-cheeked Kodi cuddled up with her e-reader. "Books that good, huh?" I flash her a lopsided grin. I need to know what caused her cheeks to turn that pink. I want to know how I can make her cheeks that color.

"Ha, very funny Big Guy. At least I can read." That response was quick witted and honestly turned me on a little bit.

Pretending to act wounded, I throw myself onto the couch beside her. "Whatcha reading?"

"Um, just a romance," she replies.

"Kodi, I have a younger sister, what kind of romance? Is it spicy? Sports? Monsters? Romantasy?" I wiggle my eyebrows at her and she giggles.

"Sports," she mumbles.

"Oh, what kind of sport?" I ask her.

"Hockey." I swear she said hockey and now I'm even more curious as to what she's reading about. Then, without thinking, I shoot up and catch her wrist in one hand and her e-reader in the other. My eyes scan briefly over the words of the page:

He has me bent over the bench pounding into me from behind. The jersey he told me to keep on, in between my teeth to keep my pleasure filled screams from echoing in the empty arena.

"Whoa. I need to borrow this when you're done. Seems fun."

"Maverick, you give that back right now!" she squeals.

"Hang out with me," I pout, holding her e-reader just out of reach. "You've been weird since we got back from Carolina."

"I have not!" She's sitting up now, arms crossed, chewing on that bottom lip. One of her dead giveaways that she is lying to herself and to me. The fun energy dissipates immediately.

"You have, Kodi. What's going on?" I push.

"I. . .I don't know Mav." She won't look me in the eyes and all I want to see is what's swimming in them. "There's a lot going on up here right now." Tapping her temple.

"Do you want to talk about it?" She doesn't share much, but if I catch her at the right moment, she might open up to me.

"No, Mav. Everything is fine. Seriously," she blurts, still

chewing on her lip. The urge to reach out and pull it from that place almost wins, but I stop myself at the last minute.

"Well, whatever it is or whenever you're ready to talk about it, I'm here for you." Something is bothering her, but I'm not going to force it any further.

"Uh yeah, thanks. Can I keep reading now please?" she asks. I just want the lighthearted, give-me-crap Kodi back, not the one that shrugs off these conversations as if how I affect her doesn't matter. In order to bring that back, I lift her e-reader back into the air and out of reach again.

"Come and get it," I taunt. This is a mistake. I'm leading us down a road of temptation. She eyes me for a moment before she's on me. Small body covering mine, arms flailing, giggles erupting from her chest and reaching for her e-reader. We continue this way until she ends up straddling my waist, still reaching above us.

As soon as we end up in this position, I harden beneath her. I know she feels it based on the way her breathing hitches and she stops fighting me. I search her eyes, I need to figure out where her mind is at. I slowly lower my arms and present her e-reader to her. She can't be sitting on my lap like this. She takes it but sets it to the side, maintaining that intense eye contact and shifting a little, making my cock twitch.

"Mav," A breathy whisper.

"Darlin." I let my hands find her waist where a sliver of skin is exposed. Her tongue darts out to wet her lips. God. I want to feel her lips on mine.

She's leaning in, like she might kiss me if I don't kiss her first.

Letting out a sigh, I say, "We shouldn't do this Kodi, but I really want to kiss you right now."

"I know, kiss me," she says on a breathy exhale. She's begun slowly circling her hips in my lap and her breathing is getting heavier.

I shouldn't do this. I shouldn't give into the need to deepen my connection with her, but my cock and her sinful hips moving under my hands is going to kill me. I let one hand glide up to grip the back of her neck and bring our lips together.

At first, our kiss is tentative. A soft exploration of our mouths meeting for the first time. Her hands snaking around my neck, keeping our connection. She lets out a soft moan and I take this opportunity to deepen our kiss, letting my tongue explore her mouth. She sucks lightly on it, as if to see what kind of reaction it will cause. I groan, lifting my hips into her core in response.

I have to stop this. We can't take it any further than this. I want to be buried deep inside her, but now is not the time. I don't know if there will ever be a good time.

It's the hardest thing to do, but I pull back from Kodi, not letting go of her face and allowing her to keep her grasp on me. She's searching my face for something, but I don't know if she'll find what she's looking for.

"What is it? Why did you stop?" she asks tentatively, but continues grinding into me. My grip on her waist doesn't loosen as I watch her mouth part into a small O shape. Seeing her lust-filled expression has me regretting my decision to pull away and I go in for one more kiss, her body melting into mine immediately. I really have to stop this now. This time I let my forehead rest against hers.

"We really shouldn't do this." *As much as I'm dying to let it happen over and over again.*

Her movement has slowed to a stop and her eyebrows are furrowed on her beautiful face as she pulls her head away from mine. "Is that really what you want, Mav?"

I don't want it at all. I want to kiss her everyday. I want to make her scream my name. I want to sleep with her wrapped in my arms. I can't though, not with Bella's heart involved too.

"I wish I had another answer, Kodi. I really fucking wish I did but we can't do this. I can't." I groan and I try to maintain eye contact to convey that this is exactly the opposite of what I want to do, but I can tell immediately that she is hurt by that statement. In the way that she pulls back, in the way that her eyes well with tears, in the way that she lifts herself off my lap, and in the way that without a word, she takes off in the direction of her bedroom

Throwing my head backwards, scrubbing my hand down my face, I groan. "Fucccck. You're an idiot."

I finally drag myself to my room and let the regret of stopping wash over me. I consider banging her door down and picking back up where we left off, but I also consider dropping to my knees and asking her to forgive me for being a monumental idiot. I'm in deep and we are towing a very thin line. A shower, a shower will definitely help. Beelining it for my bathroom, I turn my shower on hot enough that it could melt my skin.

Stepping in, I lean my head back and close my eyes under the water, but all I see are those green eyes looking back at me. I shouldn't be thinking about her, but my cock has other thoughts, getting harder by the second. Thinking of her sweet and curvy little body and how she looked wearing my sweats, the way her lips parted while she was asleep in the same bed as me. The flush of her cheeks because of whatever she was reading. I groan and reach down, giving in, just this once, stroking myself to that image, imagining what her moans would sound like if I touched her in the right places. Would they be breathy and light? Would she hold back? Fuck no. I wouldn't let her, I'd want to hear all of the noises I could drag out of her. My strokes get rougher, my balls tighten and I come with a muffled groan into my elbow. This cannot happen again.

Once I settle into my bed, I realize I desperately need to talk to someone. I text Tate. As my best friend, he will probably give me shit, but will also help me organize my thoughts.

ME

I fucked up.

I lay there in the dark of my room. I can't believe I kissed her and then sent her away. She's going to resent me. It really had nothing to do with her. I want her, but I also can't sleep with her. I know myself, I feel myself getting more attached, I won't just want sex. I want her thoughts and her tears and her affection. I'm so screwed.

TATE

What did you do? I can't handle another niece, bro.

ME

Firstly, fuck off. Secondly, we didn't have sex. But I kissed her and I let it go too far. When I stopped us going any further, she was clearly upset.

TATE

Her who?

ME

You know who.

TATE

You didn't.

Those three little dots go wild until his next message pops through.

TATE

Tell me you didn't make a move on the nanny.

ME

I can't do that.

SHOT TO THE HART

TATE

Jesus, Mav. Did you apologize?

ME

No, Tatum. I haven't apologized. I'm hiding in my room like a coward.

TATE

You're better than that dude. Give her time to cool down tonight and then talk to her. Buy her flowers or some shit.

CHAPTER 28

Wine, Cheese, And An Orgasm

Kodi

I can't believe I let myself get so hot and bothered with Maverick the other night. We can't do this. He was right, but the sting of rejection still hurt. I've been avoiding him for days. I respond to his texts and I'm cordial when we run into each other in the house, but our typical routine after Bella is down has been halted for the time being. No longer talking about our day, eating junk food in secret, and watching The *Big Bang Theory* until one of us falls asleep.

I don't know how to explain to him how I'm feeling and he is clearly just as flustered. He smiles but it's more of a grimace when we bump into each other, and he's hiding in his room when he is home. He's been so busy with practice, media and games that we haven't really had the opportunity to address it.

God, the other night was so hot. I could have come just with his tongue in my mouth and my hips rotating on his hard length. But no, he had to be the boss and stop it. This man is simultaneously the sweetest and most frustrating man I've ever interacted with. I don't have the slightest clue what to do about it.

I'm getting ready to do my nighttime routine as I watch Bella sleep on the monitor when my phone buzzes beside me.

MAVERICK
> If you're up when I get home, can we talk? I'm leaving the stadium now.

Ugh, I don't want to. I don't want to hear him reject me again, even if it's just to restate the boundary that was set after our time on the couch. We need to talk. I want to talk.

ME
> Sure. I was just getting ready to lay down but I can stay up.

MAVERICK
> Thanks. I appreciate it. See you soon.

ME
> Drive safe.

I quickly wash and moisturize my face then grab two Gatorades—as much as a beer sounds good he's going to need electrolytes after practice—and pace the back porch sipping mine until I hear the sliding glass door behind me. I turn to find Maverick in a tightfitting athletic tee, black sweats, with a black hat sitting backwards on his golden locks and—what the fuck—a dozen colorful daisies in his hand. There's no way he remembers that conversation where Dom grilled me for my favorites.

Tentatively, he pushes the flowers towards me. Taking them and handing him one of the Gatorades, I say, "Thank you. These are beautiful. Um, why did you get them?"

"Because I was a jerk the other night. I couldn't even properly explain to you why we couldn't keep going." I am getting ready to respond but he continues. "Will you sit with me?" Gesturing towards the gray, cushioned patio furniture that surrounds the fire pit. "Listen, I haven't been with anyone since Lily. We haven't even had any other women in the house aside from your friends. Not even the guys are allowed to bring women around unless they are seriously dating. You're so fucking beautiful Kodi, but I don't feel like I can have you, especially with this bond that you've formed with my daughter. Arabella's heart is more important than mine. I have to make sacrifices to keep her safe, even if it's to my detriment. I'm sorry that I didn't tell you that the other night. I felt like such a jackass and I wanted to apologize, but I felt like you were avoiding me." He sighs. It hurts me to think that he doesn't feel like he deserves happiness too but it isn't my place to tell him that, not in this moment at least.

"I was because I didn't know what to do or how to handle the rejection." He flinches. "But, I accept your apology. I understand why you didn't want to go any further. I do wish you would have been able to verbalize that the other night though." I rush to get out before he keeps apologizing or says something that might make my heart flutter in my chest.

I finally have the nerve to look into his eyes and it knocks the air out of my lungs seeing his mesmerizing blue eyes burning into me from across the pit.

"Do you think there is something else you can do for me?" He asks, never breaking eye contact.

"Sure, what's up?"

"My dad called earlier today, he asked about coming to spend a few hours with Bella this week. My schedule is super packed though. Do you think you could take her to the park or something with him one day this week?"

"Yeah, Mav. Of course, just have him text me and we can set something up. I'd love to meet him," I reply, giving him my best grin.

"Thanks, Kodi. I truly appreciate it. I don't want to be rude, but I'm exhausted. Do you mind if I head in?" he asks me with a worried expression.

I don't know if he's worried that I'm still hurt or about me meeting his Dad, or if it even has anything to do with me, but I'd love to help get rid of that expression. "Oh, of course. It's been a long week. I probably won't be too far behind you."

He pushes up from his chair and starts to head inside, but since I'm a glutton for punishment I call after him, "Hey, Mav, one question?" He turns and smiles at me, the genuine one that I can't get enough of.

"One answer, Darlin'."

"The other night, did you actually want to stop?" I almost whisper at him, nervous about what he's going to say.

He grimaces. Not a good sign. "No, I didn't want to stop."

Turning on his heels, he rushes inside, leaving me alone with the knowledge that he actually does want me. And God, do I want him too. This tension is going to burst at some point and it's either going to go really well, or it's going to end really badly.

※

Sitting at the local park, I'm watching Stu push Bella in the swings. She is giggling like a maniac, and Stu has a huge smile on his face watching his granddaughter, his smile lines more prominent because of his age I pull my phone out and snag a quick video, sending it over to Maverick.

> **MAV**
> Thanks for hanging out with them. He really needed that today, I think.

> **ME**
> Of course, Mav. *smiley face emoji*

Stu and Bella join me shortly after so Bella can have a snack before we head back to the house for her nap.

"So, Kodi, how's it been working with Maverick? He's so protective of Bella," Stu asks, breaking the silence.

"Honestly, he's been so kind and easy to work with. You raised a really good man." I can feel my cheeks blushing at the thoughts of the small moments Mav and I have shared that really showed me what a good man he is.

"Yep, I would mostly attribute that to his Ma. Bella seems to be doing really well with you." A fond smile spreading across his face, his eyes are distant like he's thinking about his wife. Thinking back to the night he told me about his Ma causes my heart to squeeze for both Maverick and his Father.

"I'm sorry about your loss, Stu. She seemed really wonderful." I smile fondly at the little girl currently stuffing quartered grapes into her mouth like a squirrel gathering nuts for hibernation. "Bella, slow down baby. They aren't going anywhere." This causes Stu to chuckle.

"She was really wonderful, I miss her. Mav doesn't often talk to others about her. He must really trust you to share those memories." I knew Mav didn't talk about his Mom passing often, but to hear Stu confirm what I know already causes my eyes to well a little bit. I think Stu notices but gives me a moment to collect myself instead of saying anything more.

We hang out for a while more, holding light conversation. Stu is so easy to talk to, it makes my heart hurt a little, wishing I had grown up with a Father like Stu. Hope blossoms that maybe I will have the opportunity to build a relationship like that with him one day.

When Stu has said goodbye to Bella, I get her home and down for her nap.

I called the girls and we decided to do a wine and charcuterie night at Harley and Sin's place. I'm packing up an overnight bag when Maverick taps softly at my bedroom door.

"Come in," I say loudly enough that he can hear me, but

Bella won't wake up from her nap. My door opens and Mav steps inside, standing by the door instead of stepping fully in.

Without even considering the consequences of my intrusive thoughts spilling out of me, I ramble, "I was just thinking how you look like a teenager trying not to get caught kissing his girlfriend in his bedroom. You can actually come into my room, Maverick. I didn't invite you in for you to stand over by the door." His cheeks turn rosy, he's embarrassed, and I kind of love it. "Come sit. What's up?"

He sits on the opposite corner of my bed, face cast downward, clears his throat, and says, "My Dad's going to take Bella this weekend so that I can go out too. I was thinking we could still ride together unless you were going to get ready with the girls or something."

I smile, knowing Stu will love this. "We haven't talked about it but I think it makes sense for us to ride together. We actually had some really great conversation about you and my time with Bella."

Mavericks head shoots up. "You guys talked about me?"

Oh, he's nervous. He thinks his Dad told me some embarrassing story about young Maverick. A devious grin spreads across my face. "Of course we did. He even mentioned a few stories about—"

Before I can finish my statement, Maverick mutters, "I don't want to know. Please don't finish that thought." The cackle that escapes me has me holding my stomach and falling over onto my bed.

"You little brat! He didn't tell you anything, did he?" he practically shouts.

Still trying to catch my breath, "No, Big Guy. He didn't, but I hope he does because with that reaction there are clearly some good stories about you available."

For a second, it's so quiet I think maybe he left the room. As I peek my eyes open, I notice Maverick is now sitting directly beside me and he's so close that I'm having flashbacks to the other night. I need to avoid this, so I jump up into a standing position. I don't know what's taken over him, maybe that tension is finally going to snap, but he looks determined.

Maverick stands just as fast, backing me into the wall next to my bed as his hand gently comes up to my throat, goosebumps erupting on my skin. He's gotten as close as he can without our lips touching. I want our lips to touch so badly, but I know he won't let that happen again. He's looking right into my eyes, like he is going to say something but shakes it off.

"Maverick," is all I get out before whatever connection we had just now is broken and he's across the room. What the fuck. He's beginning to give me whiplash.

"Have fun tonight, Kodi. See you tomorrow." And then he's gone. I finish packing my bag and drive to Harley and Sin's like a Nascar driver in the final lap.

"Hey, baby!" Sin greets me out the door with a kiss on the cheek.

"I need wine and cheese and an orgasm." Sin guffaws at this like I just announced that the Loch Ness Monster is real.

"First off, he bought me stuff when I was on my period, like what the hell kind of sweet gesture is that? Then one night last week, he comes home, snatches my e-reader and I end up in his lap with his lips on mine, but then he's telling me we can't do that. And so, naturally, I avoided him for three days and then he shows up with a bouquet of multicolored daisies and apologizes. I met his Dad today too, what a sweet guy. I wish I had a Dad like him growing up. He also backed me against my bedroom wall today like some sort of man possessed, but in a sexy way, and his lips were basically on mine again without being on mine! Then he ran away!" Taking a deep breath, I add, "And you all are definitely going out next weekend right? To make sure I'm not imagining this."

"Of course, free booze and hot men. I'm in." Sin grins.

Harley has a feral grin. "Oh my God. This is perfect."

"What do you mean this is perfect? My boss edged me and then left me alone. Now we are flirting, and it's not perfect at all," I say with frustration evident in my tone. Sometimes I wonder if they are even listening to me.

"Babe, because we can get him to give in." Sin laughs maniacally.

"I never said I wanted him to give in." Three faces break out into huge grins. I sigh, "Fine, I do. I'll hear you out, but I'm not committing."

Harley's first question is, "Who of his teammates would be willing to flirt with you to make him jealous?'

"Nik." I respond almost immediately knowing he would have fun with this.

"Call him. Now. On speaker," they demand.

I reluctantly dial Nik's number.

CHAPTER 29

Lockout

Kodi

I step out of my room at the same time Maverick does, with Bella trailing behind him in her dinosaur pajamas. He's got on a black button up with maroon dress pants and black dress shoes on, rolling up his sleeves so his thick and corded arms are showing. He looks me up and down in the same way I imagine I'm looking at him.

"You look stunning tonight, Kodi. I'm going to have to remind the guys of the no touching rule," he states matter of factly. Little does he know, that's exactly what he is going to have to do. I know I'm blushing because it feels good to have someone look at me with such hunger in his eyes.

"Thanks, Mav. You clean up pretty well yourself. Hey, Bella bear, are you ready to go see Grandpa?"

She giggles and nods her head enthusiastically and takes off down the hallway with Mav and I following. I packed her bag, so I know she has everything she needs. Spare pajamas, clothes for tomorrow, snacks, two barbies, regular diapers, and her overnight diapers.

"Does she have Floppy?" I ask, knowing this will be imperative for bedtime.

"I made sure to put him in the key bowl so we wouldn't leave him behind, but to make sure Bella could hold him in the car. I meant it when I said I wanted to have an adult night. It's been a while." I can see he's smiling out of my periphery.

"Good. I'm excited." I hop into the passenger's side after Maverick opens the door for me while he heads to the backseat with Bella in his arms, getting her settled into her carseat.

"Bella, what movie are you going to watch with Grandpa before bed?" Maverick asks, looking at Bella through his rearview mirror.

"Frozen!" She starts singing the Bella rendition of Let It Go, ad-libbing the lyrics she can't remember, causing Mav and I to both laugh. Mav queues up the movie's playlist so that Bella can sing along as we make the short drive.

Pulling up to Stu's house, I unbuckle and grab Bella's bag and Floppy while Maverick gets her out of her carseat. I follow him up the walkway and we wait for the door to open.

Stu opens the door with a huge grin on his face. "My Bella girl! How are you?"

Arabella basically throws herself out of Mavericks arms to get to Stu.

We visit for about twenty minutes, run Stu through Bella's routine and head back to the car. Maverick lets out a hefty sigh as he puts the car in reverse.

I reach over, placing a hand on his arm, "You okay?"

Maverick has very few anxious ticks but his thumb

is rapping along the steering wheel like crazy and that's a dead giveaway. "Uh, yeah, I guess I'm just a little nervous. I obviously trust my dad. Nothing's ever happened, but that doesn't mean something can't go wrong. I know he'll call if needs anything and that he probably won't need anything, but I just feel bad for choosing to go out instead of being there with her." His breathing seems to be increasing pretty rapidly, and I'm worried that if we don't get it under control, he could have a panic attack.

"Mav, maybe you should stop the car for a second." He looks surprised by my suggestion, but he throws the car into park while we're still in the driveway. I turn towards him, "Can you take a breath with me?"

He chuckles nervously, pulling on the back of his neck, "Wha—what?"

"Take a breath with me. They will be okay, you deserve a night out with your friends, and we are only going to be twenty minutes away. In three, out three. Okay?" I repeat.

"Okay, yeah, that's a good idea," he relents.

"In." *One. Two. Three.* "Out." *One. Two. Three.*

I see some of the tension leave his shoulders and watch as his chest begins to regain its steady movement. "Can we do one more?"

"Absolutely. In." *One. Two. Three.* "Out." *One. Two. Three.* "Ready to go have fun?"

His smile comes a little easier this time. "Yeah, I am actually." He puts the car in drive and we head to Lockout, where Dom wanted to celebrate his birthday.

I can see the line from the lot which gives me a little

panic. The girls texted they already found the guys at the club and were excited to see me. Once the car is in park, Mav jumps out and runs around to open my door and help me out before I can get to it myself. "Thanks, Big Guy." I grin at him, and he extends an arm to me, leading me past the line and right into the club via a flash of his smile and both our IDs to the bouncer.

Once inside, he takes my hand and leads me to the roped off corner of Lockout where all our friends wait for us. Pushing through the bodies, we ignore the looks we get whether people recognize Mav or are wondering who he's out with. Squeals erupt when my friends notice me, meaning they have probably done at least three shots, and as much as I want to drink with them, I need a clear mind going into tonight. I'm going to take one shot and then switch to water, just to give me the little kick in the butt I need to enact the plan. It'll wear off before we get home.

"Hey, everybody!" I scream over the music and I'm greeted with nods all around.

Darcy grins and waggles a finger in Mav's direction. Then her eyes slide over to Tatum, who is smirking at her.

Maverick smiles at everyone before taking a seat with the guys.

"Jesus, Kodi. You nervous or something? You're basically vibrating with anxious energy," Sin says directly into my ear so that I can hear her speaking.

"Um, absolutely I am," I say, leaning in. My knee is bouncing vigorously now and Sin takes stock of that.

"I have to pee. Let's go. Grab the other two," Sin declares.

And then we are headed to the bathroom with D and Harls in tow. Sin chooses the empty larger stall and directs us all in.

"Talk to us," that's all Darcy says. And so I do what I do best and start rambling, "He looks so handsome and what if he doesn't care if I dance with Nik, or what if all he does is pull Nik off me and then storms off. What if he doesn't want me the same way I want him? What if all I do is piss him off and he fires me? What if he does take me home and I'm not what he was expecting in the bedroom?" I let out the breath I'd been holding in all this time, not realizing how anxious I actually was. I think it had taken a backseat to getting Bella ready for the weekend and then ensuring that Mav was okay.

At this moment Harley grabs my face, making eye contact that makes me a little uncomfortable, but I can't look away from her. "Kodi James Roscoe. That man looks at you with stars in his eyes no matter how much either of you refuses to admit it. If he really pushes you away after this then we all need to go join a nunnery because hell hath frozen over at that point. I love you, you look hot, and you've got this. Let's go get your man."

CHAPTER 30

Fuck It.

Maverick

I wonder if she knows what she's doing to me in this outfit. A tight-fitting black lace corset with a green suit jacket that matches her eyes, a tight, black, fitted skirt and black combat boots drawing attention to the legs that I would love to have wrapped around my waist.

When we got into the club, after she was distracted by her friends, I turned away from her to the guys and practically growled, "You keep your hands off Kodi and her friends. If I catch any of you even looking at them with sexual intent, I will chop your dicks off. You hear me?" Mumbles ranging from "okay dad" to "it's my birthday, man" come from my closest teammates, but I take that as their agreement.

I order a whiskey and coke from one of the girls working our area, she's making eyes at me, but I just slide her a twenty and send her on her way. I only want one woman's attention tonight and I can't have it.

That woman is now staring at me as she sips water. No,

not at me, to my right just slightly, at Nik? Oh, fuck no. She and her friends are standing now, headed towards us, with an outstretched hand to Nik, and a saccharine smile, Kodi leans into Nik and with a sultry tone says, "We're headed to the dance floor. Come with us."

I know I'm glaring at Nik right now with clenched fists, he better keep to his word and say no. What does this dickhead do instead? He takes her hand and leads her and her group of giggling friends out into the dance floor. Dom and Collins follow suit, leaving me with Tatum filling the empty space on my other side of the padded bench.

Tatum is laughing like he's in on a joke I don't know about. "Dude, what are you on about?" I finally relent.

"Mav, you really aren't that dense. She's totally doing that on purpose. If you had to choose any of us to make someone jealous, who would you choose?" he asks as if it's something I've thought about.

"Nik, I guess. He's the oldest and has the most game." I shrug after a moment.

"Exactly. Look at them right now." I don't want to look but I think I need to. They are all standing in a circle, Dom is doing some weird little shimmy with Darcy and Sinclair. Collins and Harley are spinning in circles, hands entwined. When my eyes find Kodi's, she shies away from me, but I don't drop my glare. Nik has her facing away from him, face buried in her neck, hands on her waist while she moves her hips in time to the music. I see red and am grasping my glass so tight that I might shatter it. Nik catches my eyes and that asshole smiles at me then turns, giving me his back and taking my view of Kodi away, but I see her arms snake around his neck.

"I can't do anything about it man. She works for me, if she wants to date or sleep with other people she can do that. I have no claim on her." I sigh.

"Maverick, you're such a fucking idiot sometimes. You know you can let yourself have a little fun, right?"

"Yeah, of course, I know that." Logically, I know that I can have fun, but emotionally, I'm terrified. I have genuine feelings for Kodi, and I don't want to mess this up for myself or for Bella.

"Then go get your girl. We all see the way you look at each other, the way you care for her and Bella. Give it a chance," he urges.

"But what if it doesn't work out?" I ask, my anxiety is starting to peak. The music feels louder and I have to adjust my collar because I'm losing control of my breathing again.

I go back to the technique Kodi used earlier to help me calm down. In. *One, two, three.* Out. *One, two, three.*

"What if it does? You never know, and she's clearly trying to get your attention. If it all falls apart, you still have us. We won't go anywhere even if she does." Gesturing towards himself then towards the dance floor where our friends are.

"I want more than that man," I finally admit. I haven't let myself admit it because that makes this situation and these feelings that have been creeping in for Kodi real. And real means there's a possibility that I get hurt, that Kodi gets hurt, that maybe Bella gets hurt, but it also means there's an opportunity for real happiness. Happiness I haven't experienced in almost three years.

"Then work for it, bro. You love and work too hard to be alone forever. I'm going to tell you one more time, go get your girl."

With that final encouragement, I give Tatum a fist bump and head to the dance floor. It looks like Nik and Kodi have separated, giving me the opportunity to sneak up behind her. I snake my hands around her waist and lean down, nipping on her ear and speaking so only she can hear me, "What are you doing, baby? These hips are only supposed to be dancing on me. Now say goodbye to your friends, I'd like to take you home."

She sucks in a breath, but instead of moving to say goodbye, she turns to face me, wraps her arms around my neck and continues dancing. "I'm not ready to go yet. Dance with me, Mav," she says, smiling sweetly up at me.

How am I supposed to tell her no?

"Four songs and then we're out. I've been dreaming about getting you alone for weeks and I'm not wasting any time." She places a quick kiss on my cheek and then turns back to our circle of friends, guiding my hands to her hips. Sin ends up sandwiched between Nik and Dom somehow while Darcy went to sit with Tatum, while Harley and Collins are still spinning in circles. So much for my no touching rule, but since I'm breaking it, can I really get mad at them for breaking it too?

The next four songs feel like the longest eight-and-a-half minutes of my life. The only thing keeping me sane is the way that Kodi's hips sway sensually against me as her body leans into mine. As soon as those songs are over, I basically drag

Kodi out of the club towards my car after she says goodbye to her friends and I threaten mine to make sure they get home okay. I unlock and start it as we approach, quickly opening her door and getting her inside.

Leaning in, I buckle her seatbelt then jog around to my side of the car. She's looking at me with a mischievous grin on her face that makes me feel on top of the world. I decide I can't wait to kiss her until we get home, so I lean over and haul her by the back of the neck into my lips. She immediately opens up for me trying to get closer.

I need to get her home. *Now.*

Pulling away, I place my hand on her upper thigh, shifting the car into drive. Inching my hand up her thigh, she gasps when my finger finds her bare center. I tsk, "No panties and you let someone else touch you. Darlin' what were you thinking?" I've begun rubbing small circles over her clit and I know it's driving her crazy because she's fidgeting.

"I just wanted to have fun with my friends tonight. It had nothing to do with you Maverick," she breathily replies while trying to push her hips up.

"Don't lie to me, baby." I don't stop touching her but she's not going to come, not yet. Not until it's on my tongue.

She mumbles something that I can't hear so I stop touching her. "Maverick." My name comes out as a whimper.

Holy hell, I'm hard as a rock right now.

"Kodi, what were you really doing tonight? If you tell me the truth, you'll be rewarded like the good girl I know you can be. Brats don't get rewarded," I respond as if I'm not at all affected by what's happening in this car, like my cock isn't thickening uncomfortably against my zipper. "We're pulling into the neighborhood so you have about sixty seconds to tell me the truth."

She heaves an exaggerated and annoyed sound, "Jealousy, Maverick. I was trying to make you jealous. I'm tired of the back and forth, the teasing, the barely-there kisses and touches. I want it all. I want you. I want to try. Okay, there. That's the truth."

She wants this and us as badly as I do. "I do too. I'm sorry that I haven't been more straightforward, but seeing you with Nik tonight, it solidified that I don't want you to be with anyone else. I want you to be with me. When we get inside, I want you in my bed. I'm going to show you who you belong to, baby."

She whimpers and I see her rub her thighs together out of the corner of my eye. I put the car in park, walk around and help her out, sending her ahead of me. I slowly make my way down the hallway after making a detour for water that I know she'll need when I'm done with her and find Kodi sitting on the edge of my bed, already having removed her jacket, she's pulling on that hair tie she keeps on her wrist.

"Look at me," I growl. She obeys and it makes my cock twitch in my pants. I slowly unbutton and remove my shirt then remove my dress pants and boxers.

She sucks in a breath at the sight of my erect cock. "Mav, there's no way. . .You're. . .It's huge."

"Baby, you'll take every single inch so well. I know it. Stand up for me." She does and I prowl towards her, my lips immediately finding hers. Her hands intertwining around my neck. "Are you sure you want this Darlin'? I need to know you want this because once I get a taste for you, I won't be able to stop."

"Mav. I want this. I want you." To accentuate her point, she pulls me down for another kiss, slow and languid, not hurried and rushed as our previous ones were. This one isn't fleeting, this one is solidifying the potential we have here.

I work on getting her top off, pulling back from the kiss to take in her bare breasts. "Holy shit." Two pink buds with bars through them stare back at me. Leaning down, I take one in my mouth, sucking and pulling while rolling the other between my fingers. She moans and arches her chest into my touch.

My free hand moves down her back finding the zipper, squeezing her ass cheeks and letting her skirt fall to the ground. I bend slightly to lift her by her thighs that instinctively wrap around my waist and gently lay her down.

She spreads her legs wider for me, letting me rest between them.

I slowly kiss my way down her body, stopping to nip and suck at all her sensitive areas. The juncture of her neck and shoulder, her nipples, around her belly button, the place where her hips and thighs meet, stopping to pull back and admire her pretty, pink, wet pussy. I swipe a finger through her wetness. "Is all of this for me baby?"

On a gasp she responds, "Yes, Mav."

"I'm going to fuck you with my fingers and make you come on my tongue. Then you're going to come on my cock. If you don't like something, you tell me." I say before diving back into her center with slow laps and circles at her clit.

"No-oh. Oh my God. This. This is good. Don't stop Mav…"

She's so wet and she tastes like heaven. I stick one finger in, slowly pumping in and out with the rhythm of my tongue. Her hand finds its way into my hair holding me in place. She's taking what she wants from me.

I add another finger and feel her walls tighten around me. She's gasping and writhing. She's right on the edge and I want to watch her unravel for me.

I find that spot inside her that I know will set her off and whisper into her, "Come for me baby." She detonates, gasping my name, tightening around my fingers and riding out her orgasm.

Once her body begins to relax, I kiss my way back up her body.

She's got that dazed, post orgasm smile on her face and I feel the need to kiss her again. This time when we do, her hand sneaks between us and she grabs my cock, slowly stroking while we take our time exploring each other's mouths.

"Need to be inside you," I groan. "We need a condom."

She immediately shakes her head, still stroking me slowly. "No, please. I don't want anything between us, I have an IUD and I used a condom the last time I had sex, but I'm clean."

"I am too, it's been a really long time, but I am too." I've barely gotten the words out before she lines me up with her entrance and I slowly start to push in.

"Relax for me baby, I'll go slow but I'm dying here. You have to let me in."

Once fully seated, I give her a minute to adjust to my size. I need to move, it's killing me, but I don't want to hurt her. I slowly start pumping my hips and when her breathing picks up and she's grasping at my arms, I begin to move faster.

The sounds of her gasps, my groans, our skin meeting is all that I need at this moment. I'm not going to last much longer but I want her to give me one more. Leaning back on my haunches, I move my thumb back to her clit.

"Mav, I can't. I. . .It's too much." She gasps between my thrusts.

"You can. Just let go baby. You're strangling my cock. It's right there." Applying a little more pressure, she comes undone on a scream of my name, writhing beneath me.

I pick up my pace, knowing I don't have much longer. Leaning into her face and asking her, "That's my good girl. Whose are you, Kodi?"

She whimpers, "Yours."

"That's right baby." *Thrust.* "You." *Thrust.* "Are." *Thrust.* "Mine."

With one final thrust, I pull out at the last minute coming onto her stomach. Heading to the bathroom, I quickly clean myself up and grab a warm rag taking it back to Kodi.

She's a vision laying in the middle of my bed, naked, eyes partially closed, that raven hair spread around her, chest rising and falling. Leaning over, I quickly clean her up, tossing the rag aside, turning off the lamp and joining her in bed.

She snuggles into me immediately, wrapping her leg around my waist, her small hand sprawling across my chest, head tucked into my shoulder. Kissing her forehead, I mumble, "Thank you. . .one question."

She peers up at me in the dark, lit by moonlight, a small smile gracing her lips. I know she loves this little game we play. "One answer."

"Will you stay with me tonight?"

"I'd like that." She places a long, soft kiss on my lips before making herself comfortable in my side.

We lay there in the dark for a while, just taking each other's soft touches in before Kodi's breathing evens out and I let her small snores lull me to sleep.

CHAPTER 31
Definitely Freaking Out

Maverick

I wake to the sound of light footsteps and quiet music coming from my kitchen, the spot where Kodi was laying beside me is now empty and cold. Looking at my phone, I see that it's not even nine a.m. and we aren't due to pick up Bella until this afternoon, so I'm confused as to why she left me alone. We have some time and I had plans for her before I have to go and pick up Bella from my Dad's.

Dragging myself out of bed, I brush my teeth and throw on some sweats then head towards Kodi. Standing in the doorway, I notice she's making us breakfast wearing my button up from last night, hair thrown in a bun. And not just a bowl of cereal. Like coffee is brewing, pancakes are being flipped and bacon is popping on the stove top, type of breakfast. I could get used to this vision of her dancing around my kitchen. Except in my perfect world, all three of us would be in the kitchen on Saturday mornings, and I would be stealing kisses when Bella wasn't paying attention.

"Mornin' Darlin'. You left me all alone in bed this morning, I had plans for you." She jumps a little but turns to me and gives me that smile that makes me feel the need to clutch my chest.

"Hey, Big Guy. Nice of you to join me." Walking towards me, she gets up on her tiptoes and plants a kiss on my lips. She blushes a little before adding, "Sorry about that. Had to make breakfast, I woke up with a growling stomach this morning."

"Hell yeah. You're forgiven as long as you tell me there are chocolate chips in those pancakes," I practically beg.

"Um, duh. Do I look like someone who would eat pancakes without chocolate chips in them?" she teases, planting one more quick kiss on my lips and heading back towards the stove. "Get comfortable wherever you want to eat, I'll bring a plate once it's finished," she tosses over her shoulder.

"The couch sounds really good, just don't tell Arabella. I'm too old to be out all night and then to eat breakfast at the table like an adult."

She chuckles at that and retorts with,"Twenty-eight is not that old Mav."

I make my way through the kitchen, placing a chaste kiss on her neck as she continues to prepare our breakfast. "This looks delicious, thank you." I swiftly make two cups of coffee with cream and sugar then head to the couch to wait.

We need to talk about what our dynamic will look like now, what will happen if we don't work out, and how we can protect Bella before we progress our relationship further. I'd also like to take her on a proper date. I just hope that she's willing to meet me where I'm at.

"Here ya go, handsome." Kodi hands me my plate as she plops down beside me.

"Thank you, Kodi. For last night, the past couple weeks, for breakfast." Setting my plate in my lap, I pull her in for a quick kiss, feeling her smile against my lips. "As much as I want to keep kissing you, we need to eat and I want to talk to you. Don't worry though, I'll have you back in my bed before I have to go grab Bella." Looking Kodi in the eyes, I can see she's preparing herself for me to reject her again. Her shoulders are bunched to her ears, trying to keep her expression schooled, pulling on that damn hair tie again, so before I continue speaking, I place my free hand on her knee that's resting against my thigh. "Before I say anything else, I am not ending this, whatever this is. I just want to talk about where we go from here, what we both want going forward."

Kodi's shoulders drop and she lets out a long breath, nodding as she lifts her coffee mug to her lips, and if I could keep her relaxed for the rest of my life I would.

"I'm going to be entirely too honest here and I want you to do the same, Ko. Actually, I need you to be because it's not just my heart and yours at stake here. It's Bella's too." Just as I'm about to continue, my phone starts ringing, and seeing that it's my Dad has my heart dropping knowing that he would only call if it was an emergency. He wanted this time with Bella just as much as he knew Kodi and I needed a break.

"Hey, Dad."

"Son, don't freak out." Well that's the exact opposite way to keep me calm.

"What's going on?" I try to keep my voice from wavering. Kodi can hear my unsteady tone and takes our plates, setting them on the coffee table. She rushes out of the room, presumably to put on clothes that are appropriate to wear in public.

"Well, Bella woke up this morning running a bit of a fever. She's a little out of it, she's whining and she's refusing to eat. I gave her some of the Tylenol you put in her bag but I think we need to take her to see a doctor."

"How high, Dad?" I ask, and Kodi reappears wearing gray sweats and a t-shirt, holding one for me to put on myself.

"103 before the meds, 101 now. I'm getting her into her seat now." I can hear my daughter's sad cries in the background causing my heart to pound faster in my chest, my palms beginning to sweat. This isn't my dad's fault, but I'm so worried about Bella. I'm now halfway to the garage door, ready to break every law to get to my girl.

"Drive safe, we'll see y'all at the children's emergency. Thanks Dad, love you." Hanging up the phone and turning to Kodi I say, "I'm sorry, we are going to have to finish this conversation later. Bella needs me, will you come with me? I. . .I need you."

"What's going on Mav?" Kodi falters but follows me out the door. "Do you need me to drive?"

"Uh, yeah, if you don't mind." I slide into the passenger's seat of the Bronco after handing my keys over to Kodi, feeling unsteady. I know I shouldn't drive with my thoughts racing like this. I'm hoping she just caught a bug and that it doesn't progress to anything worse or that something isn't causing it.

"Mav, babe. I need to know where I'm going," Kodi's soft and tender voice breaks through my thoughts.

"It's Bella. She woke up with a fever, the Tylenol we put in her bag wasn't working. My dad doesn't know what's wrong, he's taking her to the emergency room." Reaching over, she places a hand over mine in my lap and pulls the car out of the garage. Throwing my head back into the headrest, I groan. "Fuck."

"She'll be okay, Mav. She's probably just got the flu or some other kid germ that her little body needs some extra help fighting off." She squeezes my hand in an attempt to solidify her point. "You know, Sin works at this hospital. The children's unit is really good, no matter what, she's going to be taken care of."

That's kind of reassuring, I don't know Sin very well, but I know that Kodi has a good group of women around her and I trust that Sin would be proud of the place she works.

"But what if it isn't just the flu? What if it's some deeper thing that I've missed because I'm not home enough?"

"I'm scared too. I care about her a lot, you know." I know that, I do, but aside from Ma I've never really had anyone who would notice something being wrong with Bella. "I think outside of that I would have noticed if she was acting weird or getting weaker or anything like that." I'm a fucking idiot for thinking that she doesn't pay attention to Bella like that, of course she does.

"Yeah, you're probably right." I let out a breath as we pull into the parking lot. "I know that you would notice if something was wrong, and I know you care about her just as much as I do. I'm sorry if I made you feel otherwise."

Pulling into the spot and placing the car in park, she turns towards me. Moving her hand from my lap to my cheek softly rubbing against my stubble. "I know Mav, it's okay. Let's go get our girl."

Giving my information to the receptionist, she directs us to Arabella and my dad. Taking Kodi's hand in mine, we get to the room and enter quietly. Relief floods over me when I see my little girl sprawled out on that big hospital bed with a red popsicle in her mouth. "Daddy." She's much quieter than normal and I can tell she doesn't have much energy. "Kodi!" she adds when she sees Kodi standing behind me.

"Hey, baby. How you feeling?" I approach and sit on the edge of the bed.

"She threw up on the way here, but her fever went down and the nurse convinced her that a popsicle would help her feel better." My dad chimes in from the chair on the opposite side of the bed. "I'm sorry, son, she really was fine last night, but this morning she just woke up not feeling well." His voice cracks at the end.

"Dad, it's not your fault. She's a toddler, everything goes into her mouth, she probably just picked up a virus somewhere. I'll pay to get your car cleaned out, I don't want you dealing with that." I smile at him then direct at Kodi who hasn't moved since we got here, "Come here, sit with us." She takes the chair by my side and we wait, watching Bella fall asleep with her popsicle.

A few grueling hours later, an antiviral and care instructions in hand, I'm pulling Arabella out of her carseat, fast asleep. Turns out, she had caught not one, but two viruses that her body couldn't fight off itself. I want to put her in her bed, but when I go to lay her down she cries to stay with me, so we all head to my room where I make a pillow barrier around her because I need a shower and something to eat.

"What do you want to eat? We could order something and then take showers while we wait for it to get here," Kodi whispers from behind me.

"Baby, you don't have to whisper, she's down for the count. Do you like Thai?" I ask.

"Oh, that sounds really good actually." She almost moans and if I wasn't so exhausted, I would be dragging her down the hall and into her bed because of that sound.

"Perfect, I know the place. Go turn the shower on, grab some clothes and meet me in my bathroom. I'll call it in." Pulling my phone out of my pocket as Kodi heads off in the direction of my bathroom opting to grab one of my tshirts instead of going to grab her own clothes, I place our order, let my dad know we are home, and switch the monitor app on my phone. I turn the volume all the way up and place it where I can see it from inside the shower. Closing the door behind me, I strip down and step in behind Kodi wrapping my arms around her middle and pulling her into me. She immediately wraps herself around me, letting her forehead rest on my chest. She's the perfect height that I can rest my chin on top of her head, and we stand there for a moment in silence. "Thank you for being there for me today, Darlin'. I hate that I wasn't there for her this morning when she woke up."

"You know it's not your fault right, this isn't something

you could have prevented. You were there for her and when you weren't your dad was. Don't ruminate on the fact that you weren't there as soon as she started to feel bad. You're a good daddy, Mav, and that little girl out there is surrounded by so much love because of you."

My throat tightens and I hold her tighter to my body. "Thank you, Kodi. I really appreciate you being there with us today." I didn't think I needed that confirmation but when you've been parenting by yourself for two-and-a-half years, you get used to not having someone encourage and support you when your child gets sick or reaches a milestone or is having a bad day, someone who cares about how you're doing just as much as they care about how your child is doing.

"You're welcome, but it's just the truth." She sighs, attempting to wiggle out of my hold. "Mav, we need to clean up, our food will be here soon."

"Just a little longer, please." Placing a gentle kiss on the top of her head and extending my arm to grab the shampoo, squeezing some into my hand and massaging it gently into her hair.

"Mmm, that's nice." Holding her like this, after a long and emotional day, gives me a sense of security I've never had. Knowing that we can ground each other in this moment, relax knowing Bella is okay on the other side of that door. "Alright Big Guy, your turn." She smirks up at me.

She has to get on her tiptoes and still can't reach my hair making us both laugh. "You might have to sit for this one, Mav."

I head over to the bench that runs along my shower wall

sitting down while Kodi stands in front of me running her fingers gently through my hair. Needing more contact, I let my hands find her waist pulling her closer, even with me sitting we are eye level. After a few minutes of her gently running her hands through my hair, I stand back to my full height. I can't help but pull her back into my chest, my hand resting at the nape of her neck while the other caresses her lower back and jokes, "I think you missed your calling, babe."

"As a scalp massager?" she snickers at me. "That privilege is reserved for sweet and caring, over six-foot tall hockey centers with smoking bods."

"Oh, well in that case, I will be requesting these services every night."

"Who said that I was talking about you?" She's not making any sound but I feel her small body moving up and down on her silent laugh.

"Haha, very funny." Gripping her hair and tilting her head up so she has to look me in the eyes.

"Remind me who you belong to again."

She shudders but almost immediately says, "You." With that I let my lips descend upon hers for a brief moment before I finally release my hold on her. We help each other finish washing up, nothing sexual in our touches, just soft caresses taking away the stress of the day, just in time for our food to arrive.

Snuggled into the couch with *Big Bang* playing and Bella sleeping soundly on her monitor, we devour our food. Kodi is snuggled into my side, and I can feel her dozing off. "Baby, let's go to bed."

Grabbing my hand and leading me down the hallway, stopping at her door. "I wish you were sleeping in my bed tonight."

"I know, me too."

"I could try and move her again." I give her my best Flynn Rider smolder which earns me the smile that makes me feel like the world has stopped spinning in its tracks.

"Remember what we were supposed to talk about this morning? I think this may be one of those things. Plus, if you try to move her, she might wake up and she needs rest." Grabbing my hands and pulling me closer to her. "Don't get me wrong, I don't want to sleep alone, but I think I need to. For tonight, at least."

"Fine. You're right, but I'm not happy about it," I grumble crowding her space until her back is against the wall by her room. Letting go of one hand, I run it up her side, taking my time, watching her pulse escalate until my hand is on the back of her neck. Pulling her slowly into me and kissing her gently for as long as she'll let me. When she does finally pull away, my heart is pounding and the affection I feel for her is on the tip of my tongue.

"One more question before I leave you," I whisper, worrying my bottom lip.

"One more answer."

"Can I take you on a date? A proper one where we can finish our talk and I can court you."

"Court me, Mav? This isn't the eighteen-hundreds." She chuckles. "But yes, I'd love to go on a proper date with you."

"Brat," I respond with a grin on my face.

"Goodnight, Mav. Get some sleep. We had a long day." Kodi plants one last kiss on my lips before she pulls away, heading into her room.

"Goodnight, baby." When I make it back into my room, Bella is still sound asleep in the middle of the bed. Rearranging some of the pillows and moving her small body over a little, I slide into bed, feeling the weight of the day on my body and mind. Just as I'm about to fall asleep, Bella begins moving, and next thing I know there's a tiny foot in my ribcage. I move her foot away, but it ends up right back on my side and I kiss my night of sleep goodbye.

CHAPTER 32

More Than An Inch Or Two

Kodi

> **ME**
> Why did I just get a package that I didn't order, Maverick Hart?

Imagine my surprise when I went out to check the mail today after getting Bella down for her nap and discovered a package that I definitely didn't order for myself. He isn't answering quick enough so I text again, fidgeting with my hair tie.

> **ME**
> I'm waiting.

He should be finished with practice, and honestly, I miss his voice, so I click the FaceTime button on my phone. His face transforms from straightlaced to a giant grin that has my heart stopping in its tracks when he answers. I give him my own smile in return. There's chaos in the background of what seems like a locker room. Before Mav can speak, Collins' red eyebrow comes into view wiggling up and down before he's shoved away.

"Hey, Darlin'. I miss you." Someone makes a gagging noise in the background, and Mav grabs what looks like a kneepad and chucks it at someone behind the camera. A small thud and groan tells me he hit his intended target.

"Let me guess, Dom?" I laugh.

"That would be correct. You're so pretty." He finally gets up and exits the locker room, walking with me in his hand before sliding down a gray wall and sitting on the floor. The hall is much quieter than the room he was previously in.

"Now, stop sweet-talking me and tell me what's in here." I shake the package to emphasize my point. "I miss you too."

"Why don't you just open it?" He chuckles, eliciting an exaggerated eye roll from me. I tear the package open and hear the distinct crinkle of a package echo in his phone before I pull out an assortment of rings?

"Mav, what is this?"

"Well, I thought you might like these so you don't keep snapping your hair ties. You did it the day you interviewed for the job and have done it regularly since. So, I did some research and discovered fidget rings. But I wasn't sure which one you would want, so uh. . ." He grips the back of his neck looking down. "I bought her whole stock so you could decide which one to wear each day."

I'm in disbelief that he noticed something so small about me. I didn't think that it was a noticeable habit, but the fact that he has given me specific examples means one of two things: either everyone notices, or he pays that much attention to me and the tiny details. History and recent events makes me think it's the latter.

I think I've died from a hot, sweet man overload. Darcy is going to have to put on my headstone: "Death by the most thoughtful man alive. Looking at you, Maverick Hart."

He finally looks back up from his phone screen where I am most definitely smiling like a lovesick puppy dog before I squeal, "You bought her whole stock?"

"That would be correct."

"You're crazy, Maverick Hart." I laugh lightly, going through my new collection.

"Crazy for you, Kodi Roscoe." He doesn't know, but I share the same sentiment. "Is Bella sleeping?"

"Yes, she just went down, want me to call you with her later?"

"That'd be great. I have thirty minutes around four if you can make that work?"

"Of course I can, she'll be excited to see you," I tell him, and he beams at me through the phone.

"I promised Nik I'd grab lunch with him, so I need to go."

"No problem, tell him I said hi. Talk to you later."

"Bye, baby."

❋

"Okay, little black dress or leather skirt and bodysuit?" I ask, turning to Darcy and Sin who are sprawled across my bed the night before my first official date with Mav. Between the incident with Bella, games, appearances, and other events, our date got pushed two weeks out, but we finally are able to send Bella off to Stu's and have our first official date night.

"Black dress," Darcy states just as Sin says, "Your tits look great in that dress." I don't know how that woman works in a hospital's children's unit, she has absolutely no filter.

"Alright, black dress it is then. Do we go with a leather jacket or maroon suit jacket?"

"Let us see them both," Darcy says. Stripping down I pull the black dress on my body then slide the suit jacket on first. Sin scrunches her nose at me, "You can't see your curves at all now. Put the leather one on."

"I was just trying to add some color but definitely want to show the curves off on my first official date with Mav." I slide on the leather jacket, it fits a little tighter but doesn't hug my body too closely. I twirl around in a slow circle so that Darcy and Sin can get the full picture.

"Yep, that's the outfit. What were you thinking for shoes?" Darcy asks as I change back into Mav's t-shirt and some yoga pants.

"Heels? But short ones, I only need maybe an inch or two."

"Oh, I am sure you will be getting more than an inch or two tonight," Sin purrs, and we all burst out in laughter. A throat clears from the doorway, and I look up to see Mav leaning against the frame, his gear bag slung over his shoulder and an amused smile on his face.

"Just wanted to let you know I was home." He winks at me then continues down the hallway, sending shockwaves right to my core.

Once Mav is out of earshot, we burst out in giggles again.

"Do you think he heard that?" I ask, mortified.

"Definitely," Darcy states, sending us into another giggle fit.

It takes us a few minutes to gain our composure enough to pick out my jewelry, including one of the fidget rings that Mav bought me.

CHAPTER 33

Leap Of Faith

Maverick

The restaurant around us is buzzing with people, a live pianist plays softly in the corner, but all I see is Kodi. Sitting across from me, lifting her wine to those plush, pink lips, a tight, black dress with a leather jacket covers her body that I can't wait to reacquaint myself with later. She's also wearing her silver fidget ring that has a little spinning smiley face on it. She's been wearing one every day, and I haven't seen her snapping her hair tie since. Between Bella being sick and my schedule, all I've gotten from Ko is her being asleep in my bed and stolen kisses late at night. All I've wanted to do was have her to myself, so Bella is staying with my Dad again and he is loving the extra time. This time I feel calmer, knowing no matter what happens that she will be okay.

"You're staring," she says, pulling her lip into her mouth.

"Well, you look beautiful tonight, it's hard not to stare."

"It's freaking me out. You look like you want to eat me."

Her sweet and light laugh fills my ears, her eyes crinkling in the corners.

Dropping my voice an octave lower, I say, "I do and I will." Her face immediately blushes and she drops her gaze into her lap. The waitress comes by and I place our order as Kodi takes another sip of her wine.

"I never thought that hiring someone to assist me with my daughter would lead to this." I motion between us.

"Me either, but I am glad it did. Let's talk about those boundaries." Kodi laughs but it's almost strangled. I hate that we had to push this conversation off. I've learned over our brief time together that she needs communication and reassurance. I've also learned that I want to be the only one to give that to her.

"Ko." She won't look me in the eyes now, dropping her gaze to the recently dropped off entrees. "Kodi, please look at me."

Those green eyes meet mine and show me every emotion she's experiencing. Fear. Love. Sadness. Hope.

"Baby, all we have to do is talk about what is and isn't okay around Arabella. This isn't going to change how I feel towards you."

"And what is it that you feel towards me?"

"A deep and primal need to protect you and care for you. Adoration that makes my heart jump into hyperspeed." Smiling at her, I drop my voice. "And I've never wanted to hear a woman scream my name every night this badly." She reddens immediately and I laugh at how easily I can make her flustered.

"However, you screaming my name every night could be problematic," I say, bringing us back on topic. "I have to be honest. I don't know how all of this is supposed to work. I just want to make sure Bella doesn't get confused and that if we don't work out that she could maintain a relationship with you. She's so attached to you, Kodi."

"I know she is." She sighs. "I don't want her to be hurt or confused, but I'm also not confident she would completely understand what was happening between us. Aside from the fact that now we would be kissing. As for if we don't work out, I may need a moment to collect myself, but I wouldn't want to lose my place as Bella's caregiver." She's picking at her food, this topic is clearly taking away her appetite.

"You say that, but you may change your mind if that time were to come." I add, "Eat baby. You're going to need the energy later." She reddens again but begins truly eating her meal.

"Well, Mav, that would be a bridge we would have to cross when we came to it. This really isn't a situation we can predict the outcome of or prepare for." She's right and so intuitive, it's like she knew exactly where my thoughts were going before I did.

"You're right. I just. . .I don't know, I worry and I like to be in control."

"I know you do, but there are some situations that are out of our control and this happens to be one of them. So, you have to decide if being in control is what you actually want." She lets that settle in for a second before throwing a question my way.

"Will you take this leap of faith with me?" She reaches across the table and strokes my stubbled cheek, a soft expression on her face.

CHAPTER 34

Boop

Kodi

"Absolutely I will." Mav offers me a smile that almost knocks me out of my chair. This smile. This is the smile he usually reserves for Bella and now he's offering it to me. My heart is going to explode. This sweet and kind man who was just supposed to be my boss, is giving me his heart too. I will protect and cherish it because he deserves that.

I love him. Not in the way that I loved Andy. No, this is soul deep, understanding and passionate love.

"Can I take you home now, baby?" he adds. I think he knows I was lost in my thoughts, and I wonder if he can feel them radiating off of me.

"Please do."

Mav waves down our waitress, pays our bill and we rush to the car.

My palms are sweaty. My heart thrumming with anticipation. My core is already slickening at the thought of what's to come.

As soon as we get into the house, Mav corners me against the wall, pulling my jacket off, lips all over me. My lips, down my neck, over my bare shoulders. "Too many clothes," he growls.

"Take them off then, Big Guy." My pulse quickens and I'm sure he feels it where he's nipping and biting at me. In a move that takes my breath away, he throws me over his shoulder and jogs down the hallway to his bedroom where he gently sets me on my feet, removing my clothes and tossing them aside, along with his own.

"Lay down for me baby. Show me what's mine." Instead I drop to my knees in front of him looking up at him under my lashes before taking his hard length in my hand, gripping and stroking his cock.

"Kodi, baby you look so fucking hot on your knees for me." That's all the encouragement that I need, before parting my lips and flicking my tongue over the bead of precum on the head. Then sucking him into my mouth inch by inch until I meet resistance.

"Relax your throat baby, you can take it all." Maverick groans, he wraps my hair around his hand and gently pushes my head further down his cock. I'm getting wetter by the second and my thighs are shifting, needing some sort of friction. "Darlin', I'm going to fuck your throat. I want you to touch yourself but don't you dare come. That's for me." Holy shit. This man. Gentle and kind, but here, in the bedroom, he's dominant and his dirty talk has my pussy clenching. To let him know I heard him, I spread my legs further and slide one hand down to my wetness, pushing in and out a few times before beginning to circle my clit. Mav begins thrusting in and out of my mouth, hitting the back of my throat and staying there for a moment before picking up speed again. He's groaning, his dick pulsing inside my mouth and right when I think he might come, he pulls out lifting me up off the floor and pressing his lips to mine, taking control of our kiss and thrusting his tongue into my mouth.

"On the bed now." I scramble to the bed, laying down and spreading myself open. "Dirty girl, sucking me off made you so wet, didn't it?"

Now Mav is the one on his knees, he pushes my legs open wider and takes a few languid strokes at my pussy before focusing on my clit, switching between quick flicks and sucking.

"I need more, Mav." He pushes one finger then another into me, pushing at a steady pace. I attempt to lift my hips to get him to move faster, but he pushes me back down to the bed and slows his pace.

"Ah, ah, I'm going to savor my dessert." He blows air over my center, sending shivers down my spine before bringing his mouth down on me again.

"Mav, please." At this point, I'm desperate to come. Between sitting at dinner all night with his eyes focused on me, his cock in my mouth, and now his head between my legs, the ache continues to grow, more of my wetness coating his beard and fingers.

I'm pulsing around his fingers. He must feel it because he reaches up and tweaks my nipple fast and hard. "Fuck!"

I scream as he finds that spot inside me that has my orgasm barreling in, my pussy squeezing his fingers tighter, my body writhing underneath him. His hand has moved to put pressure right above my pubic bone and holy shit that's a new feeling. He continues to fuck me with his tongue, combining with the pressure, causing me to implode, wetness gushing out of me. He lifts himself up, swiping at his mouth with his forearm, a devious smirk on his face.

"Ho. . .Holy shit. I've never done that before," I say between heavy breaths, hand thrown over my face.

"Well it was hot as fuck. Don't hide from me." My hand immediately moves back to my side at the demand. Mav is standing now, lazily stroking himself as he circles the bed, taking a seat leaning against his headboard. I follow his movement, sitting up and slowly crawling beside him. "Come here baby. I want you to ride my cock the way you so desperately wanted to that night on the couch. Do you remember that?"

My thighs clench thinking about that kiss and the way he guided my hips over him. I nod. "*Words,* Kodi."

"Yes, I do." I throw one leg over him, straddling his lap. I reach back and line his cock with my entrance, slowly sliding down him. Both of us groaning at the intrusion.

I lean in, but before I can kiss him he says, "You know I fucked my hand that night thinking about you? Those curves." I begin lifting myself off him, dropping back down. Rotating my hips. This position hits me in the perfect spot pulling a soft moan from my lips. "Your evergreen eyes. The sounds you might make. And holy fuck those sounds are more beautiful than I expected."

"Holy shit, Mav. Keep talking." Continuing the slow rotation of my hips.

"You like hearing what you do to me, baby? I can feel you squeezing me." He leans forward and sucks my nipple into his mouth, while he sneaks his hand between us to put pressure on my clit.

"God, yes!" I scream out and begin to move up and down on top of him at a quicker pace. His grip on my hips is bruising and I know his restraint is going to snap soon. I want him to let go, claim me, fuck me the way I know he wants to. I sink all the way down onto him, leaning into his ear, and whisper, "Take over, Mav. I can feel how badly you want to take control. Do what you want with me, I'm yours."

On a growl, he flips us so he's on top, putting one of my legs over his shoulder and pushing the other, spreading me open further and pushing into me agonizingly slow. "I'm going to go hard and I'm going to go fast. You're going to give me one more, Darlin'." Without another warning, he begins drilling into me over and over. The only sounds, my moans, his heavy breathing and the obscene sound of our skin coming together.

"That's so good, Mav. Don't stop, please don't stop." I gasp.

"God damn, baby. You are taking me so well." He continues to thrust into me and leans into me, claiming my lips and down my neck.

"I'm so close, Mav."

"Just let go baby. You look so beautiful when you come

for me." His voice low and tight in my ear sends me over the edge, Mav following me with a guttural groan.

He pulls back, pressing his forehead into mine, those baby blues searing into me. Our breaths synchronize as we come down. Pushing my hair out of my face, he kisses me softly then cleans us up. My body feels like jello relaxing further into the bed.

"I'm glad I let you take me out. I had a really good evening with you." I giggle as I snuggle into Mav's side.

"Me too, baby. Thank you for letting me take you out." He kisses my forehead, letting out a contented breath. We stay snuggled up like this until we both pass out.

Waking up the next morning, my body is deliciously sore and Mavericks arm is draped over my middle, his even breathing letting me know that he's still knocked out. I can't stop thinking about last night, or how I want more of that right now.

"Baby, do you want to find out what happens if you keep pushing your ass against my cock this early in the morning?" Mav's voice sounding scratchy and deep in my ear. Instead of answering him, I keep pushing backwards while taking his hand and inching it lower to the place that I ache for him.

Instead of touching me like I want him to, he stands completely from the bed and begins to leave the room. "Come on baby, I have plans for you." I trail after him and find him perched on the edge of my bed, a seductive grin on his face, with my lube and vibrator in hand.

"What's that for?" I ask slowly, approaching him and stopping between his legs.

"Do you trust me?" He replies, as his hands grip my waist and he yanks me forward so our foreheads are touching.

"Well, of course I do."

"You have one needy hole that I've yet to fill." He grins, "It's not happening yet, but I want to play a little if you'll let me."

"Definitely interested in that." He chuckles at my enthusiastic response. I've yet to have anyone fill me like that, but if there's anyone I can trust to make sure it's pleasurable and I'm comfortable, it's Maverick.

"Lay on your back, feet flat on the bed, as wide as you can for me." I move where he wants me and he continues, "I'm going to talk you through this and I need to know if anything is uncomfortable, but I want you to enjoy it baby." Maverick leans over me, kissing me softly before moving down my body to his knees, "You're going to put your vibrator on your clit and I'm going to put my fingers in your ass but first I'm going to taste you, do you want that?"

"One hundred percent, yes." Maverick spreads me with his fingers before his tongue finds my clit, sucking and nipping the way he knows I like, before inserting a finger and quickly finding my G spot. I was so riled up from this morning that I explode almost immediately.

I hear the buzz of my vibrator before Mav hands it to me, "Put it on the setting you like and then start using it." Then the click of the top of the lube bottle, "You ready?"

"I think so." I move my vibrator over my clit before Maverick's thick finger starts pushing into my ass.

"Baby take a deep breath and try to relax. Focus on the

pleasure you're giving yourself so that you can see how good it will feel to have me in your ass one day."

"Sorry." I take a deep breath and let it out, and when I do, Mav pushes in further. I gasp at the new sensation.

"How does that feel?"

"Uh, weird, but kind of good I think."

"Good, this sight is making me so hard, baby. I can't wait to fill up both your holes."

"Stroke your cock while you finger my ass, Mav." He groans, but I hear the lube bottle open one more time before I see his other arm start jacking himself.

"God, this is so hot." I lift myself to lean on an elbow so that I can see Maverick, and when we make eye contact I almost come on the spot. His gaze is filled with so much lust, his eyes drooping, and I know this is doing everything for him that it's doing for me.

We stay like this, his hand rapidly moving on his cock while his finger plunges in and out of my ass. The sound of my vibrator buzzing and our heavy breathing filling the room, but I need more, I need him inside me.

"Mav, I want you. Please." He doesn't need any more permission and quickly flips me onto my hands and knees before sliding deep and hitting a new angle that has my body feeling like a livewire. I press my vibrator to my clit as Maverick pounds into me from behind, then I feel his finger pushing into me again.

"Holy fuck, Kodi, you feel so good wrapped around my cock like this." I scream his name as all of the sensations become too much and the bomb goes off. Maverick pulls out painting my back with his cum. It takes us both a moment to catch our breath before Mav carries me into the shower where he proceeds to clean me with his tongue, before using soap, and we end up going back to sleep before starting our day.

We spend the rest of the weekend either cuddled up on the couch with takeout or fucking like animals on whatever piece of furniture is closest. By the end of the weekend, my body is the best kind of sore.

※

ME
Update, our date went well.

HARLEY
Okay, you can say it.

I roll my eyes at Harley's message knowing exactly what she wants me to say.

ME
You were right, Harls. Thanks so much. *eye roll emoji*

SIN
So, I'm assuming you had a good weekend.

SHOT TO THE HART

DARCY
> Yeah, tell us more!

ME
> We went to dinner and had fun...Lots of fun. *winky face emoji*

Before my friends can respond, I get a notification for an incoming message from Andy, of all people, and the last person I want to hear from right now. Considering he hasn't reached out in almost two months, I can only assume that Lyla came back and he's now bored of her. I consider ignoring the message but curiosity gets the best of me and I click on his name.

ANDREW
> Hey...Can we talk?

I stare at my phone shocked and angry and confused. There's no way he actually had the audacity to continue to text me. Big hands box me into the bathroom counter from behind, placing soft kisses along my shoulder. "Hi, baby."

"Hi. I didn't hear you come in."

"Yeah, you were pretty enveloped in whatever is happening on your phone." Mav is looking at me through the mirror.

I sigh, rubbing my palms into my eyelids. "My ex."

"What about him?"

"He. . ." Ugh. "He texted me. He texted a few times and even showed up at the coffee shop when I worked there." I turn to face him and shove my phone in Mav's direction showing him the thread. His grip tightens around the device as he stares at the screen.

"Are you going to text him back?"

"What if I just ignore him and pretend he doesn't exist anymore?" I sigh.

"Do you think that would actually happen or will there always be a what if?"

"There's no 'what if,' Mav. I'm done with him, but I don't know, I guess I'm just a little curious why after months he has texted me to ask if we can talk."

"Well, there's your answer." He smiles down at me.

"Are you mad?"

"That you need closure, no. That the asshole texted you, yes. But I can't do anything about it. I know you'll handle it and I trust you to do so." He hands my phone back, pulling me into him. I quickly message back to get it over with.

ME
What do you want?

ANDREW
I miss you. I fucked up Ko, forgive me.

Those words that I thought I wanted to hear that first few weeks on Darcy's couch are now making my skin crawl. I don't need or want his attention. The only person I need is encouraging me to get the closure that never came when it should have.

"What does he want?"

"'I miss you. I fucked up Ko, forgive me.' That's crap, he just couldn't get Lyla back and now he's trying me again."

"He cheated?" Mav's grip on the counter is starting to turn his knuckles white.

"Can neither confirm or deny, but I am leaning towards yes."

"Well, he didn't deserve you and he better hope I never run into him in public."

"That isn't necessary, my rejection will be a big enough blow to his overinflated ego. I'm going to text him back but then I'm done."

> **ME**
> Well, I'm sorry but the day you ended our relationship I decided I deserved better and I've found it. I forgive you but it's time we both move on.

"Why are men stupid?" I groan.

"Ouch, that hurts."

"Sorry, Big Guy, it's nothing against you. You're good to me." I look up then boop his nose. His facial expression contorts, I can't tell if I offended him or if he thinks I'm crazy.

"Did you just *boop* me, Darlin'?"

All I do in return is give him my biggest grin.

"You're so odd, Kodi Roscoe." My phone buzzes again and I glance down.

ANDREW

> Don't be like that KJ. She meant nothing, you're everything.

I laugh, actually cackling at that message, showing it to Maverick with tears in my eyes.

"What a tool," he mutters. "KJ?"

"Kodi James, and a nickname I never asked for. I prefer Darlin'." I smile up at Maverick and he pulls me in for a quick kiss before I decide Andy isn't worth it anymore. Everything I need is right here in this house, so I block his number and let the memory of Andy drift away. A weight lifted off my shoulder that I didn't even realize I was carrying around.

CHAPTER 35
The Beginning Of The End

Maverick

My blood is thrumming with anticipation. I've been away from my girls for two weeks; it's getting closer to the playoffs, and the Manta Rays have been bringing home win after win. My flight just landed and I can't wait to get home to my girls. My. Girls. Not just my daughter, but Kodi too. She sent me pictures of her and Bella around town; they grabbed dinner with my dad and Kodi's mom one night and had a living room sleepover with Kodi's friends another. "Excuse me. Coming through. Thank you." I shove my way through the people exiting the plane and through the ones waiting to board, trying to get to my suitcase and car as fast as possible.

As I'm approaching the car, my phone is buzzing with a call from Carolina, a number I don't have saved. "Hello."

"Maverick?" I instantly recognize the voice from the other end of the phone, there's no way. Not now. Not after I've finally let myself move on and have fallen for this wildly perfect woman. I'm imagining the voice I hear on the other end. "Lily?"

I'm shaking my head trying to rid myself of the shock of the call I'm receiving right now, this can't be real life. I'm just tired and delirious. "Can you meet me somewhere?"

"You're in Tampa?"

"Yes, I just want to talk, Mav." How am I supposed to trust that? It's been years, she didn't even call when she left. She's just popping up to have a friendly chat. That can't be true. She wants something, money before she signs the papers, or maybe she's found a workaround to where she can take our daughter, which is why she never sent the papers back, or another chance with me. No, she can't have any of that.

I need to get to my car, I can't fall apart in the airport parking lot where there are eyes everywhere.

Once the door to my Bronco is closed, I realize that I am about to agree to meet with a woman I haven't seen in three years and every emotion that I felt when Lily left Bella and I suddenly hits me like a tidal wave. The abandonment, the fear, the anger, the sadness, the regret, all wash over me, my head barely staying above water. Bella's soft cries from that night crash in with the waves, the panic that overtook me as I ran through the house looking for the woman who didn't want me. . .or her daughter.

"I'll text you a place and time." I quickly hang up the phone, jumping into my car and dialing my dad from bluetooth.

"Hey son! Great—"

"Dad." My throat constricts and my heart is racing.

"What's wrong?" My dad's voice is calm but barely holding it together, kind of like the day he called to tell us Mom had passed.

"Lily called." Letting my head rest against the steering wheel, tapping my fingers anxiously against my legs. Attempting to keep my breath in check.

"Wh...What?" he sputters.

"She's in town. She..." I'm beginning to gulp in breaths. "She wants to talk. It's happening, Dad. She's going to try and take her from me." My hands and forehead are clammy, I can't breathe. I want to scream and cry and punch something all at the same time. The logical part of my brain is telling me that I know she can't do that, but the illogical part has taken over, every synapse in my brain screaming that this is the moment I've been dreading since she walked out of our lives.

"Maverick," my dad's voice booms from the other end of the phone. "Take a breath son, I can hear you struggling."

In. *One. Two. Three.* Out. *One. Two. Three.* I repeat this cycle five times before my heart rate is back to a semi-normal pace.

"I don't know what to do, Dad."

"Son, go home. Talk to Kodi, plan a time without Bella to meet Lily, call your lawyers. Figure out what she wants and then go from there."

Oh no, I have to tell Kodi.

"Thanks, Dad. I'll keep you updated." I hang up the phone and drive. I don't know how or when I got home, driving on autopilot. My brain is everywhere but on my drive from the airport to the house.

The front door opens before I have the chance to put in the key and when I see Kodi's smiling face waiting for me, I can't do anything except pull her into me, wrapping my arms around her in a vise grip. My knees want to buckle beneath me and tears I had been holding back fall freely down my cheeks. Kodi's hand rubs soothing circles on my back.

"Mav, hey, talk to me. What happened?" She steps back a little, lifting my head with her hands so she can see my face, wiping at my tears.

"Lily." I exhale. Her body tenses and face pales. "She called, she's in town and she wants to meet up. I. . .I don't know what to do, Ko."

"You should talk to her. It might be important," she states plainly with a terse nod and tears welling in her own eyes. Oh God, I'm going to lose her because of this. She thinks Lily showing up means I'm going back to her. I'm not, I can't, I won't. I can't even explain that to her right now, my head beginning to pound.

"I. . ." Taking a shaky breath. "What if she found a way to take her from us, Kodi?"

CHAPTER 36
The Aftermath

Kodi

What if she found a way to take her from us, Kodi? That question plays on repeat in my head. Take her. From us. Not him, but us.

Bella and Maverick mean so much to me at this point that this heartbreak would hurt worse than any I've ever experienced. If I lose Maverick, I don't think I could keep working for him, especially if I had to watch him with another woman. We said that if we didn't work out that I would continue to care for Bella, but we didn't account for her mother coming back. There's no way they would want me around, and if Lily found out about us then she definitely wouldn't want me in the house.

All I can do at this moment is support Maverick. His face is filled with anguish, eyes wildly searching mine for an answer that I don't have. I wish I did. I wish that I could take that fear and anger out of his eyes, but I can't.

"Let's go to the couch, babe." That's all I manage to get

out through my own clogged throat. Taking his hand and guiding him into the living room.

Sitting down, I pull Maverick down between my legs, his head resting on my chest so that I can run my fingers through his hair and rub his back.

"I know that you're freaking out, but remember she can't just swoop in and take her from you." I finally answer his question from earlier. I don't want to lose Bella either, I love her just as much as I love Maverick. The thought of losing them both is almost unbearable. "She—"

"But she could have found a loophole in the paperwork she sent. She could demand something if I want her to sign the papers."

"And if she did, then you have a really great legal team that will help you through it. Maybe you should call your lawyer."

"I don't know, baby." His breathing slowly began to even out. "I'll call them before I talk to her."

He blows out a loud sigh after a moment. "I can't. . .I can't see her Kodi. Hearing her voice took me right back to that night."

"I know it seems like you can't handle seeing her, but I know you and you can."

"I'm just. . .I don't know what she wants, and this situation feels totally out of my control. I think that's why I feel like I can't see her."

"You have to, Mav. If you want to guarantee a future for all of us, you have to go see what she wants. And I'll be here when you get back to help you process whatever that conversation entails. When do you have to meet her?"

Blowing out a breath after a few strained moments, he says, "I haven't told her yet. I told her I would text her. I just needed to get home to you." He finally looks at me. His hair is disheveled, his eyes red rimmed and puffy. The light that normally shines through his baby blues has gone dim. My heart aches for the pain that he is experiencing in these moments. I would shoulder that burden for him if I could.

Grabbing his cheeks, I place a gentle kiss on his lips. "It'll be okay, Mav. We will get through whatever this is about. Call Jeremy and then text her, might as well get it over with."

He grabs his phone and dials Jeremy. He doesn't put it on speaker, so I only hear his half of the conversation. "Hey Jeremy, sorry for calling on a Sunday."

"So, Arabella's mom called today. I don't know what she wants yet, but I want to make sure that you guys are available in case I need help."

"No, I don't want to bring her into the office. I want to talk to her first by myself."

"I understand that she can use what I say against me if we aren't sitting in front of you, but it's been three years, I don't want our first conversation on display for a room full of legal counsel." He sounds like he's getting agitated.

"Thank you, I will call you afterwards."

I watch him type out a text to Lily after he hung up the phone with Jeremy.

MAVERICK

3:30 PM. Wake, Bake, Repeat.

She immediately responds.

LILY
See you soon.

It's already one o'clock, which means that Bella will be waking up soon and he will have to leave us. . .Again.

"It'll be okay, Mav. When you get back, we can all snuggle up and watch Simba together." He lets out a defeated laugh before pulling himself to a sitting position and pulling me into his side. We breathe together for a few moments, neither of us saying anything.

He's the one to break the silence between us. "Kodi?"

"Yeah, Mav?"

"Can you promise me you'll be here when I get back?" He gently lifts my chin, gaze to his, those deep blues portraying everything he can't find the strength to say to me.

"I promise."

CHAPTER 37
Rainclouds

Maverick

Walking into Wake, Bake, Repeat, the aroma of coffee and pastries floats around me. My body feels rigid as I look around the small cafe for the woman that I remember. Sitting at a table near the window, Lily waves to me. Her once jet-black hair that she passed to our daughter is streaked with blonde highlights. As I approach, I notice that her eyes seem to have sunken in as if she doesn't sleep much.

"Mav." She gives me a smile and stands, opening her arms for me. I decline that option, sticking my hand out stiffly. She steps back, her lips pressing into a firm line, taking my offered hand in a firm shake.

"Lily. How have you been?" It takes her a moment to respond as we sit, fiddling with the straw of her coffee. Sitting in silence with Lily used to be comfortable, but now it makes my skin itchy.

"Honestly, I've been fine. Been better, been worse. Can't

complain. How are you?"

"I'm fine and so is Bella."

"That's great, really." She smiles at me but it's filled with tension.

"So Lily, what is it that you want?" I'm not here for pleasantries, and I really only want to know why she showed up and called me out of the blue.

" I just wanted to see how you guys were doing."

"So, you call me out of nowhere just to see how I'm doing? This could have been a phone call Lillian." She jolts back at my use of her full name, and for long moments she doesn't respond, looking into her coffee cup like the answer to solve an impossible equation lies within.

"And how is Bella doing?" I ball my fists at my side, her daughter by blood maybe, but her daughter that she raised and loved and cared for, absolutely not.

"To be quite honest, I don't think you deserve to know how I've been or how my daughter has been. You lost that right when you walked out on us without so much as a note." I take a deep breath so that I don't let my temper get the best of me. "You know she'll be three in less than a month and you've missed every birthday, every milestone, every sickness, every smile and giggle that comes from that beautiful little face."

"Maverick, that's not fair. I had to leave." I'm not even sure how to respond to this because she didn't have to leave, she chose to leave. "Listen, I know that I missed out on those moments, and I know that I will continue to do so."

"You didn't have to do anything, you chose to leave!" my voice rises just a bit, my fists still tightly balled at my side.

"I did, Maverick." Her eyes are starting to water and I'm trying to keep those walls up, but it's hard to watch her cry, so I slide her a few napkins across the small, round table. "I wasn't good for her or for you. You guys are better off without me."

She wasn't good for us? We are better off without her? It's been years and she's just now offering this information to me.

"How could you think that we were better off without you?"

"I. . ." Her eyebrows furrow as she tries to find the words she wants to use, maybe second guessing her decision to call me. "I didn't know what I was doing. I was suffering Maverick, it got to a point where my parents forced me to seek help. When I started therapy, I was diagnosed with PPD. When I left, the only way I saw Bella turning out okay was if I left, so that's what I did."

"Wait, I was at your follow-up appointment when they screened you for it. Did they not catch it?"

"I. . .I wasn't truthful with the doctor or you. I couldn't bring myself to tell anyone I needed help. I hid behind the guise of hormonal changes when I knew it was so much deeper than that. I had thought about telling them and you what I was feeling, but I couldn't. I wanted to believe so badly that those feelings of sadness and anger and not feeling like I was a good mom would leave as Bella got older. They just never did." I am hit with a wave of guilt, feeling like I should have noticed. She purposefully kept this from me and still waited three years to tell me, my anger warring with the guilt.

"Well, I wish you would have talked to me instead of just

disappearing, and I'm sorry that I didn't put more effort into checking in with you. I know we were just together for her, but I was worried, and then one day I just assumed you were either dead or living the life you always wanted without us."

"I regret the way that I handled everything. I should have talked to you, I wish that I would have been honest with myself about how I was feeling. I wanted to call once I was stable, but I've backed out everytime." Her tears are freely falling now.

"You should have." My first thought is that I don't want to allow her to come back into our daughter's life and then leave again. That's not fair to her or Bella though. Pushing my resentment aside, I continue after a minute of silence. "You know, it's not too late. She can still get to know you. I think we'd have to set some serious boundaries, but my intention even after you left has never been to keep her away from you. We can arrange that."

"I know that it's not too late because you're a good person and I don't deserve your forgiveness, but through my therapy I realized something else. When we stripped it down to the bare bones of who I am and what I want out of life after I got past the PPD and the guilt of leaving unannounced, which I know now was prompted by something I had no control over, being a mom was never a part of that plan. I didn't *really* want to be a mom, I never did. That's actually what I wanted to talk to you about." She sucks in a deep breath, leaning into her bag and pulling out a stack of papers before continuing. "I signed the papers. I. . .Well, I don't want you worried that I'm going to pop up and try to take her or your money like you probably thought I was doing today. I know that holding onto them for this long was wrong, and I apologize for that."

My heart drops into my stomach. It's relief and anguish swirling in my gut. I thought Lily would be here for my daughter or my money, but she wants neither. She never will. I can't tell if I'm relieved or devastated. Bella will never know her mother, but I won't have to worry about this happening again.

"Are you sure that's what you want? What if she wants to get to know you one day?" I ask.

"It is. I've thought about it, I've talked to my therapist extensively. Each time I got a new set of papers making me feel worse about holding onto them." She sighs. As if she's been hanging onto this weight forever. "If she wants to know me one day, I'd be open to that, but I don't see her wanting that to happen." I think about arguing with her, but what's the point? She has clearly made up her mind. I've raised Bella on my own for the past three years, and I have Kodi now. We can show Bella a healthy relationship and give her a positive maternal figure, even if it's not her mother. I wouldn't want it to be anyone but Kodi if I'm being honest.

"Well, alright. I'll get these taken care of then." I hesitate for a moment, considering if I want to mention this next part. "You know I won't hide you from her. If she has questions, I'll answer them. If she wants to know you, I won't stop that from happening. Again, I never wanted her to not know you, but I needed to protect her."

"I know that." She smiles at me, genuinely this time, though a little wobbly. "I know you wouldn't do that. You both deserved the truth, tell her everything when she's ready. I think I should head out."

I'm considering letting her go, but I have one more question that I feel like I need an answer to for this door to truly be closed. "Wait, can I ask you something?"

"Anything."

"Why didn't you at least talk to me before you left?" I'm not sure if I actually want to know the answer, but it's the only thing I'm stuck on after our conversation.

"I didn't want you trying to convince me to stay or forcing me to talk to someone when truly I wasn't ready, Maverick. Every day I would look at our daughter and care for her on autopilot, sometimes not remembering what our days looked like. I'm sorry that I didn't handle leaving properly, but at that moment it felt like the only option I had." I open my mouth to tell her I would never have done that, but she continues before I get the chance. "Don't tell me you wouldn't have, Maverick. You wanted to have the perfect family, you would have done anything to maintain that, and you would have grown to resent me even more than you already do. You didn't do anything wrong, I just realized too late that I wouldn't be the mom that little girl deserves and the partner that you deserved. But I knew from the moment you stepped up to take care of not only her, but me too, that you were meant to be a dad and a partner to someone who deserves it. That person wasn't and would never be me."

Her words hit me like a truth bomb. She's right, I would have done anything to keep our family together which wouldn't have been fair to any of us. It doesn't change the fact that I wish she would have talked to me before leaving, not leaving me to wonder what I did wrong to make her leave and never come back.

"Well, I guess that's it then. Thanks for clearing that all up for me. I know it wasn't easy to admit all of that to me today."

"It feels good to get it out. I should have done it sooner. Thank you for meeting me today."

I stand and walk with her out of Wake, Bake, Repeat. Finally letting go of my past and moving into my future.

The feeling of sadness lingers over me like a raincloud on a sunny day. I've got the answers I've needed for years, the relief of knowing my daughter isn't going anywhere, and the woman I love waiting for me at home. But it doesn't feel like enough to push that cloud away right now.

CHAPTER 38

You're Fired

Kodi

The front door clicks open as I'm sitting on my bed debating if I should pack the duffle bag that sits on the floor at my feet while Bella plays quietly in the corner with her farmhouse. Since Mav left to meet Lily, my fidget ring has been spinning as fast as those tilt-a-whirl rides at the fair. I don't know what Lily wants, but I need to be ready to go. Back to Darcy's couch, back to working at the coffee shop, back to feeling unwanted and unloved.

"What are you doing?" I hear the panic in Mav's voice before I turn to see his face. When I do turn to him, his eyes are wide, zeroed in on my bag, and he's got a palm pressed to his chest.

"Mav, it's not what you think." I jump up, taking a step closer and he takes one back. "Please, just let me explain. But maybe not right now."

Bella jumps to her feet when Maverick enters the room, leaping into his arms. I watch as he embraces his daughter, clutching her tightly to his chest and breathing in her presence as if it's a lifeline. "Bella, do you want to watch Bluey? Then Daddy and Kodi will join you and we can watch Simba!"

She nods enthusiastically, he settles her on the couch and then leads me to the dining room where we can still have eyes on Bella, but she won't be able to hear us speaking. "Go ahead Kodi because it looked a lot like you were going to run away before you even knew what was happening after you promised to be here when I got back." His sternness is like a shot to the chest. It hits me in the heart, ricocheting throughout the rest of my body making me feel weak and lightheaded.

"I. . ." Words have escaped me. I'm choking. I can't do that right now. He needs to hear what I have to say. I venture a step forward again and this time he stays put. "I just, if she wanted you back, I wouldn't be able to stay here. I wanted to be ready to go. I was going to pack a bag just in case, but I couldn't bring myself to do it."

"She didn't want that, Kodi." He sucks in a deep breath, letting it loose on a shaky exhale. "She doesn't want anything. Not me. Not Bella. Not my money." His voice becomes more unsteady with each confession.

"Let's sit down and talk about it. I want to know everything." I hope by telling him this, he believes that I have no intention of leaving. He pulls out a chair for me then himself at the table, I reach for his hand and he places it in mine. That one gesture grounding me in this moment with all of my fear and anxiety here.

"She doesn't want any of it. She wants to sign over her rights, and gave me me the paperwork. How can she just not want anything to do with that beautiful little girl we created together? Claimed she isn't and was never meant to be a mom, but couldn't bring herself to tell me that, which is why she just disappeared on us."

"Do you want me to listen, or do you want my opinions?" I ask. Support comes in so many different ways, I don't know if at this moment he just wants to get everything out or hear what I have to say.

"Just listen for a second. Thank you for asking." He gives my hand a reassuring squeeze. "I mean she just shows up out of nowhere to dump all of this on me. No phone calls or texts for almost three years. Fucking unbelievable."

I don't blame him for being upset. Everything he expected to happen didn't, instead he got hit with something that's arguably bigger.

"I can't even describe if I'm relieved that she doesn't want anything from me or anything to do with Bella. Or, if I hurt for my daughter, who might one day grow up and ask me why her Mom didn't want her." Tears are falling down his face now and I feel my own welling in my eyes.

"Can I say something?"

He doesn't answer but nods, wiping at his tears then at my own. Gentle hands swiping the tears away as I begin to speak. "That little girl is never going to feel unloved or unwanted, Maverick. This family that you have created for her is going to supply her with more love and support than she can ever ask for. I uh. . .You know that my dad left me too, and he has a family that got everything I didn't. What you've given Bella is everything that I could have ever asked and wished for. My mom is wonderful, don't get me wrong, but she didn't have people supporting her the way that you do. Bella might ask questions about Lily as she gets older, and when she's old enough you can tell her the truth, you can leave the door open for her to know Lily. In the end, it's up to you and your partner when that time comes."

"You, it'll be up to me and you." My heart stutters, those blue eyes piercing into my own. "I don't care that she doesn't want me. I have everything I need in a woman right here. I don't need anyone else, Darlin'. I need you. I need that hair fanned out over my pillow while you snore. I need your nervous rambles. I need you caring for Bella. I need chocolate chip pancakes. I need Big Bang Theory and your head on my shoulder." He peers over at Bella before pulling me into his lap, each of my legs resting outside of his, tears falling down my face as he confesses everything he needs and wants from me.

"Mav—" A gentle finger comes up to my lips before I get the chance to respond.

"I'm not done. I love you, Kodi Roscoe. I've realized I don't need anyone else, but I can't fight it anymore, I don't want to."

"Oh, wow." I could feel Mavericks love before he admitted it. In the way he cares for me, the way he remembers the little things, and cares what I think even when it feels miniscule, the way that my happiness is just as important as his, the way he apologizes to me, and the way he's looking at me right now.

One golden brow lifts at me. I giggle realizing that he caught me so off guard that I haven't said it back.

"I love you too, Mav." Pressing my lips into his gently at first but quickly deepening it, pouring every ounce of affection I have for him into it.

"Oh, one more thing baby. You're fired."

"Wha-what?" I stutter, confused and taken aback.

"You can't be my girlfriend and my employee, Darlin'." He's smiling at me now. The tension from earlier has left his shoulders.

"Girlfriend, huh?" I cock a brow at him. "I don't remember you asking me to go steady, Mr. Hart."

"So, are you going to ask me to be yours or are you going to assume my answer is yes?" I feel my lips tip up into a sexy little grin.

"Will you go steady with me Kodi?" he asks, and now I know that I am full-blown smiling.

"I'd like that old man." I giggle, and a smile I was so desperate for spreads across Mav's face.

"You're a brat, you know that?"

"But, I'm your brat." A thought hits me just then, "Uh, how am I going to pay my bills?"

"That you are." A contented sigh leaves my lips. "And as far as bills go, you can keep helping with Bella and I'll give you money for whatever you need or want. *If* that's something you'd be okay with."

"Wait a minute, I can get my streaming services again?" I joke.

"I take it back," he smiles, pushing my hair behind my ear and holding my cheeks so that I can't look away from him he whispers, "But seriously, thank you for today and everyday

Ko. I love you."

"You're welcome, Mav. I like it when you tell me that you love me." That earth shattering smile growing even wider.

"Baby?" Gently he nips at my bottom lip.

"Yes, Mav."

"I love you." I'm giggling again, Mav is laughing, and fuck, I love that sound. I wish I could bottle it up to play on a bad day. "Let's go watch Simba with our girl."

CHAPTER 39

You Didn't Let Me Fall

Maverick

We have a bye-week since the playoffs are next weekend, so the team is hosting family skate night at the rink. It took a lot of persuasion, meaning six orgasms and chicken nuggets, but I convinced Kodi to come and try to skate with us. I've never had anyone to bring to these except my dad and Bella. Kodi is holding Bella on her hip, her free hand wrapped in mine, and I don't attempt to suppress my goofy grin as we all walk into the arena. Kodi's best friends, Tatum, my dad, and Kodi's mom are following behind us.

The lights of the arena are bright, a hot chocolate bar set up on one side, and skates of all sizes on the other. I spot Dom and Collins tying up their skates on a bench and guide everyone in that direction.

"Hey, you all made it!" Dom, as usual, is super enthused to see everyone. "Let me take my niece for a spin." He makes grabby hands towards Bella who giggles and reaches back to him.

"Perfect, I can focus on getting everyone set up and teaching Kodi how to skate circles around you guys."

"That's never going to happen." Collins is right, but I give him that look that lets him know to shut up, so he adds in, "Sorry Kodi."

She crinkles her nose but says, "Trust me Collins, I wouldn't even attempt to move that quickly on the ice."

Collins, Dom, and Bella head onto the ice while the rest of us grab our skates, everyone gets tied up and heads out except for Kodi and I. She's sitting on the bench as I get my skates on, her leg bouncing, fidgeting with the rip in her jeans. "Baby, why are you so anxious about this?"

"I don't want to embarrass myself out there." She gestures towards the ice where almost everyone is gracefully moving around the rink.

Placing my hand gently on her knee, I say, "Hey, I'm not gonna let you fall or get hurt. If you fall, I'll just go down with you."

She laughs at that. "You don't have to do that for me."

"Well I want to, we'll go down together." I shrug and move to my knees in front of her to help her get her skates on and laced up. "Just trust me to catch you when you lose your balance, Darlin'." I don't know if she catches my double meaning there, but I mean it literally and in whatever time we have together going forward.

"You ready?" I stand, reaching a hand out to her.

"As ready as I'll ever be." She takes my hand and we walk out onto the ice. I place her on the wall for a second before I show her how to get started, but I notice her knuckles turn white almost immediately with the grip she has on edge.

"Okay, so don't think of it as stepping, think of it more like gliding. Don't lift your foot, just push it back. Like this." I glide a little ahead and then make my way back to her. "Take my hands and I'll get us moving, then you just focus on staying upright. Make sure you use your core then, when you're ready, push yourself forward."

She grabs my hands and I slowly move backwards, she wobbles a little bit but finds a steady position. After a moment, she attempts to move her feet, and like a baby deer they immediately crumple beneath her, but I'm able to catch and steady her before we go down. Holding her close to me, her eyes are closed and her nose crumpled like she was preparing for an impact that never came.

"Kodi, open your eyes."

"Oh." She nervously laughs. "You didn't let me fall."

"I told you I wasn't going to." I place a gentle kiss on the tip of her nose that's turned pink from the cool air in the arena.

"You guys are disgusting," Sin says as she glides by for what feels like the fifth time since we got on the ice. Kodi sticks her tongue out at her. "I'm ready to try again."

The more time that passes, the more steady she's becoming on her feet. "Are you ready to let go?" I know that she can do it, I can see how easily she's moving with my support.

She gives me an apprehensive smile but nods her head. Letting go of her hands, I stay close enough she can grab me if she needs me. She's beaming at me as she skates towards me, following my lead around the rink. Nik has joined us with Bella in his arms, but when she sees me she starts reaching for me, so I scoop her up and skate beside Kodi hand in hand. We make it around the rink twice before Kodi almost falls, Collins just happened to be nearby and helped her regain her balance before she calls it quits.

"I'm proud of you," I say as we take a seat with our hot chocolates. "Thanks for trusting me."

She beams at me. "Thank you for being confident enough for both of us."

She doesn't realize that if it means I get to keep her by my side, I will continue to be confident enough for both of us. Or that I would swim across an ocean every day to have her smile at me the way she did when she was skating without my assistance.

CHAPTER 40

The Jersey Stays on

Maverick

The arena is loud and boisterous. We made it to the Stanley Cup by the skin of our teeth and get to play on our home ice.

Our music begins to play, screams erupting throughout the stadium, and we skate out being led by Nik onto the ice. I make it around the rink looking to where my girls are seated. Kodi and Bella are both wearing their jerseys, huge smiles on both of their faces. My dad and Grace sit on one side with Tate, while Darcy, Sin, and Harley sit on Kodi's other side with her mom. Pointing my stick to my girls, I place a hand over my heart and take my position on the ice.

The first two periods fly by, Collins and I are so in sync tonight that we haven't had one mishap on the ice, but the Vegas Flyers are pushing hard to keep Collins and I away from each other. It's the final period, we are tied three-to-three and the tension between the teams could melt the ice beneath our feet. When the puck drops, we spring into action.

SHOT TO THE HART

Collins and I chase the puck down the ice, keeping it away from our opponents. The one time it gets away from us, Nik ensures that it doesn't make it into the net. In the last two minutes, everyone is on the edge of their seats. Dom gets the puck after blocking the shot from the opposing team, and we pass it back and forth speeding down the ice. We knock it to an open Collins and he shoots, making it directly through the goalie's feet.

Chaos erupts on the ice, the crowd whooping as we tackle Collins in excitement. Then Nik and Dom do a victory lap with him on their shoulders, his helmet and stick raised high in the air. When we've shaken the opposing team's hands and they are cleared off the ice, our loved ones join us. Spotting Bella and Kodi across the rink, I skate over as quickly as I can, scooping them both off the ground kissing Kodi. "You were so good out there tonight, Mav," Kodi mumbles against my lips and I kiss her some more.

Setting them gently back down, I hug my dad. "Great game, son. Your first Stanley Cup win, Jane would be so proud of you."

"Thanks, Dad." I was already teary eyed over the win, but that sends me over the edge.

"Yo Mav, get over here. We gotta get these pics and get off the ice," Dom hollers from behind me. I wipe the tears from my eyes before I turn to Kodi again.

Kissing her one last time, I whisper to her, "When we get home, the jersey stays on and everything else comes off." She blushes, nodding her head at me. I knew that if we won, the adrenaline would have me buried inside her most of the night, and I knew that if we lost, I would probably still be buried in her, but that her consoling me would be exactly what I needed.

After the photos, we all shower quickly, some of us running out without a shower. The adrenaline is pumping through our veins. Some of us are going home with or to our wives and girlfriends, others like Dom and Nik are running to Lockout to seek out companionship. Then there's people like Collins, who will go home and go to sleep because adrenaline has a draining effect on them. I head to my Bronco where I asked Kodi to take Bella and get her changed into her pajamas and into her seat before we make the drive home. Walking up to the Bronco, Kodi is leaning against the car and I can see through the window that Bella is already knocked out. I eat the distance between us, dropping my gear to the ground and supporting her weight when she jumps into my arms, wrapping her legs around my middle. I kiss her furiously, the way I wanted to on the ice but would've been inappropriate given the audience. Our tongues meet in battle for dominance and her little breathy moans are carried away with the night air.

"We need to get home and we need to get there fast," she says with a giggle before biting my lip and unwrapping her legs from me. I jog to her side, opening the door for her before tossing my gear into the trunk and driving us home safely but quickly.

Rather than celebrating tonight, especially because we need to get Bella home and in bed, we are having everyone over tomorrow for a family barbeque. It would have happened regardless of how this game went, we wanted to get everyone together to either celebrate our win or support each other after a loss.

<hr>

"Oh fuck, Mav." Kodi groans as I press into her from behind where I've leaned her over our bathroom counter, her hands bracing her on the marble countertop. As soon as I made her my girlfriend, I insisted that she move into my room with me.

"I just won the fucking Stanley Cup and I couldn't imagine celebrating any other way." I'm looking at her through the mirror, her jersey still on, one hand playing with her nipple underneath it while the other rubs slow circles on her clit.

I'm thrusting into her hard and fast. Kodi's orgasm is building quickly and I can tell my groans are spurring her on.

"Mav, I'm so close." She throws her head back in pleasure. "Come for me." I groan long and hard at her encouragement, my thrusts are becoming erratic and I know I'm not too far behind her as she erupts around my cock. My name escapes her lips on a scream as I spill inside her.

"Fuck," I mumble, pulling out of her and kissing her softly. "That was the perfect way to end my day. Let's get cleaned up and get to bed."

Snuggled in bed, my phone begins to ring. It's Jeremy, my lawyer calling this late must mean that he got the paperwork processed. We combed through everything to make sure it was signed and notarized properly. I told Jeremy to call no matter the time of day once everything was finalized.

"Put it on speaker, babe," Kodi's sleepy voice comes from

beside me.

"Jeremy."

"Mr. Hart. Congratulations by the way."

"Thank you. Do you have good news for me?"

"I do. Everything was sent to the judge yesterday, but I was advised not to call you until after the game. It should be approved by the end of the month and then you'll officially be the sole guardian to Arabella Hart." I let out a whoosh of air that I think I've been holding in since Lily swooped into town unexpectedly.

"Thank you, Jeremy. Call if you need anything else." Ending the call and smiling, I place a kiss on Kodi's lips. "Now my night really can't get any better."

CHAPTER 41

The End

Kodi

Celebrating the win of the Cup with our favorite people, I can't help but reflect on the past few months. I was sleeping on Darcy's couch with no idea what I was doing with my life. Working in a coffee shop. Single and feeling sorry for myself.

Now, I'm sitting in the lap of the man I love while our closest family and friends swim and mingle. The smells of beer, chlorine, and grilled burgers floating around us. Nik and Dom are manning the grill while Collins is in a deep conversation with Sin and Harley. Tatum and Darcy sit by the fire, knees barely grazing. The little girl that I've grown to love just as much sitting on my mom's lap with Fwoppy in hand. Dale, Stu and Grace sit with them, casually chatting. This is everything that I ever could have dreamed and hoped for, but wasn't sure I would ever have.

I feel more loved than I could have ever imagined. I didn't know that this type of love existed. The type of love that makes you forget all of the hurt, the betrayal, and the feeling less than. The type of love that is all consuming and squashes any type of doubt that creeps in.

"What are you thinking about, baby?" Maverick asks, kissing my exposed shoulder.

"Just about how life has a funny way of working out. I didn't think I would end up here a few months ago, but I wouldn't have it any other way." I turn to smile at him.

"I didn't think so either. We deserve this moment filled with love and these people who helped us come together."

"I love you, Mav."

"And I love you, Darlin." That nickname still gives me butterflies, and I imagine it will for many years to come.

EPILOGUE

One Question

Kodi

6 months later

It's been six months since Mav and I gave into our feelings, Lily made her surprise appearance and the guys won the cup, and I've settled into this new life with ease. I love caring for Bella and being by Mavericks side for all the ups and downs of parenting and hockey.

Firm footsteps cross the threshold onto the porch behind me as I listen to Bella's little snores through her monitor. Gentle hands lifting my gaze to his as Mav places a kiss on my lips.

"I missed you," he says from above me.

"I missed you, too." I smile up at him.

He wanders over to the edge of the porch looking up at the stars. "Come here, baby."

I walk over, squeezing myself in between Mav and the railing. I lean my head back on his shoulder looking up at the stars with him.

"How was the game?" I ask him, knowing they lost by a point but checking in anyways.

"It was fine. Collins and I could have done better, but it is what it is. I'm glad to be home with you and Bella now." He sighs.

"I'm glad you're here now, too. I don't like sleeping alone."

"I know, I don't either. How has this week been?"

"Well, like I told you, Bella is loving preschool. She's such a little social butterfly. She didn't even cry when I dropped her off. It kind of hurt my heart." I chuckle. "Other than that, same old, same old. Just wishing you were here with us."

"Sounds like our girl."

We stand in silence, just soaking up this moment in each other's arms, when he breaks the silence.

"Darlin'."

"Yeah, Mav."

"One question." He sounds a little nervous, which is odd. We play this game all the time. It's become a staple in our relationship.

"One answer." I smile, even though I know he can't see it. His body heat has suddenly disappeared from behind me. I turn around to see where he went, and he's still there, just on one knee.

I gasp seeing an oval diamond with marquise diamonds jutting out the sides sitting on a rose gold band in his shaky hands. The tears are already sitting in my eyes as he begins to speak.

"Kodi Roscoe. When Bella ran into you all those months

ago, I didn't think that you would be the woman I ended up falling for. I regretted not asking for your number that day, but fate brought you back into my life." He swallows, his own tears falling with mine. "You've brought so much joy and love into not only my life, but also Bella's. I need to spend the rest of my life with you. Will you marry me?"

"Maverick, yes! This is perfect!" I squeal, tears rolling down my cheeks as he places the ring on my left hand. "I can't wait to spend the rest of my life with you. I love you so much."

"I didn't think I would ever get this, and I'm so glad I get it with you Ko. I love you."

※

I didn't think that Maverick and I would be on a joint bach trip so soon after his proposal, but he is of course ready to get married tomorrow, so we join our friends on a private plane bound for a week in Bora Bora . I convinced him that he at least needed to let me have a bach trip and plan the wedding I've been dreaming about since I was a little girl. And because that man is literally perfect, we settled on six months from the proposal. When I say settled, I mean that I attempted to bargain for a year, but he tricked me into agreeing while he had his tongue on my clit and two fingers working me over.

"Are you ready to drink Sex on the Beach and watch these gorgeous men attempt to throw a football on the beach?" Sin asks as she plops down across from me, the floppy matching bridesmaids hats that Darcy bought the girls abandoned in the seat beside her. Harley promptly picks up said hat and plops it back onto Sin's head so she can take a seat beside her.

"Hey! I'll have you know that I played football in high school and am very well adept with my hands." Dom winks at Sin as he walks by, throwing his duffle into the overhead compartment and taking a seat with Mav, Nik, and Collins at the back of the plane.

"God, he is insufferable." Sin groans once Dom is out of ear shot.

"Yeah. . .insufferable." I chuckle. "Anyways, yes I am ready for sex on the beach, in more than one way." My phone pings at that moment, and Sin grumbles something along the lines of, "Disgusting. If I ever speak like that, please sedate me Harley. I'm begging you."

> **MAVERICK**
> I heard that and you bet your sweet ass I will be making that happen. *winky face*

> **ME**
> Can't wait. *smirk emoji*

Just as I'm wondering where Darcy and Tate are when the plane is supposed to leave in ten minutes, I hear Tate grumbling as he drags Darcy's suitcase behind him, her walking in front of him without a singular care in the world. "Jesus, Darcy, did you put fifteen bricks in your suitcase?"

"Hi, babies!" Darcy squeals, plopping down beside me. "Thanks Tate."

"I'm so glad you're all here. I can't believe I'm getting married!"

One day and two fuel stops later, we are stepping out of the plane and into a van to take us to the private beach house that Maverick rented. Apparently the house opens onto a private beach, but despite our seclusion, we're still only a short ride away from the cultural hub of the island.

"Holy shit." I gasp as we pull into the driveway of what Maverick described as a "small beach house" but is actually a mansion. We all pile out of the car, rushing inside with our bags and looking around our home for the next week.

"Kodi gets the first pick of rooms! Nobody get settled in yet!" Maverick yells, approaching me from behind and wrapping his arms around my middle while lowering his voice which sends shivers down my spine, "I want to show you the room that I think you'll enjoy most."

"Lead the way then Big Guy." He lets go of me, sliding one hand into mine and leading me upstairs and across the home. Opening the door, I'm greeted by a king-sized lush bed, a small reading corner complete with a swinging egg chair, and a bathroom bigger than my car with two vanities. The thing that halts my breath though are the floor-to-ceiling windows that look onto the water and the balcony connected to it. Not only is there a giant, outdoor soaking tub, but there is also a swinging daybed that I can't wait to drink my morning coffee on.

"Yeah, no, this is definitely our room. I don't even want to sleep inside, like I could live on this balcony." I make my way outside and take a seat on the day bed, taking in the lush greenery on both sides of the house and the white sands stretching out into oceans that match Mav's eyes. Mav chuckles as he takes a seat beside me placing an arm around my shoulder, and I take this moment to lean into him, soaking up this quiet moment we have together.

"I thought you would enjoy this view at sunset but also thought that your screams mixed with the sound of the ocean crashing against the shore would be music to my ears later tonight." I can feel the pink staining my cheeks, I am still in awe of the mouth on this man. He says things to me sometimes that leave me somehow embarrassed and soaking wet at the same time. This would be one of those times. "It's okay, baby, you don't have to say anything. Your cheeks are telling me everything I need to know."

"Hey, lovebirds! Get down here, let's go check out the beach!" Nik bellows from the pool deck. I can't see him, which is good considering what Mav has in store for me later.

"We'll be down in a second, let me get my bathing suit on!" I holler back down. "Let's go, Mr. Hart, I'm all yours later." I stand up and make my way to my suitcase.

"Can't wait." He places a chaste kiss on my lips. Snatching up his trunks, we change quickly and meet our friends on the pool deck. We spend the rest of the afternoon drinking on the beach, take a short nap, and then have a catered dinner on the most beautiful sushi boat I've ever seen.

Everyone has since gone to their respective rooms and I'm sitting with my glass of wine on the day bed while Mav showers up.

Strong hands land on my shoulders and I instantly feel myself relax into the touch. "Hey, baby."

"Hi, Mr. Hart."

"Did you enjoy yourself today?"

"Mhhhmm, thank you for this trip." I plop my wine glass onto the ground, turning myself, propping up on my knees and wrapping my arms around his neck. Kissing him slowly, I run my hands down his chest and under his shirt. He growls into our kiss, pushing me slowly onto my back and hovering above me.

"How can I take my future wife tonight?" he asks as he nips at the sensitive spot beneath my ear. His hand trailing my body as he continues, "Should I fuck your throat while your head dangles off the edge? Should I take your ass bent over the balcony? Or, I could take your pretty little pussy with that toy I know you packed, while my cock is buried deep inside your ass?"

"Mouth first, then toy and ass." I sigh.

"Move to the edge for me baby, open that pretty mouth nice and wide." His weight is lifted off me and then he's standing above me, looking at me with pure lust in his eyes, the light from the room illuminating his hard body. I follow his directions, waiting as he undresses. He doesn't take his time, hitting the back of my throat, which just makes me want him more. I moan, wriggling my hips a little trying to relieve some of the pressure between my legs.

"Touch yourself baby, it's okay." That's all the permission I need as he continues thrusting in and out of my mouth, my hand finding my clit. "Fuck, Kodi. Your mouth is heaven. I need to be inside you soon."

He quickly pulls out of my mouth, running inside to grab my toy and the lube. Hopping back onto the daybed, spreading my legs open, he gently works the toy into me letting it slide in and out while a finger finds my clit. "Give me one, Darlin'."

He ramps up the vibration on the toy, causing my back to arch off the bed and a scream to escape my lips as the orgasm that I was holding back breaks free. "I told you that your screams and the ocean would be a beautiful sound," he says, smirking at me.

Lowering the setting, but keeping the toy inside me, Mav slowly starts to push his lubed cock into my ass. The feeling of fullness once he's completely seated has me seeing stars as another orgasm builds.

"Mav. Holy fuck, it's so much."

"And yet, you love it. You're soaked baby." His thrusts match the rhythm of the vibrator and I'm teetering closer to the edge by the second.

"Kodi, give me another, baby. I can't hold out much longer. You feel too good." The erotic sound of our bodies coming together and Mav's encouragement send me over the edge again, him following not too far behind me on a growl. His large body blankets me for a moment, my nails running along his back as our breathing returns to a normal pace.

One minute I was dozing off to sleep, and the next, corded arms lifted me and set me on the plush bedding inside, a wet towel being run along my body. I can feel my post-orgasm, loopy smile on my face when I peek my eyes at Mav as he cares for me. He smiles back at me, throwing the rag and joining me in bed, pulling me closer to his body.

"Best bachelorette trip ever." I lift my head up to smile at him and kiss him hastily one last time before sleep takes us both.

I hear him whisper, "I can't wait to marry you, Kodi James."

EXTENDED EPILOGUE

Our Happily Ever After

Maverick

4 years later

I sit on the patio rocking Aurora as Kodi and Bella splash around in the pool. Our sweet Aurora joined us a year ago. It took us some time to get pregnant, even though we decided that we wanted to start trying right after our wedding. Arabella has been the best big sister, and we assumed that it would take a while for us to get pregnant again, but to our surprise, in another six months, right around my mom's birthday, a little boy will be joining our family as well. Kodi looks absolutely radiant, her little bump has just started to pop out and she's managed to chase a seven and one year old around everyday while growing another human. I am in awe of her and how she does it. When I'm home, I can't keep up with those kids and pass out almost as soon as my head hits the pillow.

"Darlin', I'm going to lay Rory down. I'll be right back!" I holler at her as I stand and turn into the house.

When I come back outside, Bella is laid out on a lounge chair with remnants of a PB&J on her face and Floppy sitting next to her. When she started calling him Floppy instead of Fwoppy, Kodi and I both cried because our little girl was growing up. Kodi sits next to her, chewing on a sandwich of her own.

"Mama, can I get back in the water now?" she asks Kodi. When Bella was four, she started calling Kodi 'Mama' of her own free will. When she turned six, we explained adoption and let Bella decide if she wanted Kodi to be her Mama legally, to which Bella said yes.

"No baby, twenty minutes so you don't get a tummy ache." Kodi smiles at her with so much adoration in her eyes.

Arabella huffs but nods her head. I approach Kodi's chair and motion for her to scoot forward so I can sit behind her. We sit there for twenty minutes soaking up the sun, but when we look to Bella to tell her she can go back into the pool, she's knocked out.

"How are you feeling?" I ask, running my fingers through Kodi's long locks.

"Honestly?" She relaxes back into me, head resting on my chest.

"Yes, honestly."

"Pretty good, but there's one thing I am struggling with."

"And that would be what, Darlin'?"

"I'm so horny. Like unbearably," she whispers. It's been four years and she still hasn't grasped the fact that our daughter sleeps like the dead. Baby screams, moans, sirens, none of it wakes her up.

My light grip in her hair turns tight, angling her head so she's looking at me. "Well we can't have that can we?" Her cheeks are tinged with my favorite shade of pink. "I'll take care of dinner, bedtime, and then you tonight. Sound good?"

Her sultry smile spreads across her face and she places a gentle kiss on my lips. "Sounds wonderful, actually."

The rest of the day flies by, Rory and Bella play in the living room while Kodi watches from the couch as I prepped tacos in the kitchen. Arabella passed out as soon as I shut her light off, while Rory had a hard time going down for bedtime, but I'm finally headed to our room.

The sight that greets me when I open our door has me hardening in my pants almost immediately. My wife lays in the middle of our bed, naked, a hand snaked in between her legs, rubbing her clit in small circles, her chest rising and falling rapidly.

"What happened to I would take care of you?" I say, shutting and locking the door then stripping as I approach the bed.

"I just needed some relief. You were gone and I haven't gotten any time with you. Then today, you were just so you and I couldn't wait any longer," she rasps, her hand still between her legs. I want to tell her to stop but she's so fucking sexy touching herself and thinking about me.

"I'm here now. Let me take over." I position myself between her legs, pushing her hands out of the way replacing it with mine while leaning down and kissing her roughly. "God, I missed you."

"I missed you too." She gasps as I push two fingers into her pussy. "Shit, Mav."

"So wet for me already?"

"All day."

"Fuck, I love that." I growl rocking my hips into her but I'm not going to fuck her yet. She needs to come for me first. Moving myself down her body, I work my tongue over her clit with the motion of my fingers. Her wetness is dripping down my hands, she is so much wetter when she's pregnant and if I drowned in it, I would be a happy man. She's clenching around me, writhing with her fingers grasping my hair holding me in place.

"Mav. Mav. Mav," she chants, tightening around me as I continue to devour her. She continues to rock her hips up with the rhythm of my fingers and tongue before she comes on a curse, wetness gushing out of her. I lap it up like a starved man until her body relaxes for me.

Coming up to my knees, I smirk at her as I wipe my forearm across my glistening face. "Are you ready for my cock, Darlin'?"

"Please." Lining up, I slowly push into her.

"You okay?" I need to make sure she isn't in pain.

"So good. I need you, Mav." Those evergreens boaring into mine to make sure I know what she wants. With that permission I push the rest of the way into her, groaning at the feeling of her wrapped around me that I will never tire of. I thrust into her over and over, holding her gaze, her puffy pink lips in a small o shape as I rub her clit with one hand and grasp her hip with the other. When she tightens around me again, I spill into her on a grunt.

After cleaning her up, I pull her into my side, placing a hand over her stomach and kissing her forehead softly.

"So I think I found a name we might both like while you were gone." She says into the darkness. We had been going back and forth about names; ultimately I will choose whatever makes her happy, but I drew a line in the sand when she suggested we name our son Waylon because my name "gives North Carolina vibes and our sons should too".

"Okay, hit me with it." Nervous for what is about to come out of her mouth.

"I know we have the A thing going with the girls, so I figured if we have more boys we could also stick with this letter. Gives us lots of options." She's twiddling her thumbs like she's nervous.

"Out with it then, babe, I'm sure I'll love it."

"Theodore, Teddy, Stuart Hart." She sucks in a breath and does my favorite thing, rambles. "Listen, I know it is giving old man vibes, but it's cute and the girls have classic names that have cute nicknames, so I thought he deserved one too. And well, I thought we should honor dad, especially if he might come on your mom's birthday."

My eyes are watering before I lift her gaze to mine to tell her, "Kodi, I love it. It's perfect."

"Wait, really?"

"Yes. Thank you for wanting to honor my parents in that way. Mom would have loved you and Dad is going to feel so special when we tell him." Now we're both crying.

She lifts herself onto her elbow and kisses me slowly and

sweetly.

"Thank you for loving me these past four years and making me a mama. I love you."

"I wouldn't want it with anyone else. I love you most."

ABOUT THE AUTHOR:

Katelyn is a Florida native, born and raised. She lives with her long term partner, Adam and their two dogs, Yogi the goldendood and Smoosh the pocket pittie mix. She's not a fan of being outdoors but enjoys the occasional excursion to the mountains, hoping to one day experience life there. Returning to her love of reading when the COVID pandemic struck, she rediscovered she's a fan of all genres and all things spicy. She gravitates most towards hockey romances while ironically enough she isn't a follower of hockey. Her writing is a labor of love outside of her full time Nanny job to the cutest two under two. If she's not reading or writing, you can find her playing cozy games on the Nintendo switch, in a Dungeons & Dragons campaign, or binge watching bad reality TV.

ACKNOWLEDGMENTS:

I'd like to first say, holy frickin crap I published a book. I wish I had a cool story to tell but one day in November of 2023, I decided I wanted to try and write a book and like I did it??? So first, I'd like to thank me because if you know me, I don't step outside of my comfort zone, I don't put myself out there, I don't challenge myself but I did the fucking thing. I'm so damn proud of myself. Now onto the people that helped me get here in no particular order.

To my critique partners, Kristin Marzullo and Mindy Pettengill. Kristin, you were the first to lay eyes on my baby all while writing one book and promoting another. Your encouragement and feedback helped to flip Shot to the Hart on its axis, helping me to evoke more emotion into my characters and reminding me to show not tell. Mindy, not only did you provide helpful feedback but I lived for your feral reactions, they brought me joy when I felt like I was losing steam. You also helped me with promotion, hyping up my posts and being an all around support system since our goldfish brains get along so well. Thank you for bringing my characters to life via art, I am in love! I love and appreciate you both more than you know.

To my editors, Cait, owner of Caitlin Lengerich Editing and Chelsey, @theimperfectionist . Cait, thank you for talking this baby author through everything, for respectfully tearing my book apart and helping me put it back together for an even better story. Thank you for answering my anxiety ridden messages and ensuring me that everything would be okay and for the ENDLESS communication which I needed because again anxiety. Are you ready for the next one? Chelsey, thank you for stepping in and helping push my first book baby over the finish line while Cait focused on her family.

To Dee, my unofficially official PA, my graphics guru and one of my first ever book besties. Thank you. THANK you. THANK YOU. From helping me plot, letting me bounce a million character names off of you before I chose one, volunteering to help me run my street team and reorganizing my google forms when they didn't make sense. Everything you've done has helped me get the word out about Shot to the Hart and I can't say thank you enough so here's some silly little words.

To my parents, I'm sorry that you can't read this book even though I know you'll have a signed copy on your shelf. Ps. My offer still stands to tab the parts you can't read if you want to experience the story without the fun stuff. I can't thank you enough for your love and support my whole life, like when I decided to play softball or joined the winterguard team with no athletic ability you encouraged me to practice and grow everyday. That encouragement is what led me to finish this book and publish it knowing you would be proud of me.

To Adam, my boyfriend, the sunshine to my grumpy and my knight in shining tin foil. When I looked at you and said I'm writing a book, you simply said you were proud of me and couldn't wait to read it. That's how I knew you loved me because in our entire relationship, I've never seen you read a book. When I was stressing deadlines, costs of services and about actually publishing for people to see my book with their eyeballs, you continued to tell me how proud of me you were and that no matter what people thought, I did it and I should be proud of that too. I love you so many.

To my real life Darcy, aka Em. When I told you I was writing a book, you immediately were ready for it to be in your hands without knowing what it's about. You've constantly checked in and been a shoulder to laugh and cry on. Half of our lives and you still give me unconditional support and I couldn't do it without you.

To Gaven and Carly. Gaven, thank you for taking photos of me to make me look more put together than I am. Carly, thank you for designing my stickers, I love them all.

To my Chaos Crew, thank you all for sharing, liking, and reposting. For letting me bounce ideas off of you, for hyping me and Shot to the Hart up before it was even in your hands, for deciding where spicy scenes should take place and helping expand the book playlist. You all are amazing!

Lastly to my readers, this is my debut novel and if you've read it well I can't thank you enough. I didn't think people would be excited about my book but there were more people than I could imagine who wanted to meet my characters and you being one of them just makes my day! I hope you stick around for what's next in the Scoring with Love series.

Wondering what book Kodi was reading in Chapter 25? Check out Timber Hollow by M. Pettengill!

Made in the USA
Monee, IL
22 February 2025